Raynesha Pittman Quincey Bowen

TOXIN

Conglomerate Ink

PO BOX 512 Shelbyville, TN 37162
www.RayneshaPittman.com

ISBN13: 978-0-9967856-2-4

ISBN10: 0996785624

Facebook: www.facebook.com/ConglomerateInk

Twitter: @ConglomerateInk

Instagram: @author_rayneshapittman

DEDICATION

There's no way to dedicate this book to life and the character building toxins within it without first taking a step back to dedicate it to Jehovah, the true creator of all life. We know there is no such thing as peace without knowledge of toxins and where there are toxins lays an opportunity to choose his peace. Thank you, father God, for the right to choose even after we've made the wrong choices. We also dedicate this book to the two Angels that you gave us on Earth, our grandmothers. Mrs. Shirley Mae Wilson, Raynesha's Angel may have gotten her wings but I know she still watches and protects her like she did in the flesh and Mrs. Garnita Beard aka Meme, Quincey's epitome of strength, roots and the first to introduce him to God, he thanks you for never wavering. There's no love like the love a grandmother gives. We thank you God, for two of the best grandmothers to walk this cruel Earth. Jehovah, you are worthy to be king, to God be the glory!

ACKNOWLEDGMENTS

From Raynesha Pittman:

There are hundreds of people that I would love to acknowledge. Starting with my supportive family to the people who've crossed my path with lesson, reasons and those who stuck around for a few seasons. Honestly, I dislike writing acknowledgments so instead of listing names and accidentally leaving some one very important to me off, I'll only acknowledge the resources we used to write this book.

It's only right that the one name I drop be somewhat of cliché. Quincey, from the moment we spent 72 hours talking with neither one of us needing to sleep, I knew our chemistry was extraordinary. You reactivated my mind and forced it out of the dormant state I had gotten comfortable with it being in. You made me understand the importance of having a why in my life and helped me hunt for it. It was a pleasure to write Toxin with you but with all the hours we spend talking, we've already written ten books together. Thanks to love, ten is only the beginning. I love you, Mr. Bowen.

Life, thank you for never missing a beat when it came to beating me up. Those beatings have always fueled my strength like a ball of yarn building momentum, I've learned to stop questioning them. I now know it's okay to be beaten up. The true goal in life is to never accept being beaten down.

Social media outlets, thank you for granting me the

opportunity to interact with people all over the world. I've met some of the strongest willed, strong minded, geniuses that act as if they don't know the definition of stop nor regard it as a word. I love being able to speak with my readers anywhere, anytime but for everything social media has to offer that is not positive, I thank you for allowing me to witness it. It helped me to push my creativity beyond my personal understanding while writing this book.

Google, you came into this nerd's life and it's never been the same. Any thought that crosses my mind, I no longer feel weird or too different to have. You've helped me see that I'm not the only one who thinks without restraints. The content found on your engine was useful in dissecting these scattered thoughts so I could put them on the pages of this book.

In the process of researching for the writing of this book, I strengthened my relationship with God. The NIV (New International Version) never left my side. I read the scriptures using Bible Gateway online. Although Toxin is a work of fiction, only those who've read the Bible will understand what I referenced from the NIV. I've enjoyed reading a lot of books but none of them hold a candle to the Bible.

Lastly, if you're reading this book please know that I appreciate you. There are millions of books in this world, you didn't have to pick up mine. I'm thankful and blessed to have you. You're the reason I continue to share my god given gift. I don't have to meet you for you to know that I love you and there's nothing you can do about!

From Quincey Bowen:

I would like to acknowledge Jehovah- God, the head of my life, Jesus Christ, and the holy spirit for giving me the vision and allowing the joining of two intelligent minds to create this work.

To my children, Q7, and to my beautiful fiancée for her love, support, and the faith in me she stepped out on when it came to finishing our first book together. Author Raynesha Pittman soon to be my Rayn Bowen, this is Kismet baby. How we are and how we've been living our lives together since we met, I know Jehovah put us together. What he put together, let no man put asunder.

Seeing that this is my first book I want to thank all the others who have been in my life. To my mother also known as my twin, Janice, thank you for supporting me through it all. I'm glad to know you're always there with a listening ear. Darryl, my dad, and the most down to Earth man I know, thank you for always being the voice of reason in my life. I have to thank my baby sister, Chelcee, for believing in my dreams and cheering me on even when she didn't understand them. Dondra, my little brother, and my granddaddy, Major, thank you for being the comedy in my life. It never feels like it's raining on me with the two of you around. Finally, to all my uncles, aunts, cousins which there are too many of you to name. Thank you for not forgetting that family always comes first, I love all of you and to my favorite niece in the world, Mariah thank you for always lighting up when you see me. Your smile is a joy and know that uncle QB loves you.

There are two honorable mentions that are also references we used in writing the book. Robert T. Kiyosaki and Napoleon Hill. Besides reading your books, I implemented some of your teachings/suggestions in my life. Thank you for making them clear and concise.

To all of you reading this, I hope this book brings you the same joy I felt when writing it. May God bless you.

Dwayne Hollingswell

This isn't the outline for a get rich quick scheme nor is it a read this book and tomorrow you'll become successful prophecy. I've made sure to remove the hard work meets opportunity, luck syndrome most people bank on to make it through until retirement age and I'm telling my life and love story in manual form like the laws of success. I'm a strategic man, a logical thinker and a mathematical type of guy who knows to question if one plus one truly equates to two. Utilizing this logic in every category of my life is how I make it through, love isn't excluded.

What is life? Whether you call life a scientific creation or a gift from God, it's the living we do within the 24 hours that makeup days, years, decades, and centuries while our hearts pump. There were traditions we used to follow to help us with living but the nontraditional ways of maneuvering through life have become the new tradition. Let me slow down, I don't want to lose your attention without convincing you to pay attention for free. Don't misunderstand; there are levels to nontraditional thinking and the level I'm on was built for me to gain success.

The road to success is paved with rags to riches stories, we've done away with walking on failure. The word failure doesn't motivate traditional thinking people, it solidifies it as a possibility they face on the road to success. Non-traditional thinkers don't comprehend the word failure because we never give up and accept failure. What traditional thinking people don't understand is there are laws and principle set by the universe that gets you whatever you want whether you are just or unjust. Nontraditional thinking people learn that money is just a toxic tool that aids health to wealth and we use it to gain true success which is freedom. Life and love are filled with toxins to keep people from freedom, success, and power. Over time, traditional thinking people get enlightened. I'm not talking about that sitting on the pulpit holy spirit talk that brings tears to our eyes as we reflect on our wrong doings against the rules laced in the book they've nicknamed the "good book." I'm talking about that independent reading of the Bible that dropped the jewels on finance like when Solomon asked for wisdom and then money came to him. We bust our asses in the flesh but for what? Think about it, what's so good about the world telling you that you're a hard worker? If you've read Ecclesiastes chapters 1 and 2 then you'd know to take it as an insult. We should all work hard like we're working for the lord but the truth is, we should be working hard for ourselves.

I've study money and the means of getting it without hard work and it's lead me to the gateway to the white man's world, which is investing. I'm not saying those of us with bronze skin don't invest but we prefer to invest in tangible items like homes, cars and in business ventures while those who lack bronze invest in what can't be seen, the stock market. I don't want to make the stock market seem like an easy game to play, it's not. It's filled with a lot of losses but the gains are worth the risk.

Like with everything else in the world you must

learn the craft of investing and master it. If you're thinking you can just pick a stock and everything will come in to play, you're foolish. If it was that easy the laws of investment wouldn't be needed. There wouldn't be 21 laws to money, 48 laws to power, 105 laws governing the universe and life itself and 17 laws to success. You see, we've been taught that we can look upon the good book, follow all the 10 commandments perfectly and everything will fall into our laps but there are 65 other books within the Bible, both new and old testaments that house over 1,663 life lessons that we pay no attention to. Let's be real, how many have truly been successful in following those commandments to get success while on earth in the flesh? I'll wait while you Google the information as if it's going to be factual and free from human error but If I can recall correctly, following those commandments earns us the right to sit with the father, after the flesh in our true forms. So, common sense which is only common to those who don't see the obvious, should teach us there must be a method to the madness before judgment day but then again, intelligence isn't that common but smarts are…

The late Napoleon Hill said, "Study wealth and get wealth." Which is the reason why one of my favorite scriptures in the good book is, "Study wisdom and learn about fools." Which equates to, foolish is what foolish does. Insanity is doing the same thing repeatedly and expecting a different outcome yet there are so many people who fall into that trap. I'm not into being caught up in anything. While the majority are reading the good book in search of the rules on life and love I'm reading it to seek the Kingdom and to learn the true history of finance.

I know I'm at the age where I should be looking for a wife and planting seeds that will carry my DNA to leave my legacy per the world's standards. I'm 37, plenty of women have given me the alias handsome in view of my physical attributes, my bank statements label me successful, and I've somewhat beat the odds of a black man by staying out of jail and still being alive. Honestly, none of that means a thing in this color powered world we live in. For example, I'm 5'8 and weight 145 lbs., there are 12 years old girls bigger than me but that doesn't stop white women from clutching their purses when I walk by nor does it stop the police from pulling me over for driving an expensive car that they think no black person but Oprah or Tyler could afford in a suburban area. I'm black, a black man at that and even with my foot in the door, the fact remains it's only small progress in this white man's world.

Some could label me angry due to me getting upset behind the treatment of my people over the last 500 plus years but that doesn't mean I walk around with hate in my heart like our arch enemy. If Batman has The Joker to keep his stock going, Superman has Lex-Luther to keep him valuable then I hope the truth doesn't piss anyone off when I say the Bronze man has ignorant racist White men trying to suppress us, giving us a reason to soar or end up dead for trying to do so.

I didn't mean to get too far off subject but I do agree with the scripture in the good book that says, "He who finds a wife finds a good thing." But I'm more motivated in hunting for my missing rib for reasons other than love because of the scripture that says, "A good man leaves an inheritance for their children's, children..." I want to be looked upon as a good man by the almighty but I'm not settling for having a headache giving baby mama to do so. The woman to bear the pain of birthing my seed must be my wife and since I'm not romantic, I'm not going to force myself into a vain romance trying to place a ring on a finger. That's not a contract I'm willing to invest in.

The cold showers, bottles of warm lotion and condoms used on women who can't spell Stock Exchange do get boring but the drama-free, non-conditional bond I have with the three makes them priceless. You can keep all the Toxins that build like plaque on the cavity of love and I'll take my money first in a heartbeat. You see, I know the love of money is the root of all evil, so I don't love it... I respect it like the good book instructs, I give respect to whom respect is owed. If money can divide families, can be used as a tool for happiness and control the flow of the world, I'd be foolish not to respect it.

For S and G (Shits and giggles), if you hear that I'm in love with a woman check her hands for that fruit ole girl slid to Adam and my digestive track for traces of it. It's going to take a set up and some poison to get me to trust a woman enough to hand out my heart again. No offense ladies but I've been vaccinated from your toxins. Just give me both sets of those juicy lips and you can keep everything else...

Nivea Bowen

What's my take on love? Well, think of condoms. You can have sex without one but nine months and no prescriptions later, you'd be thankful you didn't. What I'm saying is, you can exist without love if you're one of those people who prefer to only exist and not live. That's just my opinion but seriously, who living in the age of sexting wants to hear the tainted opinion of an outspoken, college educated, 36 years old angry black woman who doesn't know what in the lovely fuck I'm mad at in the first place?

Furthermore, I don't know if my take on love would do you any good seeing that I haven't had a man since a man had me. Nevertheless, I've dusted the spider webs off my Vicky secrets, copped me a cute lace bra to match and I've been on the prowl for one. Like a crack pipe to a pair of ashy lips, I'm close to locking down on one or so I hope I am. I'm tired of sleeping and sexing alone. I usually keep myself busy with anything that has a tie to the stock market but that isn't working anymore. I've tried to stay patient and wait for the right man to choose me but my perception of a good man is becoming extinct and before they die off I'm snatching one of them up, fuck waiting on being chosen.

I'm all too familiar with those love stories where the boy meets girl, he realizes he likes her, she makes him chase her until he wins her heart, they fuck like dogs, she has his litter, and then they live happily ever after... BULLSHIT! I call bullshit on the entire romantic fantasy and now that I'm thinking back, I always have. I can remember when Mama used to put on cartoon movies that were supposed to teach me lessons and display morals to help build and strengthen my core. They were made to make parenting easy and for the enjoyment of innocent children but I watched Mama go through so much bullshit with niggas, not men, but grown ass thoroughbred niggas, that my innocents were gone long before Cinderella's shoes were upgraded to glass stilettos.

Nah, I don't do make-believe and farfetched love stories; I prefer to take my bullshit the smelly way, funky! However, there is a story of love I read years ago, that's written so well that it must be true. It's about a man, his rib, some powerful fruit, and a fake friend. I believe the first author out of the 40 who wrote the book called the friend a serpent... Anyways, the man and his rib which he eventually named woman and their story is one that is well-known. It starts with dust and a breath of life and goes on to talk about bruised heels and eating by the sweat of our brow.

That probably wasn't the best summary of the story suffice it to say, that's about the best I can do with my weed stained memory. What I do know is, that same story has been credited as the story of our creation. It was written thousands of years ago and is the reason why men side-eye the hell out of us now. I mean damn, almost every man's downfall in the book had something to do with their weakness over a woman. David's did, so did Adam's, Job's, Moses', Abraham's, and the list continues. It also holds the explanation on why women bring forth kids in sorrow and it sheds light on why women end up calling more than one-man daddy. So, how do you expect me to believe in love at first sight and finding your soul mate when the first relationship story ever written didn't mention the two?

There are other stories in the book but I don't remember any of them mentioning the foolishness I see people calling love today. Like titling each other, "Bae" like it's a badge of honor. What in the hell is a Bae, anyways? Could you see Coretta Scott-King calling Dr. King, Bae? But we let that bae shit roll off our tongues as we profess with our mouths that we want the King's kind of love. Now let's be real, how many women of this generation could handle being married to a man that was never home and smothered in death threats on civilian and government levels? Some of us won't even hold a man down while he's in jail nowadays, even if he's serving time for trying to take care of our asses.

Then we ask for that Will and Jada sense of understanding but how can we get it when we forget that we have one mouth and two ears? Don't you have to listen to obtain and understanding? Oh, and my favorite thing to hear these simple-minded chicks asking for is that Jay and Bey hard time hustling love A.KA. The Power Couple love but how about stepping outside of the box of music they brainwash us with for a second and let's allow Bill and Hillary to use that title for a moment or should we be calling what both couples have, saving face? My thing is, would they still be together if there wasn't a gain involved but what does that matter when we're calling it quits over direct messages and Facebook pokes? We aren't giving out passes on our mates getting oral pleasure from anyone other than ourselves no matter what the gain is. WAIT! Let me clear that up. That wasn't confirmation that my presidential vote was for Hillary. It was solely based on my views of her marriage. Politically, I thought we should have taken a presidential election off. Maybe we should have used the time off to huddle up and rethink this Democracy thing. Giving us the right to vote in the days where everything found on social media and trending is the truth seems a little scary to me, hence President Donald J. Trump but that's just my opinion…

Getting back to the book, it holds the prologue to love, marriage and the biblical laws that bind them. If you take the time to read it from front to back, you'll learn a thing or two like how unconditional love works. Life would be a lot better and less bitter if we did. Listen to me preaching without practicing the lessons I teach, that makes me ten times worse off than you. Although I'm smart, determined and will Rhino over anyone or anything to get what I want out of life, I'm not bright enough to apply the shit I know to get my ring finger encircled in gold. I've chopped it up to it coming with the territory of being a deep thinker. I see and hear a lot, dissect it, and make my own theories from it. Will, I ever apply what I know? Hell, who knows…

What's disheartening to me is, that story, our founding story has fallen off the radar with the rest of the good book. It once was law and now people treat it as a bestselling work of fiction. Without giving love a notice we've turned it into a light switch and depending on what side of the bed we wake up on we're switching love off and on too easy while forgetting our hearts are paying the bill.

I can't speak for the powerful man or the ruler over women like the main character in that old book appointed them, but I know the ways of the world has fucked me and my sister's minds up. We've rolled around listening to music that subliminally makes us feel like we love thugs, money, brand name clothing and that it's okay to be a side piece. It seemed innocent, the beat was hot and our round browns jumped to the baseline as we sang along to the hook but then it happens. That subliminal we weren't paying attention to sends us in a new brand name outfit with a thousand-dollar bag on our shoulder to the club with our girls. We meet the sexiest thug since Tupac and since he hit that thang right that same very night, we're moving him in within a week's time. Next, we're combining our work incomes with his street hustle, adding our struggles and baggage together while we keep doing it raw like we've checked their medical history for red flags and they've checked out with a clean bill of health. Now we're crying on the phone to our fake ass sister who was with us at the club when we met him about the positive pregnancy test and how he lied about not having a main bitch. We're screaming, "he ain't shit" but his ain't shit ass still manages to have us stressing and our "sister" isn't shooting us nothing uplifting back. She's more comfortable with dealing with us while we're in a negative space anyways. We don't recognize the hate she has for us in her heart until two years later when she's at child support court dressed like and standing next to our child's father as his woman and as the key witness on why our club going ass is an unfit mother.

On the other hand, we can't keep blaming it on the music nor the television shows. We are supposed to be individuals with strong minds and willpower to overlook it... or so they say but facts are the only truth. When we had television shows like Good Times, The Wonder Years and The Cosby show on air their subliminal messages promoted uplifting in the family and friendships. Now they have been replaced with reality shows and their subliminal messages are coming to tear apart the power of those throwback shows. If you think I'm wrong how do you explain Doctor Heathcliff Huxtable being pulled into the accused actions of Bill Cosby? Let that marinate.

Man, I love that old moral filled story about Adam and Eve, it used to keep me grounded, but the story I'm about to tell isn't it. Nor is this that February 14th flowers, cards and candy romance that includes a dinner and movie. I gave the naked baby in the diaper with pretty hair and arrows the day off. Sorry, there's no love at first sex in here but there will always be someone willing to play pussy and end up losing and fucked, it's called life. If you really want to know my take on love, there's only one way I can explain it to you, in the form of a story. So, if it's a love story you're looking for I'll try to create the fantasy for you with these few words to tell you about mine,

Once upon a time...

Raynesha Pittman Quincey Bowen

TOXIN

Dwayne

The Mississippi river was at visual perfection during the darkest hours of the night. The normal beer cans filled with cigarette butts and latex condoms oddly floating at full capacity were nowhere in sight. All you could see was stars beyond arm's reach and spread out by threes. They not only freckled the sky like the face of a red-haired underdeveloped and shaky voiced boy, their reflection also illuminated the watery floor. More surprisingly, the steady flow of traffic going in both directions on Riverside Drive managed to remain silent as the river did its job of separating Memphis, Tennessee from West Memphis, Arkansas or to be frank, one state's scraps from the next state's.

There I was standing in my picture window admiring the sight of a peaceful downtown Memphis night while my mind was in its usual gear of overdrive. It wasn't like me to become frustrated with anything easily yet, the fact that I couldn't remember Arkansas sales tax with my eyes locked on the Welcome to Tennessee/Arkansas arced bridge had taken me there. I'd known the states sales taxes by heart and kept up with both of their financial changes. It hurt my ego to have to pull out my phone and ask the computerized chic for the answer.

"Suki, what's Arkansas sales tax?

"6.5%" The almost human voice answered.

"Oh yeah, that bullshit!"

"No search results found for, oh yeah that bullshit. Would you like to refine your search? or use the closest match... No Bullshit, artist... Chris Brown?"

"No thank you, Suki I'm done."

Suki was gone causing the light on my cell phone's screen to go out and instantly the bulb in my head turned on. It made me remember the $1.07 I spent at the Dollar store in Arkansas for paper towels versus $1.09 I paid for them here in Memphis. I wasn't going to sweat it seeing that retail tax was the only taxes I paid thanks to having my company set up as Limited Liability Limited Partnership in Delaware. The United States Commercial law also known as the Universal Commercial Code modified the Limited Partnership, now I'll never and so will other Hedge Fund managers pay taxes again at the end of the year and it's 100% legal.

Shaking my head disgusted I looked towards the opposite end of the river. I didn't know what turned my stomach the most, the fact that the bridge was the only obstacle causing Tennessee's tax to be 9.25% or the fact that I paid my maid good money to clean my condo and she wasn't cleaning the windows. It was obvious that I purchased the condo for its beautiful view. She had to be flat foot stupid to cut corners on the windows unless she didn't care and wanted me to know. It made me wonder what else she wasn't cleaning?

I turned my back to the murky view of the outside world provided by the glass, clutched the papers in my hand and started walking down the hall to my home office.

TOXIN

I had printed off the prices for commodities like energy, agriculture, and livestock from Bloomberg on every index of the day. It was my nightly routine to review the technical analyst of every index but tonight was thrown off from the dimming of the sun. My T1 service was down and I couldn't get on the internet. After waiting close to two months to have it installed seeing that the FBI decided they not only wanted to watch my private equity firm but my private individual investments as well, down time always felt like it was under their control. My MacBook was two seconds away from being slung off the desk thanks to the installation of updates. Candlesticks and moving averages were permanent images in my mind but tonight I needed the online visual. I wanted to review the results to find the next commodity I could bank on to make my investment fund a handsome return. The president was announced only hours ago but I knew change was going to make its first appearance at 9 o'clock the morning after at the New York Stock Exchange. Bull president elect, bull market and history can prove me right. All that meant to me was invest opposite, invest bear. The market will rise high, break records, this I'm sure of but what goes up must come down and every balloon filled with hot air will stretch to its limits before it burst. It's going to be a sad day watching my countries economy fall. Anyways, no matter which way I decide to invest I mostly invest in commodities on the account that they're natural, come from God and if we lose them we've lost our rights, both biblically and scientifically to live comfortably on this Earth.

My eyes were locked on some potentials as the high-speed service kicked back in until hard knocks rocked my door. The knocks were a surprise seeing that I invested a pretty penny to stay beyond arm's reach like the stars. I don't entertain company and on the rare occasions that I did, it was by invitation only and the guest knew it. I'm an introverted realist and I am sound with the title and the life style that came along with it, I don't do people.

"It has to be a drunk neighbor…" I mumbled but, *it better be a drunk neighbor,* is what I was thinking reading the time on the grandfather clock that was seconds away from striking 11pm. I bypassed my 4K security system's video surveillance, the peep hole on the door, and went straight for the lock and handle. Besides wishing someone would be stupid enough to test me and being confident it was a lost guest of a neighbor, I knew no one else could get past the doorman, not even food deliveries.

"What's up, cuzzo?"

Chauncey stood in a runway model pose in the hallway. He was looking every bit the mirror image of what I had worn the last time he and I hung out with each other. He had on a wool slim fit suit with a London collar and a Milano pressed dress shirt. Seeing it on him made me think of a Brooks Brothers catalog or the front two rows in church on Easter Sunday. Those really expensive looking suits were made like the one he wore.

Chauncey finessed the suit with cuff links filled with 1/10 ounce of 24k United States gold, shaped into American Bald Eagle coins. I was sure those were mine. I had ordered them online for shits and giggles. They were a hint to what I really invest in gold and silver, in the physical. I had them custom made. How Chauncey got his greasy hands on them was the real question.

Although not as expensive as the Santory Tristan sleek leather penny loafers I had worn, the cheap replicas he probably got from Payless were still a nice piece of garnishment on his look. If I didn't know he was a starving player and small-time weed dealer, I would have thought he'd walked straight out of the New York Stock Exchange. But the red lipstick kiss, tattooed on his bright yellow chest that hid behind his shirt, said he couldn't be more than a low-budget ambulance chaser.

"Tell me why I shouldn't slam the door in your face for popping up without calling first?"

"'Cause we're family."

"Not good enough!" I said using force to slam the door in his face. I couldn't help but shake my head after a few seconds of staring at him adjusting his tie like a trial lawyer through my peep hole. As the curiosity of what prompted Chauncey to make an unscheduled visit grew I reopened the door.

"What!" I asked permitting him entrance.

"Damn, I can't check on you? If you wouldn't have changed your locks over that petty shit I would have used my key."

"You stole from me, how is changing my locks being petty?"

"Cause, I didn't steal shit important," he said with way too much vigor in his voice.

"But you thought you were. You assumed you could snatch a hundred trillion-dollar bill out of my currency scrap book, sell it, probably to trick off after a skeezer, and I wouldn't know it was missing."

"I was trying to pay my phone bill so I could call a skeezer but the fact of the matter remains...You're a petty ass nigga. You knew I'd try to steal the biggest bill in that bitch and you let me make a fool out of myself."

Chauncey looked pissed and I couldn't help but to laugh and rub it in his face. "What happened when you walked in the bank with it again?" I tried to straighten my face like I was asking him a serious question but my muscles were too comfortable in the smile to stop.

"Fuck you, you know what that ho said at the bank. She handed it back to me when I asked her how much it was worth and said for me to roll my next blunt with it or I could wipe my ass with it."

I roared with laughter and eventually, he joined in.

"What happened to Africa's money anyway?" he asked genuinely looking interested.

"Close and lock my door," I instructed and once he did, I schooled him, "It wasn't Africa's currency, it was Zimbabwe's, a country in Africa. Now that you've got the geography part of it straight, this is what happened. Long story short, the politicians as crooked as we know they can

6

be, stole the farm land, thought they could operate it since they think being rich equals being smart, and they killed the GDP."

"Hold up nigga, what's GDP? Sounds like a gang rivalry to me," he said cutting me off.

"Only you would say some shit like that. The GDP is the Gross Domestic Product for the country, which is the final market value of what a country is producing and the labor that comes with it. So, since the country couldn't produce a product, no one made money from the goods and services. It forced the money to go bad; they didn't have a product to fully represent its land. Just like the United States doesn't produce anything. Yeah, we have factories and shit that's labeled made in the U.S.A but 99% of the pieces used to make the items come from other countries. Check anybody's house you know and 99% of the stuff in it was made in China."

"Alright stop right there, I already know where you're going to go with the shit next. Some kind of way you're going to end this by telling me I need to be investing my money in commodities."

"Aw, you know me a little bit. You're exactly right. The U.S claims our GDP is 2.2% but the truth is it's -0.5% so before we end up like Zimbabwe, you better cover your ass by investing in something from Jehovah!"

"Well like I said, I came to check on you Mr. Don't Need Nobody. I didn't come for another drawn out lesson on how I'm fucking up my money. I had gone to see your pops about some money he owed me." I looked at him to let him know I knew he was lying and he quickly straightened up. "I mean, to see if he would loan me some money and he said him and your moms haven't heard from you in months."

"They don't need to; they get the deposit I make every month. My parents know I'm straight."

To hell with what they thought, my standoffish behavior with my family was warranted. One by one, my family members jumped off the roller coaster ride to my success. They were doctors and lawyers, careers that required vast hours of education and had stability but that wasn't the road I'd taken. I wanted to be more than a college educated, hardworking, successful man. I wanted to be rich without the hard work so at the age of 15 I decided to search for the means of doing so. I started with research at public libraries and then began reading the *Rich Dad, Poor Dad* books. It may have started there but thanks to my grandmother teaching me to search for more knowledge, books in the same genre became my tools.

From, *The Laws of Success* to *Think and Grow Rich*, if it was about working less and earning more I not only read it, I incorporated the teachings into my life. Seeing that those books never forced a college education into my brain I didn't immediately pursue one after high school which labeled me as a bad seed to those linked to my string of DNA. I asked my parents for the money to open my first brokerage account so I could trade and they didn't give me a dime. Instead, my dad told me to get a real job which meant overworking myself in a warehouse or flipping burgers for crumbs. My mother had supported my decision at the early start of it, but she didn't offer me her pocket lint neither. It wasn't until I made my first $50,000 that they decided to write me a check as investors but it didn't last long. When my venture cost her and my dad money, her support dwindled away. Now that I had perfected my craft, I chose to love my family monetarily. I still have bruises from being black balled by those I loved most and it wouldn't heal with their vain band aid like apologies nor their kind words of congratulations. I wasn't in my feelings about the cut, but I didn't like seeing the nasty ass scar that it left behind.

"Money don't mean you're straight, cuzzo, but since we're talking dollars it only makes sense that I ask you to let me hold three hundred dollars to take baby out on a nice date. I'll run you your money back when I get this work off."

"Now there goes the truth. That suit only shields the South Memphis nigga in you. If you can afford Brooks Brothers, why are you hitting me up for cash?"

Chauncey didn't answer. Instead, he made his way over to my white contemporary sofa that sat in the middle of the room.

"DON'T YOU SIT ON MY COUCH! That suit doesn't grant you access, you know the drill, go sit at the bar."

Chauncey gave me a look that said, 'fuck you' but

did as he was told.

"My baby bought me this suit and took me to one of those expensive barbershops that puts the hot rag on your face after they trim it. You know, that bullshit you be over paying for when I keep telling you my boy Juan can tighten you up for the low. Anyways, she's trying to open my mind up to a different world and shit, I'm down with the plan." He began to doze off in his thoughts. "As a matter of fact, let me use your phone to call her."

He snatched my cordless phone off its cradle without consent and punched in the numbers that displayed on his government issued food stamp phone which was more than likely currently out of free monthly minutes.

"Vicky, hey, baby, it's me. I was just calling to tell you that I'm done fucking with your fat ass. The pussy is garbage and your head game ain't about shit. Yo' fat, black neck having ass needs to lose my number, bye bitch!"

He put the phone back on its cradle after ending the call and quickly put the woman on his block caller list as I stared at him in awe.

"Did I miss something? A minute ago, she sound like the best thing that could happen to your low life ass and then you pull that. What did I miss?"

"She was until I met Trina. See Vicky is a high school principal, fat, ugly, and always smelling like a fast-food drive-through but Trina, Trina got ass. She has a cute face to go with it and she's a CEO for some big ass watch company. She's making almost four times more a year than the fat bitch and her pussy smells like water. I've been hitting that for a week now and she's damn near in love with me. She asked me to move in and I'm thinking about it since my moms is talking about I need to give her more than just food stamps each month; she wants rent money and gambling money too. Who in the fuck do she think I am, her man? But peep this, I told Trina I was into investments and shit like you and those panties melted away like butter on granny's biscuits when I started talking about ETFs. I may not do what you tell me to do with my money but I listen to all that shit about gold and commodities you be spitting like it's the Bible."

I had to laugh. "You're a fool. How did you meet her?"

"I stayed the night at the fat bitch's house and couldn't sleep. She was snoring like a bear in hibernation so I went through the bitch's purse. I snatched me up a twenty-dollar bill for the pipe I laid and then used her credit card to upgrade my subscription on Black Professionals Meet Dot Love. You know that website all the lonely rich hoes needing some dick get on? I used your bio from your website to complete my profile and them hoes came running. I don't understand how your ass is a 37 years old virgin. Those hoes ate your bio up. I had 20 meet requests in less than five minutes."

"I keep telling you I'm not a virgin."

"Then who did you lose your virginity to then, nigga?" Silence took over the room and Chauncey started back up, "Exactly, you ain't never had a bitch or no pussy. That lotion and hand shit don't count, cuzzo!"

I wasn't feeling being put on the spot and his joke didn't compliment me but what joke ever does? When people joke, take heed to it. It's coming from their perception of you. If you want to know how a person really feels about you, listen to the content of their jokes. It's rare to hear one that doesn't shed light on a flaw. I don't think I've ever heard anyone say, "You're too smart and handsome, nigga." And then bust out laughing hysterically. If they do, you might want to get them checked out for Tourette's.

Chauncey's attack was partially true but it wouldn't pass an accuracy check. No one in my family knew the truth about my virginity but me, God, and my mom's best friend, Vivica. I lost my virginity to her at 16 years old in her basement she had hired me to help clean.

I couldn't blame her for wanting me; I was advanced for my age. Reading all those books had expanded my vocabulary causing me to become a rare commodity in Memphis. Being intelligent, young, black, handsome, with a steady income and had the makings of becoming a successful man of finance in Memphis. It was like watching a unicorn drink rainbow colored water out of a rambling stream flowing peacefully through the hood. To top it all off I could dance. Not the average two stepping or a copycat of what I saw on Soul Train but a natural. I was becoming known as one of the best gangster walkers Memphis had ever laid eyes on and being the proud supporter my mother, Charlene was, she had me performing for her friends whenever there was music playing.

Vivica had enjoyed watching me dance for years. She would give me $5.00 when I was done entertaining them and I'd thank her with a peck on her cheek. She was the auntie I wished I had and I was her nephew until my manhood kicked in. Those dry pecks on the cheeks began to do something to her, I could see it in her eyes. It seemed to moisturize the space between her legs as the stubble grew around my face with each kiss. Facial hair wasn't the only thing she noticed that I had grown as she walked in on me stepping out of the shower with no towel in sight. She tried to ignore it but it was like my body found its way into her dreams, day dreams, thoughts, and eventually into her two fingers as she masturbated to the vision of me. I'm not gassing myself up, she told me this out of her mouth and her plan of attack. She knew getting me to her house would be easy but seducing a virgin with both Seventh day Adventist and Jehovah Witness upbringing would be the challenge.

At 36 years old, she didn't look a day over 21. She didn't have kids to stress her nor an unhappy marriage to age her. She was a social worker for the state and cut thick like a fine grade of steak. Vivica had the kind of breasts that couldn't be hidden behind a sweater and although she dressed business professionally seven days a week she always had plummer's crack showing when she sat. Her butt was too heavy for the restraints of the material holding it.

I copped a look or two from time to time but that's all it was. I thought she was fine but at 16, the age 36 marked her as old and it didn't matter what she looked like, she was Auntie V. When I arrived at her door she had her stage set perfectly making sure to let me in wearing nothing but a bra and cutoff shorts. She wanted to see if she could create a lustful reaction from me and she did. I looked at her breasts as if I needed to suck on them to survive twice before turning my head out of respect while she retrieved her v-cut t-shirt off the couch. As we worked on the basement to the sounds of slow jams she made sure to do one too many unnecessary bends and squats to keep my attention on her assets.

"This is my jam!" she squealed as Freddie Jackson's voice blared through the speakers. "Come dance with me, Dwayne. Let me show you how us grown folks do it," she concluded with an innocent laugh and I obliged.

"You got to loosen up, baby. Here, let me help you out," she said grabbing my left arm then putting it around her waist. She placed my right hand on her butt. "You have to pretend that I'm one of those high school girls you have your eyes on. You don't have to be scared, you can rub it."

"But, Auntie V…"

"Hush, I'm not your auntie right now and I'm giving you permission to practice on me. How will you know what to do when the time comes without a little practice?" she whispered the words into my ear like she was serving lyrical sex.

TOXIN

My dick began to rise as I gripped her meat and in that same moment my grandmother's words about lust and marriage ran through my thoughts but they were instantly mowed down as Vivica's tongue made its way into my mouth. I thought, *I have to be dreaming*. It felt real but there was no way it could be so I decided to enjoy my first kiss even if it was fictional.

We stayed tongue tied until the song ended and when Toni, Tony, Tone's voices replaced the previous song, she fell to her knees and quickly unbuckled my pants.

"Can I?" she asked.

"Can you what?" I asked puzzled.

"Can I suck on all of this dick you have?"

"If...if you want to, I guess..." I said shrugging my shoulders.

Vivica proved she wanted to as she took me deep into her throat and nestled her lips in my fuzzy pubic hairs. She didn't bob her head as she used her tongue and oral muscles to give me pleasure. She swallowed my first shot of baby fluids without complaining about the urine I released thinking I was still nutting.

"Now, it's your turn to please me. I don't want your tongue, ram me with your dick," she purred her words to force them to sound sexy and less pedophilic.

I looked at my deflated meat wondering what I could do with it in its current soft state but when she took her shorts off and bent over to allow her lower lips to smile at me, my meat stood back up like she had a magnet between her legs.

"Do you have a condom?"

The words felt funny coming out of my mouth but sex education and the commercials on the AIDS/HIV epidemic forced me to ask the question. I had seen the announcements about Easy-E and Magic Johnson, and I knew it was real.

"We don't need one, baby. I keep her clean and healthier than a dog's mouth."

The analogy didn't make sense to me and almost scared me out of her house but the magnet forced me to point my dick in the direction of the mouth of her south and I penetrated her raw. I didn't stroke nor move as the feeling brought mist to my eyes. I was in heaven until she began throwing it back. At the fifth slap of her butt smacking at my thighs I released again. This time my release was much more powerful and longer. The freeing of the buildup caused me to curl over her back like a dog out of breath.

"Did you like it?"

"Hell yeah!" I said cupping my hands over my mouth. It was the first time I had cursed and the first moment I realized I knew how.

"You don't have to apologize for letting it slip out of your mouth..." Vivica started but I quickly interrupted.

16

"I wasn't going to apologize. I was going to ask my mom if it was okay to sleep over here so I can help you..." I grabbed her by the jaw softly, forced her to face me, and scooted closer. I wasn't really allowed to watch TV but I had a hunch of where my smoothness might have come from, my estranged biological father. "... and I need you to help me with something too."

She blew a laugh through her nostrils, "What can I possibly help you with?"

"Investing, I'm not 18 yet but you can do it for me and I can make us both money." I reached her harden nipple and gave it a twist. My smoothness was on a roll.

"I'm listening, keep going," she purred.

The more we had sex, the bigger the returns we got. At 16 I took her five hundred dollars and turned it into twenty-eight hundred in hours. She called me over the next night and remained fully dressed.

"Look, I put my life savings in the account. That's $72,000 plus what is already in there. If you can turn it into $120,000 I can save my mother's house and move back home to Georgia. I know we've been having fun but..."

"How's your credit?"

"Excuse me?" she was holding the pockets on each side of her sweater like she was sixty.

"I can do it and possibly double it if I can margin call it but you'll have to set up a brokerage account which requires good credit."

"I have a few small things on there but nothing major. But you don't have a lot of time, I need it done within a year to save it."

It felt good when she called me crying six months later.

"$142,000!" she screamed in a mixture of joy filled tears. After squaring up the money, which I wasn't really okay with, and how could I be knowing we could have made a lot more? I pecked Auntie V good bye for the last time.

"This man ready to lie on his dick," Chauncey broke out laughing and then asked, "Who you fucked, cuzzo?"

"Man…if I told you, you wouldn't believe me so I'll save us both the time."

Chauncey crossed his arms in front of his chest.

"Auntie did tell me you were living with a bitch a few years back. I bet you didn't even stick a finger in the pussy, though."

His laugh took me back to waters I didn't want to travel. I'd been in relationships after Vivica, five of them. My first was at 18 with a Hispanic chick named Esme, pronounced, Es-May. I met her at the coffee shop. She was there studying for a midterm and our friendship took off like a rocket. She was smart, although I prefer intelligent.

Smart is textbook; read it, learn it, and remember it, but intelligence is biblical and a step away from wise. It's still textbook but with added insight and the desire to learn more about it. Now that's sexy to me. Yes, Esme was smart but she was also oh so dumb, in my eyes. She stressed over good grades, worried about making tuition payments, and getting her education was her life. That would be a plus for most men but to me, her time spent educating herself only to work for someone else didn't make sense. Even if she made the big bucks at a company she would only receive a small percentage of their gross profit, making her a nicely paid slave. After letting her suck on me a few times as we drove around the city I called it quits without ever getting the opportunity to rip open a condom on her sexy Latin ass. My relationship with her was unknown to those around me thanks to the language barrier, she didn't speak my type of English.

The next fly by night relationship was at 23 with Kim. She was a black chick with an aggressive attitude but her go-getter personality had my nose wide open. I met her at the Memphis small business expo that I spoke at regarding the financial achievements I'd made as a college student. She was there selling her homemade line of cosmetics and her marketing strategies peeked my interest. After agreeing to meet for small talk over lunch I fell for her entrepreneurship when she disclosed that the cosmetics were only one of her business ventures. Almost instantly I wanted her to be my woman and she solidified the yearning to court with her when she gave me a sample of how wet both of her mouths could get, but in the 36 days the opportunity to cuff her never presented itself. We both were too goal focused to make time for a real relationship. Even when I stayed the night at her house our time was spent working on our individual dreams. The hustle and bustle of our success separated us to the point where we didn't have time to pick up the phone to say hi anymore. Now she's the owner of the biggest African American line of makeup on the market and when I see her booth in Macy's I smile, forcing me to label the time we shared together as a damn good dream.

At 25 I met Samantha and quickly dived into the title of being her man. I knew better than to jump into an emotional tie before getting to know her but I was lust driven. She cowboy rode her way into my heart the first time she mounted my lap and sucked the soul out of me, which made her become my number one priority. I gave up investing just to clock in as assistant manager at the burger spot she worked at so I could hit it on our lunch breaks. I was secretly fighting depression over not being able to spend my days trading but whenever she touched me, I got lost in her toxins and all I could think about was being inside of her. Working with her became the antidote to cure me of her. I wasn't there a week and was still in training when I found out she had spread her toxins to all the male employees I was about to manage. I tried to chop it up to it being her past and I was the right man to come along and change her, but a month later I found out a few of the loyal male customers had gotten a taste of her happy toxins with their meals too. I tried to come up with an excuse for her on that one but when I picked up my check on my day off and saw her blowing the owner of the franchise in the back of the building, it was a wrap. At first, I couldn't understand why my dick kept craving the trap in between her thighs but I eventually realized she chased cheese, baby girl was a fast food rat. I didn't waste my time telling her it was over and the saddest part about it was that she never picked up a phone to ask why she hadn't heard from me. I guess I was only one of the millions she served.

Going through that with her made me implement a 30, 60, 90, 120-day rule. I give myself a 30-day warm-up period to get to know a woman. That doesn't mean I'm not going to have sex with her during that time if she's willing to, but if she gives it up, I'm going to add it to the profile I build on her. By 60 days in I should be able to determine if she's worthy of a title or not. If you can get under my skin in two months, there's no way I'm planning on dealing with it for the rest of my life, that's crazy. If a woman can make it 90 days without me raising an eyebrow, she's got me. The additional 30 days is to monitor for change. Like I said, titles change people and with the smallest bit of power that comes with title ownership, I needed to see what changes came with it. If her new title went to her head in a negative way I would get a new title. Call me the repo man. I was going to repossess the title I gave.

Implementing this rule is what lead me into almost marrying Cynthia, the CEO of a fortune 500 company I was thinking of investing in, and to this day, we had the longest relationship I've been in. Once I quit the burger spot, I invested my last few paychecks into stocks yielding high dividends. I wanted to ensure a great return on my investment and its steady growth was promising if the Dow

Jones industrial average continued moving to the bull side, the upside. I grabbed the newest books I could find on investing and researched the internet to elevate my knowledge. I could see my growth as I stepped up to the financial learning curve and I didn't need recognition from an outsider that I was getting good at picking stocks to invest in, my brokerage account funds acknowledged it. But the day I met Cynthia and took the time away from watching the market to contribute to the flirting session she had started, I lost everything.

I had done massive research and was sure the stocks I'd selected would be lucrative. I was so certain that I convinced my parents to invest 70% of their life savings to go in with me on it. My parents were against it until I told them I would be investing the two hundred thousand I had in the bank from the success of my endeavors. I transferred every dollar out of the account except for the original $5,000 I had opened it with and my parents' 70% totaled to another $200,000. Sad to say I took the almost half a million dollars and like the game of roulette, I placed it all on black. Black being the fail-proof, always needed, real estate market. As I chatted with Cynthia at 8:30am central time, here in Memphis those on the floor at 9:30am Eastern time at The New York Stock Exchange were seconds away from hanging themselves with the ties that encircled and hung from their necks. On September 29th, 2008, the stock market lost 1.2 trillion dollars and while I thought meeting her had to be a gift from God, the ball stopped spinning around the roulette wheel and like the magnets they use in Las Vegas, the ball abruptly landed on red and my life changed.

Meeting Cynthia was the only roadblock that stopped me from climbing up the Tennessee/ Arkansas bridge and jumping into the 5 o'clock traffic to ensure death met me there. It was like God had given her to me at the right second and she never left my side. From the moment I checked Bloomberg on my phone and got the bad news, she made me her priority which had to be heaven sent. I couldn't believe that our first time meeting was only an hour before that.

Once she got me back to my apartment in Raleigh, calmed me down with softly spoken questions, yet was firm about forcing me to answer them, she came up with my next moves for me.

With only $5,000 to my name, no job lined up as a backup, and knowing almost for certain I was about to be disowned by my parents for losing their money it was nice to have a stranger hold me down. She moved me in and financially covered all my day to day needs. Cynthia threw out all the jeans, khakis, and t-shirts I owned and replaced them with bags of clothing from Brooks Brothers, Jos A. Banks, and Banana Republic. If it wasn't classy or so original that it deemed positive attention Cynthia didn't allow it in her presence. Before I could give her the title in 90 days she had sent me to the dentist for work, paid for my eye exam and designer frames, and I had a consultation with a body builder on gaining weight and building muscle which was manifested by her wants for me. In 90 days, she earned the right to have the title wife, but I had learned 60 days prior that she was still legally married to some rich guy on paper. That was a red flag, but it was something that could be fixed. Since she didn't like my response to her nuptials she only covered me in saliva and vowed not to let me penetrate her until her divorce was final which was fine by me.

I was completely satisfied by her head and the techniques her mouth practiced on me but above all, she was more intelligent than anyone I had ever met. She provided the lifestyle I yearned to have and it didn't cost me a dime...all it took was my freedom. Cynthia was a full-time control freak and although she could give me the money I needed to bounce back she'd rather die than to give me financial or any other independence from her. She was very strategic in her moves and I was vulnerable so by the time I realized I was her boy toy, it was way too late.

On September 29th, I really met the devil wearing a D-cup bra full of silicone under an Armani cocaine-white suit but I didn't recognize the demon for what she was until 92 days in. On December 31st, 2008, she introduced me to the real her as we left her job's New Year's Eve party that she invited both me and her husband to as her dates.

"That was foul!" I yelled when we got out of her Benz G-wagon at her house.

"Stop crying about it, Dwayne. I invited my husband, so fucking what! Cry when I decide to leave the party with him instead of you..."

"No, I'm going to leave you alone before that ever

happens. I'm about to grab my stuff and leave. Thanks for letting me stay at your place but it's time for me to move on."

"It's time for you to move on?" she mimicked me and then bellowed a laugh that was on the dark side. The look on her face and the words that came out of her mouth when she was done laughing was my true introduction to the devil. She said, "If you walk your nothing ass out that door I'll make sure you regret it for the rest of your life!"

"Yeah, is that right? Well if I stay here with you, I'll regret it too so I'm gone!"

With my parents still upset with me and nowhere else to go I took off walking with only the clothes on my back. I walked ten blocks away from her place before the police cars came flying past me. It was strange to see them in the upscale neighborhood but it was New Year's Eve so their visit could be looked at as somewhat warranted until they made U-turns and forced me to the ground at gun point. I was arrested for domestic assault and trespassing in a fucking three-piece suit. My mugshot looked like Saks 5th Avenue sent me there on a photo shoot. She made me out to be a stalker she couldn't get rid of and even her husband backed her story up with his own lies about confrontations with me over his wife. Finding out her husband was riding for her in her time of need made me call my mama but they didn't have access to receive collect calls. I was shocked that my mother knew to come and visit me.

"Dwayne, I don't know anything about what happened besides what that girl called my house saying you did. You haven't picked up a phone since you lost our life savings as if we didn't forgive you and we did. You haven't dialed my number in months and now you have some girl that I've never heard of calling my house saying she's your fiancée and you're in jail. I know we raised you right but no matter what we did to ensure a fruitful future for you, you went the opposite way. I've been praying for you all your life and I know God is listening but if you don't follow and live by his words my prayers won't protect you. Look at where turning a cold ear to the Lord has gotten you!"

"Mama, I didn't do whatever she is saying that I..." My mother silenced me by holding up her index finger like she needed to excuse herself in church.

"I know her truth isn't the truth. I know I raised you not to put your hands on a woman and I know a lie when I hear one but you are now at that woman's mercy. If you play this smart you can get off on this, son. Little miss rich and crazy gave me the money to bail you out but she wants you to come back home to her. The courts granted her a restraining order against you but she wants you there while you wait on the court so she can make you jump through hoops for her in order to keep your freedom." My mother looked around and finally rested her eyes on the jail house ceiling as she shook her head.

"I must be losing my mind to even fix my mouth to say this to you but you need to play by her rules. When you make bail, go home and play puppet for your puppet master until you go to court and get this dropped. I raised you by the Bible but I need you to improvise some of what you read and listen to me really good... Dwayne, I'm talking to you as a woman. Lay that woman down when you walk through that door and satisfy her in the bed like none of this ever happened." I shook my head no and she spoke on it. "Yes, you must and you can, baby, it's in your DNA. I don't talk about him much but your daddy, the biological one, could talk a nun out of her panties while she signed over the church's bank account to him. I prayed you didn't inherit his smoothness but you did and this is the only time I'm going to encourage you to use it. Mind fuck her until you own your freedom, Dwayne. If you weren't in love with her before all of this, you better pretend jail made you realize you were!"

She placed the phone back on the wall, prayed for me through the glass, and left as fast as she came. I did exactly what she told me to do when I made bail. I evolved from her boy toy to her lap dog and on to her slave. My court date was two weeks away which wasn't long to put up the act for but the court date was reset and I soon learned I was on a journey that would take 9 months to complete.

I kept a smile on my face as I did whatever she asked of me which now included dicking her down at her demand. I went for the gusto when I laid pipe the first time and now she craved it all the time. I couldn't judge if I liked what she had between her legs or not. I hated her which meant she was dead to me. I know it's a strong word but I'd never profess love for the devil. She lived like she hadn't lied on me and even told me I wouldn't be going through none of this if I knew how to keep my hands to myself. For a half of second, I had to replay the night in my head to make sure I didn't hit her. She believed her lies and every night when she went to sleep I hoped to be the only one to wake up in the house the next morning.

I had made it two months pretending to be in love and my mother's plan would have worked if I wouldn't have snuck on the house phone I wasn't allowed to use to check on her.

"I took your mother to the hospital yesterday and they kept her…the cancer is back, son." I hung up the phone and dressed hurriedly, I didn't need to hear another one of my father's words.

"Where do you think you're going?" Cynthia asked walking in the door with take-out for the both of us.

"To see my mom. I called my dad and he said she isn't doing well, the cancer is back."

"You're not going anywhere tonight! I brought take out and grabbed some movies. You can deal with her tomorrow, the cancer ain't going nowhere."

She laughed and I looked her square in her eyes and said, "Bitch, you're stupid." And closed the living room door behind me as I left her house for good.

The urge to choke her off her feet was too grand to stay and check her for disrespecting my first lady. And like clockwork, I was arrested before I could reach the hospital. This time I was charged with violating the restraining order, aggravated assault, and property destruction since she took the time to bust out the screen on her television before the police arrived. Good had gone bad and bad became worst. I spent 30 days in jail researching, exercising, and writing every hedge fund manager that had a listed mailing address, which wasn't a lot of them. The four arrests that followed my release from her lying to the police claiming I violated the restraining order she had on me was more than enough time for me to realize I was done with relationships. Insanity is the repetition of a failed behavior in hope of a different outcome. Unlike the men I've read about in the Bible, I refused to allow insanity or my downfall to occur from being weak over a woman, again.

Quick casual sexual encounters were the only way I interacted with women until loneliness kicked in at 33. I had gotten back on my feet and they were now deeply rooted in finance. I learned from all of my previous investing mistakes from a seven-page letter postmarked from China. It was from one of the hedge fund managers I had written while I was in jail and now I had all of the finer things in life but no one to share them with. I became a master at stroking my meat and the process only took four minutes from start to finish. I felt pathetic. I got a gym membership to burn off some of the ill feelings I had about myself and messed around and met Renee. She was a 27-year-old customer service representative with the body of a dark chocolate African goddess. She wasn't all that smart and her way of dress read discount racks but her smile was contagious and she had made it 180 days without one incident.

It was time for me to invest in making her what I wanted to be. A helpful trick I learned from the devil, Cynthia. Thanks to modern technology you can make a person look however you want them to look on the outside. All you had to do nowadays was hunt for the right stuff on the inside. I took her to the best plastic surgeon in Memphis and changed her right B-cup and crooked left C-cup into identical double D twins. I had the gap in her teeth filled, her nappy short naturally curly hair changed into 22 inches of straight weave, changed her wardrobe, and made trips to get her hair, nails, eyebrows, and lashes done a weekly reoccurring event.

I had turned my quarter into a silver dollar and planned a trip to Mexico. For the first time, I would get to play with the investment I put on her chest. I was so excited by the thought of running my meat in between her cleavage as she sucked away that I passed my exit on the interstate and had to merge on a connecting interstate to turn around. I exited at the first available exit and made the U-turn to get back on the on-ramp, but Renee's pink Cadillac CTS I had bought her caught my attention. Pulling up next to it I couldn't get a full view of what was going on behind the tint but I'd have to be blind not to be able to tell she was riding some dread-headed guy's lap on the passenger side. I blew the horn and they scattered like I was Donald Trump and the INS at Texas' lower border.

"So, this is how you do me?" I asked once she had climbed off his lap and got out of the car. I prepared for a weak apology or at the very least an explanation but instead, I got, "Fuck you, robot ass nigga. I'm tired of all that logic, step by step, 90-day rule bullshit. You ain't shit but a trick to me!"

I wanted to say something in my defense but instead, I nodded my head in peace, drove off, and went to my condo to pack her things for the Salvation Army. How I wished I could have repossessed those titties I bought her!

In truth, Chauncey was wrong about me being a virgin and dead wrong if he thought it was hard for me to get some.

"Whatever, I'm stingy with my Johnson. I'm not trying to end up with four bad ass kids by four crazy chicks who like knives like you, cuzzo. While you were stealing that girl's money you should have been stealing enough for you to invest in some trust funds for them kids or buy a farm to secure them a future," I started up and Chauncey quickly stopped me.

"Don't speak on my seeds and you can save that old Mc Donald had a farm conspiracy theory you always prophesying on. Black men freed themselves from slave work on farms. If that's the only way to live in the future, I'll be dead. I'm not doing it!"

"You need to lose that half researched negro-spiritual mentality you have and learn that there's no security in the American dollar. Do you not know who was just elected as our president? I've been telling you about Donald Trump for years. I told you that I read all of his books on real estate and how infatuated he is with gold. He wrote a book with Robert T. Kiyosaki about real estate and money but I'm talking about the real money, gold. That paper stuff you're hustling for isn't the real money, that's a form of fiat currency…remember what the lady told you to do with the Zimbabwe money right?" Chauncey nodded in agreement so I continued, "President or should I say y'alls president since I'm governed by God doesn't even accept paper as money, he has to be paid in gold on leases for the Trump towers. If you're not intelligent enough to move like your country's leaders you'll wish you did when the stock market crashes, the dollar will lose its value, and it won't even be worth the tree it was printed on. I'll be telling you to wipe your ass with that next!"

"Ok, Dwayne, after you lend me the bread I asked you for I'll plant some weed seeds or something to keep me alive when the weed heads let the markets crash." He laughed and walked away from the bar to my guest bedroom and sat at the computer desk.

I followed him and said, "Well once you make your profit from selling it in the street bring me your money so I can help you invest in the marijuana industry. I wasn't going to tell you this, but weed is a commodity too. I'm only telling you knowing that it's probably the only way I can get you to invest."

"Hell yeah, I'll invest in weed, it's my life and I'll die for this shit. It's connected to God too. Go ahead and let me borrow a thousand dollars instead. I need five for my pockets and five for the stock market."

"I'm not giving you shit but a handful of knowledge I sell for free, you're welcome," I said laughing and he joined in turning the power on my MacBook.

"Look, cuzzo, but let's be real. You are the man in Memphis. You got bread, you're smart as fuck, and you look like me which is a triple plus. I would be a sorry excuse for a cousin if I don't find something thick, cute, wet, and warm for you to strap that Trojan on for. I'm not comfortable with you lying on your dick, and your stock in pussy is a reflection on me, so I'm getting yo' ass some pussy tonight."

Chauncey logged onto his account on Black Professionals Meet Dot Love with the look of an important mission on his face and then said, "Pull up a chair, cuzzo, time to teach you your first lesson in getting pussy off the internet, let's call it World Wide Pussy 101." He laughed and I took a seat deciding to play his game.

Nivea

Sitting in the hospital's waiting room reminded me of what I hated most about being born with a pussy. You'd think it would be my irregular monthly periods that seemed to pop up minutes before I was scheduled to get some dick or the bloating that comes with it when I'm trying to find the perfect tight pair of jeans in my closet to flaunt my ass in without ending up with a yeast infection or my camel toe saying hi to the world. I can deal with both of those. What I can't keep dealing with is these other pussy owners who lose their minds over a hard dick.

I'm not talking about the ones who've lucked up and married the right man. If he's treating you like his queen, crowned you the title with a ring, and has the dick to top life's perfect sundae like a cherry, you're winning. You have every right to be a little 51/50 over him but those other chicks who fall short of real love into that gray area of uncertainty of not knowing if they are the main chick or side piece. Those women who have to play code cracker to decrypt the truth in their man's words, or those dating Milton Bradley, a boy in grown man's clothing who loves playing games, those heffas got to get the fuck from around me.

There isn't anything wrong with being excited about having someone special in your life. I applaud those who pair up to make it work but when the perfume can no longer cover the scent of shit they've gotten themselves into, I'm flushing the toilet before they can offer me a

35

whiff.

I was going through my own shit and my misery was too stingy to share me with company. If I wasn't tired of checking my phone for any form of contact from Evol's nothing ass, I'd have my butt in bed watching movies that would make me cry instead of playing the supportive friend role for Miya.

"Visitors for Ms. Jackson." The CNA called it out and I stood to my feet. As he approached, something about him reminded me of Peter Pan, the black, less masculine version. "She said you could come back and visit her now."

I followed his lead and even mirrored the switch in his walk. I wasn't hurtfully mocking the blue-black king who looked like he'd prefer the title queen walking before me. He actually looked good in the amber colored contacts and extra popping lip gloss. In all honesty, I was taking lessons and tightening up on my femininity at the same time. If my grandmother would have seen me copying him she would have said, "You know we're living in the last days when it takes a man to teach a woman how to be a woman." I'd agree with her but if mirroring him helped my future husband to find me faster, then so be it.

"Wasn't y'all just here for the same thing not too long ago? Both of y'all look familiar and I don't forget pretty faces."

I had to stop myself from laughing at his attempt to hide his sexuality through an empty flirt. He was a dog lover like me, he knew he didn't want to pet this cat.

"Yes, we were here two months ago and two months before that." I rolled my eyes disgusted at all the hours I calculated being wasted with Miya at the hospital that I'd never get back.

"So, what are the doctors saying? If her menstruation is that heavy, why doesn't she elect to have a hysterectomy and save herself the trouble?"

My eyebrow raised and I shrugged but I didn't respond my disdain verbally. I'd known Miya for four years so her lies and the levels she went with them, no longer shocked me. I'd learned over time how to brace myself for her next nose growing tale and when I walked into her room, Pinocchio was ready for her wooden microphone.

"Did you get in touch with Man-Man and tell him what happened to me?" Miya managed to ask through forced sniffles and spit made tears.

"Bitch, you're not crying, you're dehydrated. Your spit tears need some water. They look like dried up patches of foam underneath your eyes. You can save the show you're putting on for Man-Man when he gets here...that's if he comes. I called and texted and he didn't respond to either."

"That's okay, my mama said he told her he was on his way here and for your information, tramp, I was crying. You don't understand what I'm going through, anyway, you've never miscarried before!"

I bit my tongue and decided to be a friend and not

put her period miscarriages on blast. Did she really think I didn't notice that she always miscarried at the same time of the month? I wanted to slap the stupid out of her and yell, 'BITCH I BLEED ONCE A MONTH TOO!' but a strange part of me knew the medical condition she was going through. I once was diagnosed with the, "He ain't shit but got good dick," disease too.

I caught the illness from Evol, a neighborhood scumbag, and drug retailer. With a name that spelled love backward, I should have known he wasn't going to amount to shit and that love would be the last emotion he'd know how to display. He had his hands in a little bit of everything bad in Harlem and his dick in a little bit of every chick in the city too. Of course, that information wasn't made available to me until after I had been diagnosed with the disease and even then, the infection had me doubting that it could be true.

I had to give it to Evol, he kept his game tight and he had me fooled into thinking that he was the only person on this Earth that understood me. From the late nights to the early mornings I spent consumed in the research of penny stocks, to the vast upgrades of speed I had placed on my internet service whenever new options became available. He acted as if he understood that every move I made was calculated and a part of my plan. I disclosed the plan that I made when I was in college to him and he'd gas me up like a lawnmower in spring time pretending to understand it. You see, I knew way back then that a college education wasn't necessary for the career pool I was jumping into but I wasn't foolish enough not to get one.

The way I saw it, if I got into Yale, graduated in the top 5% of my class, and took the expensive classes at New York Institute of Finance for every professional certificate they offered, the big fishes in the world of finance would have to see that I had the potential to be one of the best straight out of the gate. The odds were already against me from the start. I'm black and sad to say but that's strike one being born in America. I was raised by my mother who was a gung-ho welfare recipient who thought the more information she shared with the census bureau the more government assistance she'd received. And having no family with a background in finance was strike three. Truthfully, the only investments I'd seen my mother make was lottery tickets and turnaround trips to Las Vegas with the church which never sat right with me after reading what the Bible said about gambling. It doesn't say that gambling is a sin but look at all the sins that can be created from and linger around it.

I proudly came from nothing so the world should have known not only would I set out to beat the odds and erase the strikes, I'd conquer everything my mind allowed mc to envision.

Evol knew this about me and self-appointed himself a role in helping me reach my goals. He had me sprung off the massacres he placed on me in bed and all the time I was enjoying him; I knew without a doubt that he wasn't shit. He didn't qualify to be nothing more than a biologically functioning piece of shit and for me to try to acknowledge him as the streaks left in the floor of the toilet bowl after a muddy use would have been giving him too much honor.

At our first encounter, his words came off real smooth like verbal satin-silk with the looks to match. We met as I was exiting and he was entering the bodega on 125th street. Besides noticing the perfection of his curves on his chest and upper abdomen as I held my hand out to prevent our collision, I noticed the perfection of his dreads. The twigs of matted hair had been freshly twisted in boxes of perfectly even squares and tied back in a manly ponytail. He was wearing Timbs, untied, his 501 jeans were the perfect amount of saggy, and his T-shirt was so bright that it caused the Jesus piece around his neck to look like a cross of welded ice cubes. Evol was a few shades darker than me but he couldn't be considered dark. The pumpkin orange glow in his face dubbed him bronze and he was light enough to still see the rosiness of his cheeks when he smiled. His color reminded me of warmed honey seconds before it burned. Wild like the hairs of a wet dog after attempting to shake himself dry, his eyebrows sat like broken dashes on his oblong face. Peach fuzz trimmed his thick lips from the regrowth of hair from yesterday's shave and arched like a rainbow over his mouth that held a slight over bite. The longer I stood in the door admiring his look the more he began to look like Future from the movie *8 Mile* if his dreads were real. As a matter of fact, he was the non-fictional visual version of the character Dre from this book *Kismet* by Raynesha Pittman I read. Except Evol wasn't southern and I could tell by the confidence in his stance he wasn't weak over the opposite sex like the character in that book.

Instantly, I bit down on my bottom lip and my teeth

slowly scraped it until it was released. It was an uncontrollable habit of mine that happens when I had to have something and when the emptiness of his eyes met the growing lust in mine, I knew I had to have him.

"Excuse me."

"No, excuse me, beautiful."

That was all that we said as I removed my hand from his body and walked out the door. I continued my stroll up the block pretending that I didn't see him walk out behind me. He was following me and there was only a small distance of space between us. He could have said whatever he wanted to me without yelling and I would have heard him but he let me get all the way to the light on Lexington Avenue before he said a word.

"I had to make sure you didn't have a man out here sitting in the cut waiting on you, beautiful. So, you mean to tell me that he lets your sexy self roam these Harlem streets without him?" he asked using his hand to brush my hair clear of my face.

I knew he was spitting game but like I said, I had to have him.

"Who's he? You must be speaking in third-person."

"Damn, I like that. You already know it's daddy's," he said lustfully checking me out from head to toe. "So, when can daddy and mommy play house?"

"Oh, mommy doesn't play house, I build homes."

Thirty minutes later daddy was ripping open a condom and I, mommy, was snatching that white t-shirt off him. Three hours later we were in my kitchen laughing as I cooked for him wearing nothing but his t-shirt. Three minutes after our food digested we were back in bed and his t-shirt draped over my skin made me the white chocolate he ate for dessert.

That round of applause, take a bow shit Rihanna sang about described my sentiments towards him perfectly. On day three of us being locked away in our love nest, he earned a teary-eyed, standing ovation, for the award-winning line of bullshit he presented me.

"Look, I have to be real with you." He pulled me closer into his chest before continuing, "I'm about to get married in a week but I want you in my life too. Yo, I know it sounds crazy and the shit feels crazy coming out of my mouth but I can't act like meeting you was just a fun time. Keep whatever you have going on with the next hard head, just say you're mine too. I ain't worried about the next man as long as you know who you really belong to."

I was awed but loved the lies he mixed in honesty and I might have agreed with him but I didn't have anybody on the side. See, Mama had taught me to wear a slip so you'd never know what I hid under my skirt. Before meeting Evol I didn't allow overnight stays nor were men given my address. I got fucked in hotels, motels, back seats, and if the coast was clear bent over outside somewhere. I didn't ask for names and telephone numbers and I never offered mine unless I made up new information for myself.

I moved to New York to be a model, that was the lie that I told, and I was going to stick to it until I no longer needed it. I refused to date until my company went public and I decided not to lead anyone on during the process. Call me a ho if you like, I called myself worse when I wrote into my plan.

I heard Evol out before I put him out of my apartment and I tried to put him out of my thoughts but how could I when I aimed to be at the same bodega I met him at, at the same time of day I met him, secretly hoping to have the pleasure of meeting him again.

For three months straight, I went to that bodega at eleven o'clock hoping to see him. I knew his toxins were in my respiratory system when I realized every second spent with him made me want to scrap my plan. I didn't let the snow stop me from getting to that bodega either and I still hadn't adjusted to a Northeast winter from a Southern California one. I had only lived in New York two years yet that was the first winter I spent there. I was smarter than a bird and knew to fly south or southwest during those months but my cat perched in my panties had me dick dumb. My nose was frozen yet running and my pussy lips felt like twin pop popsicles stuck together as I pranced back and forth to the store. It was in that moment I realized I had fucked around and caught the disease.

On the 3rd day of the month, at the 3rd minute following the striking of eleven o'clock, Evol walked in and looked at me as if he'd missed me. Apart of me expected that fairy tale reunion where he would run over to me, scoop me off my feet, kiss me deeply, and then carry me away. I could see that he had a lot he wanted to say to me, screaming at me through his eyes, and I believed he would have said it all and a lot more if his pregnant wife wouldn't have waddled into the bodega behind him.

I couldn't knock her for wanting to shadow her king, if he were mine, I'd do the same. I was sure it was her by the timing and even if I weren't, the necklace she rocked with his name in the same ice as his Jesus piece, confirmed it. She was cute, even more so since she was with child but what hurt most was when she grabbed his hand and he pulled her in for a hug, that they looked good together. I left the store with my head high and went home to trade.

Living on 127th in Harlem wasn't my ideal place to lay my head but it was a part of the plan and saving the extra money by living in the hood made it flow easier. I had lived in the hood in Los Angeles which was similar to the ones in the big apple, yet very different at the same time. In L.A, the streets of the hood were filled with gangs but in N.Y.C, the streets were filled with hustlers more than anything else. It was like everyone had a hustle or two, even those who made beds out of cardboard boxes in public streets had a hustle about them. The atmosphere alone was motivational to me, I absorbed the energy like a sponge.

Normally, I listened to jazz as I traded or neo soul but there was something about crushed feelings that will allow an artist to zone in. I was able to trade to the sounds of my breathing and heartbeat alone. I was wired in and if he wouldn't have laid on my doorbell I wouldn't have heard him.

"Did you bring your wife with you?" I asked and rolled my eyes so hard I'm lucky they didn't get stuck.

"Shut up!"

"Why should I? You fuck me for three days, make me think we have something special, and then drop the bomb that…"

He didn't let me put the truth in the air. It would have made him look bad so instead, he grabbed me by my neck and kissed me until I was in a full ballerina stance. I didn't fight him off and as his lips kissed mine like he had hungered for them I thought, *fuck his wife!* We both started moving each other in the direction of my room which reminded me I was trading.

"I can't right now; I'm trading."

"I'm not stopping you from getting your bread, pretty lady, keep trading. Here, let me help you out, baby."

He rearranged the pillows on my bed until they sat against the headboard enticing me to sit in a seated position on them. When I did, he laid my body pillow across my lap like a high school desk, sat my MacBook on it, and gaped my legs open. I went back to trading while he sloppily tongue kissed my pearl and lips.

We kept this up for a nice length of time, me the side bitch of a married man but it never felt right and he never felt like mine. So, in the third year of me playing the in love side bitch, I called it quits and came straight to the hospital to watch Miya's latest blockbuster performance in part 5 of, "Miscarriage Periods." It wouldn't be right to call her bluff in her current mental state nor in mine.

The door opened, the doctor came in, and before he could close it, Man-Man's sorry ass came walking in. He mugged me like he made it his business to do every time he saw me and that day he put more stank on it than usual.

"We have your test results, is it okay to share them with your visitors in the room?"

Miya yelled, "NO!" and Man-Man and I finally saw eye to eye saying our yes' in perfect harmony. The doctor looked at us individually and doubled back on Man-Man.

"Sir, the maternity ward is upstairs but I thought your lady and baby were released this morning? Is there something I can help you with?"

I cut my eyes at Miya not shocked at all by the doctor's words but her Hollywood actress butt looked like an in-love cartoon cat. While she sat there with her Tom and Jerry look the doctor had poured the tea on her so-called Man-Man, but the illness made her miss it.

"Nah, I'm good. I...I came up here to see what's up with this baby." I could smell a hit of weed with each word he said. It made me remember that two hours ago, I had cut up my side bitch membership for life. I now wanted a blunt and a bottle of organic wine to put me on my back.

"With this baby?" the doctor asked him and his

words peaked my interest. We had finally reached the plot twist in the movie, where's a bucket of white cheddar popcorn when you need one?

"Yeah, nigga, my baby that's in her stomach!" The muscles in Man-Man's face tightened as he spoke and the doctor gave him a puzzled look. The word EXPOSE kept crossing my mind but to my surprise, Miya's dumb ass was smarter than that.

"Can y'all just please get out so the doctor can tell me what's going on? You know I'm going to tell y'all." Her face held so much devastation properly mixed with hurt and pain that you believed it was the real reason she requested privacy. I had seen and heard enough, she wouldn't have to ask me twice. What did irritate me was that Man-Man followed me out. I wanted to put my hand in his chest like I was a sexy upgraded version of the Oracle from *The Matrix* or *The Never-Ending Story* and say, "Dumb ass, stay in the room and hear the real!" but you can't tell these grown boys pretending to be men anything. That's why they still accept being called 6- letter words that start with the letter N that isn't their names.

"You must have felt like finally being a friend I see." His words were like listening to DMX's voice but he borrowed his laugh from Ja Rule.

"Um...Boy-Boy, Tink-Tink, or whatever your name is, your opinion of me burns like small debris and around my planet. Don't speak to me, peasant!"

"Bougie bitch! I keep telling Miya those moves

you're making on Wall Street don't compare to the ho-ing you do on 125th street. Sucking my nigga Evol's dick like it was a fast-acting asthma inhaler..." He laughed when he saw my eye's buck at his words. "Close your mouth before I put something in it, yeah I know it all. Now you're up here mad at the world since my nigga cut your nut supply off. He didn't want to but he had to start keeping it at home with his wife. But I know you'll bounce back from it like you always do. Ho's don't go without dick long." He made sure we were now face to face. "All that big talking you do about energy, investing money, and popping herbs but none of the shit you're doing to better self, like yo' weak ass be spitting to Miya is taming the ho in you."

"FUCK YOU!"

"That big ass vocabulary and that's the best you can do?"

"Yes, why waste my big ass vocabulary on the nothing of you?"

"From what my boy told me, you keep your mouth too full to use that big ass vocabulary, anyway."

"Fuck you!"

"Damn, Miya said you might try to get me too but I told her I don't do everybody's pussy." He shrugged his shoulders like he was above it. "Yeah, she told me how you've fucked every nigga she's broken up with...on accident." He laughed again and then spoke...again. "It doesn't surprise me that rich freaks like you don't mind playing in other folks' garbage. Look, I'm going to tell you like this, slow them frequent flyer miles down on that pussy and I got some dick for you, and if Miya acts right, I might just let her watch me fuck you."

His eyes rolled up to the ceiling as he considered his words. That's when I took the opportunity to throw blows below the belt so I could go on about my day.

"Congratulations on your new bundle of joy. Miya might have slept on the doctor's words but I didn't and I'm also sorry for your latest loss. But, Boy-Boy, you don't find it strange that we get called to the hospital at the same time of month every miscarriage? Or that Miya never has a follow-up doctor's visit? You'd think the doctors would make her visits mandatory with her having three miscarriages in the last six months." I took a step closer. I wanted to ensure he heard me good. "While you're out here checking on my mileage, Jiffy Lube, you should be in there learning the truth about these emergency room trips; but to each its own. You have your priorities and I have mine. Tell Miya to call me after she gets some rest. Miscarrying can be hard on the body."

"Fuck you, bitch, you still a ho!"

I walked off laughing with my ho-ish ass.

*****

"Nivea, you know that baby the doctor was talking about was really his, right?"

When Miya left the hospital to go home with Man-

Man I knew it wouldn't be for long. He knew the truth about the period miscarriages and she had finally woken up about his first-born son. I gave it to them for trying to keep whatever they had going on flourishing for another two weeks but eventually, she made her way into my guest room.

She was in my house for a month which was three weeks and six days longer than she originally asked to be there. If she wasn't eating up everything while complaining about me not having red meat and pork she was leaving weave glue on the hallway bathroom sink. After making her confess to me about her foolishness while going through the illness I let her stay the night and she hadn't left yet.

"I'm so over Man-Man, I swear. There's a world full of good men. I thought I was going to have to wait until I got my CNA so I could hook up with sexy doctors but I hit the jackpot online. Have you ever been on Black Professionals Meet Dot Love? Girl, all them heavy pocket niggas be on it."

Miya turned the single monitor around like it wasn't attached to a $7,000 system with T1 streaming into it.

"Watch how you're handling my monitor and no, I haven't heard of it. Plus, I don't want a nigga anyways."

"There you go with your philosophy on the difference between niggas and men. I don't care what you say, I've dated both and they both ain't about shit!"

"You saying that proves you don't know the difference between the two. You keep getting with these niggas and calling them men. You're helping men become extinct. One day soon we'll have to read a history book just to hear about one."

"I don't know why I'm handing you the microphone but go ahead. Tell me the difference between a man and a nigga."

"You already know what a nigga is, you've been with plenty of them. It's a man that you know nothing about but I'll spare you the reality trip and hit you with one jewel you can find in the Bible."

"Um, before you get all holier than thou I'm holding my index finger up to be excused from it. I'm going to need you to try and break it down without putting God all up in it. Don't forget I'm about to try and find you some internet dick."

"You're pathetic but you already know that don't you?"

"Yep, pathetic and synthetic baby. Now tell me how to spot a real man without baptizing me first, heffa," she said rubbing her fingers through her matted weave.

"You can't spot them with the eye, you have to get to know them to see into their souls. You win this round, student. I can't think of a way to explain qualities in a real man without those qualities mirroring those of God. Don't get me wrong, there are good men out there that might have never stepped into a church or read the Bible themselves but I think whoever raised them had to have done some heavy praying."

"Yes! It's about damn time I finally won one. Now we can get back to what I was saying, the site has men on it too. I mean, you have to weed them out, like you said. I thought I found one. He seemed cool but lied about being an investment banker or something like that. He lived down south and I had to give it to him, he had his game tight. He said all the right shit and made all the right promises he had no intentions of keeping. If you didn't know shit about investing, he'd easily impress you. He had me mesmerized but thanks to all those unwanted trading lessons from you I asked him something simple about holding a position versus buying in and out of stocks. He started rambling so I asked him about tax laws surrounding trading...crickets. I cut him off quickly!"

It made me smile to hear her repeat the knowledge I had dropped on her. Now if she just utilized it for more than show and tell she'd be onto something.

"Aw shit, I see I got your preaching ass to smile. Why don't you pull your superhero cape off for a second, put away your nerd role, jump on this dating site, and be a woman for a while? I know you're tired of fucking yourself!"

"I get some when I want some and being driven doesn't make me less of a woman."

"Yes, it does. All that independent, don't need a man shit, is man repellent. You're going to fuck around and end up being a lesbian. How tough you act I'm sure that's what you're attracting. I love you and all that good stuff but this thick bitch is off limits."

"You must have lost your mind and didn't realize it. I'd never lay up with a woman not even for a threesome but I'm the only one in this room who can say that so I'm sure you don't understand."

"Now you sound like you're in your feelings. Does baby want to suck a tittie until she feels better? Might as well suck on my nipples since I'll have to teach you how to lick monkey, Miss Independent," she laughed and then said, "And yeah you get some dick every now and then from random dudes whose names you don't remember, Nivea. I'm starting to worry about you."

She had concern in her eyes and I'm the one who fed her the lies that put it there. I couldn't tell her I was creeping with Evol so I couldn't be mad about her nicely calling me a ho. I gave myself that title. What did surprise me was Man-Man hadn't told her I was creeping with his boy. I wondered why he hadn't.

"You don't have to worry about me, I promise. Once my company is exactly where I need it to be I'll start accepting applications from potential kings."

"You do know you don't have to be filthy rich or have broken every record on Wall Street for a king to crown you queen, right? And speaking of wall street whatever happened to that white dude from Bank of America who wanted to give you the dick and his banking account? I liked him."

I knew it was coming but it had been over a year since she had brought Isaac up. Isaac Britton, white, fine, rich, and would have done anything in his power to make me his. He was an equity research associate which was a cross between a corporate finance analyst and a statistician. In other words, money on top of money. His yearly salary starting out was $196,607 but his bonuses easily doubled his yearly compensation.

We met at the New York Institute of Finance while taking the same five-day Capital Markets class and became lunch time buddies. The goal was to try to persuade him to teach me more of what he knew about the future of derivatives but he ended up being best at the art of persuasion as he got me to teach him how to sexually satisfy my needs.

It was funny but being treated like a queen by him made me feel like I was cheating on my married man, Evol, now that Isaac had pulled out all the stops. From trips to expensive cars and the trying of foods I couldn't pronounce, he wanted me to have the world. My company and my growing income didn't mean a thing to him, all that mattered to him was making sure he left me with a bigger smile than I had at his arrival…until.

"Baby, I got you something and it's a little different than the other gifts but I hope you accept it."

He handed me a small box. It was too big to hold a ring but small enough that it just might. I declined without opening it.

"I can't accept. It's been a beautiful two months and I'm enjoying our time together but I have to be honest with you, I have a man."

"Are you referring to Evol Garcia, the unemployed drug dealer you're committing adultery with?" My jaw dropped at his words and he kept going. "Of course, I hired a private investigator, I did it day four of our class together. I was sold and I decided then that you'd be mine. I mean, you have a few other things I'll have to clean up but besides that, I'm sure you're the one."

I could have called him crazy but when you have money like that you'd be crazy not to hire investigators to check out those around you, especially if it's a potential partner. I decided to question the latter of the two.

"What few other things do you feel need to be cleaned up?"

"They're small things, baby, and my gift fixes one of them." He opened the box and inside was a key ring full of keys. "These are the keys to all of the properties I own in New York. You can have whichever place you want as long as you get out of this dump, I don't care."

"This dump?"

"Yes, this dump, baby. I also think it's cute that you set these little goals of being a big fish in finance but let's be real, your kind doesn't get that far in this world and you'd be better off as a wife of an investor than trying to be something that isn't naturally in you. I'm sure you understand what I'm saying to you, right?"

"I do, you're saying that I'm black and…"

"Oh no, black is no longer an issue, a lot of you colored people pass through and do just fine but nothing will ever change the fact that you were born a beautiful woman and meant to be a strong powerful man's wife. Why kill that beauty to end up as some third-rate broker's secretary?"

There were a lot of colorful words thrown from a wordsmith like myself so I couldn't get mad when the sheriffs served me the order of restraint he had placed on me.

"I told you, Miya, a man with money isn't everything and a white boy can still be a nigga too!"

"Well can you call Vanilla Ice up and tell him I'm interested in his nigga-rich ass!"

"Shut your crazy ass up and scoot over. I want to see what this website you're talking about is like. Create my profile but don't tell all my business. Make me an owner of a small flower shop in China Town or something. I don't want anyone to be able to tell who I am."

"Bitch, I got you. Welcome to my world!"

Dwayne

I had the opportunity to get in another five minutes of sleep before the alarm sounded to start my day but that day I didn't need it. For the first time in a long time, I woke up completely happy. It was also the first time in a long time I didn't go to sleep alone.

"Good morning, beautiful."

I tried to put on my sexist rendition of Barry White's voice without killing the mood with the loud smell of warm morning breath. I didn't wait to hear sweet pleasantries back, the way my heart was beating against my chest if I didn't hurry up and get the words out of my mouth, I would have died.

"Baby, I know we've been hanging out for a while now and you know I've never crossed the line when it came to getting you in my bed. I had to make sure you were the one and after waking up feeling like this, I'm positive you're it for me." An uncomfortable silence took over the room and all I could hear was my heart beating like a drum being stroked in my ears before I continued, "I've had my heart stomped on, I've been played, and I've even had my character destroyed but you're different and I trust that you're not out to hurt me. Before I get to the point of all this, I need to confess…"

I held my finger up quickly to prevent interruption before I got the monkey off my back. Now that I had built up the courage to break one of the man code rules, I couldn't let my boo stop me from being honest.

"Please hear me out, baby. Last night my cousin Chauncey came over and I messed up. I won't try to sugar coat it, I'm human and my flesh is weakened by things like pretty women. He showed me page after page of beautiful faces, fat asses, and titties so perfect that I can't lie, I drooled over them. I don't know what I was thinking to consider stepping out on what we have but I knew I had to lay you down, respect you for who you are, and who you aren't, until the sun came up. I decided to confess my wrong doings for breakfast, say something."

It was like I had been put on mute. I could feel my mouth moving, I could hear my voice, but I wasn't getting a response. I scooted over and baby didn't move an inch. I took it as my cue to finish.

"I'm sorry and I'm going to make it right. You've been good to me since the day we hooked back up and I know you love me. I don't have a ring for you right now but um…well…will you grow old with me and be my true source of happiness?"

I was nervous but the loyalty, honesty, and respect I was receiving were one of a kind. Baby was a curly fry in a bag of French-cut ones. I didn't order it but it was definitely a keeper.

"Will you marry me?"

Where you'd think I'd hear an answer the words were replaced by my alarm clock. I could have been hurt by it, but the crooked smile continued to grow on my face and so did the beast who lived in my pants. Like a thief creeping in an open window, I eased to the other side of the bed, hovered for a few seconds, and then kissed the stack of Benjamin Franklins in the center of his big face.

That was a $10,000 kiss and I was glad I decided to get it. I didn't idolize money nor did I have any love for it, but I did respect it. It's a green piece of paper that has the power to make and break lives, damn right I respect it.

I put the money in bed with me when I saw how long it would take for Chauncey to build my profile. I could have knocked out the pages of questions faster than him but he had already used my bio on his account so if everything was going to be fictional I let the self-renowned player do it. I gave him an idea to run just in case I accidentally ran across the real thing. I wouldn't want her to know my true net worth, I'm too diabetic to play sugar daddy.

My new alias is Mr. Raymond Brown of Nashville, Tennessee. Ray, better known as me, is self-employed and has three hard-working employees. I lowered my income drastically and made sure to tell Chauncey to make him a fun people person, the exact opposite of everything that makes me. I confessed lust to my money but last night was the only time I would ever get on the site. As for Ray, that's a different story. He planned to log on as soon as we made it through the day.

I parted with my money at 5am and got in as many miles as I could run until 6. By 6:30 the jets from my shower were shooting all over my body. I lathered my body the best I could with my black soap and only used the rag for my face and my nuts onto the rear, in that order. I wanted to be 100% cotton soft and keep my skin free of anything that could taint it. If it wasn't for the centaur, the half human half horse Sagittarius zodiac symbol tattooed on my left pec my body would be blemish free. I'm not conceited but I do love my body. I have muscle etched into every inch of my 5'8" frame and only 10% of my body could be considered fat. That's my full-sized soup coolers and the all-beef link sausage and meatballs sitting heavy in my drawers.

I didn't restrict myself to a timed schedule but there was a strategy to every move I made and I made sure my execution of it was tight. My hair, the s-curl low with tapered sides brushed down giving me waves instantly that men walked around in stocking caps for at least six months to get. It too is a part of my strategy to always look my best. I took my time getting ready as if when I stepped out onto Memphis' blues and bar-b-que filled streets I was going to bump into the President. You never know but there was no way I'm leaving anything up to chance.

It was blazing outside and I had on the wrong suit for the heat. Thanks to Chauncey flashing his suit on me last night I decided to wear mine to show him how it's supposed to be hung but it was too hot for it. I doubled back and threw on a Fitzgerald fit plaid print suit. It was thinner and it still showed off the business professional I strived to continue to be.

I walked a block to the parking garage and jumped

in the CL 63 AMG for a much needed trip to the car wash before I hit the office. Two right turns, a left, and the longest red light in history, and I was pulling into Zion Venture Capital, my company. My office was 5 blocks from the condo and if I didn't have to make the trip to the car wash I would have walked like I normally did.

The lot was packed as I expected it to be since my office manager hadn't called to say that anyone had called off. I pulled my Benz into my designated parking space and smiled at the cars surrounding me. The Maybach to the right of me belonged to Elliott, my senior investment manager, and a well-thought-out purchase, but the newly purchased Aston Martin on my left was a disappointment to see. It was parked in the junior investment manager of the month's spot and belonged to Edward for the next 26 days as he reigned supreme. It was time to have a talk with the youngster about sound investments.

"Good morning, Mr. Hollingswell. You have four messages I've already placed on your desk, one is from your mother. She said you've given them more than enough money and she'd rather see your face at Sunday dinner then another cashier's check in the mail." Heather stood up from her receptionist's chair and handed me my stack of newspapers. The *New York Times* sat on top, the *Wall Street Journal, Financial Times,* and Monday's edition of *Barron's* were sandwiched in the middle with the *Los Angeles Times* on the bottom.

"You know my mom says that every month but it hasn't stopped her from cashing the check." I laughed and she gave a heart filled smile. "Send Edward to my office in 15 minutes and good morning to you as well, Heather."

I placed seven floor seat tickets to the Memphis Grizzles basketball game for later that night on her desk. She was a huge fan and deserved the bonus.

"Thank you, sir!" Her smile turned to a show all teeth as she scanned the tickets and then screamed, "Oh my God, they are playing the Cavs tonight. The boys love the Cavs!"

I continued walking away without saying 'you're welcome.' She worked hard to earn it and shouldn't have to be thankful for excelling in her role. It wasn't a gift for a job well done, it was payment for it.

My office smelled like a funeral home with all the flowers covering my desk from clients thanking me for doing my job of making them money. I wanted to throw them away every time I received them but just in case the client decided to come thank me in person I kept them and sat the papers next to them. I started reading the messages Heather left on my desk when the sideline header of the Wall Street Journal caught my attention.

BOWEN CAPITAL MANAGEMENT FILES FOR A STOCK OFFERING

The hour glass has been flipped and the sands of time are now running for one of the most awaited debuts of 2017. Bowen Capital Management LLLP, a hedge fund management company founded by Nivea

Bowen, is the first African American and the first 100% female owned and operated company to IPO this year…

"You asked to see me?" Edward asked walking into my office without knocking on the door first.

"I did but what happened to you knocking and waiting for me to tell you to come in?"

He took a seat in front of me like my words held no weight until his eyes met my face. When he saw the stone cold expression locked on my face he stood up, sighed, and walked back out.

"Knock, knock…" he said placing two taps on the door. I didn't respond immediately to pour a little salt in his open ego wound. I finished reading the moves of Bowen Capital Management first with the promise to research the New York based company, folded the paper, and put it away.

"Come in and have a seat. I wanted to talk to you about a few things. First, congratulations on earning the junior investment manager parking spot. That bonus must have been real nice; I see you went to that spot I took you to in Atlanta and copped you an Ashton Martin."

"Yeah, I scored big. I snatched up a couple of suits with that bread too." He stood up and hit me with a GQ magazine pose and then crossed his arms in front of him, while his chin balanced on his index finger. He looked like a picture of Malcolm X except he was missing glasses and sporting a Mohawk.

"Hmm…are you still living in North Memphis with your mom?"

He shook his head, "Nah, not really. I've been staying with this chick I met out in White Haven but I still pay all my mom's bills for her. Do you like my new ride?"

Fishing for answers wasn't my style so I got to the point.

"Yes, I do and I might swap cars with you from time to time but how much did Atlanta Motor Sport and Luxury Rides charge you to drive off with it?"

"It was a steal, I put $40,000 down and pay $2,675.00 a month."

"WHAT? For how long?" I cut him off, it was a habitual reflex from hearing money spent poorly.

"I don't remember off the top of my head but I think like 6 or 7 years. That might not be right…"

My jaw would have dropped if I hadn't prepared for the outcome. I knew Edward was new to money and those who weren't used to having it didn't know to keep it. When I made the decision to take Edward under my wing I knew it would take a lot of work to transform him into the man he had potential to become.

I saw his potential at our first meeting. I was at a financial expo at the University of Memphis with the odds against me. By sight alone, I could tell that 30% of the audience had given me their full attention but the other

70% were ready for me to finish. They were only near the stage to await the CEO of FedEx, who was scheduled to speak next. When the expo came to an end I took a walk around the campus to relive my backpacking days as a student and that's when Edward approached me smelling like a walking marijuana field.

"Aye, how much did you say you made last year off dividends alone?"

I hadn't decided if he was asking as an inquiring investor or if he wanted the information to size me up to rob me. I did a quick visual analysis of him. Young, no more than 21, he was wearing what I assumed were the latest Jordan's to come out with a dingy U of M jogging suit. Besides being higher than Whiz Khalifa leaving Snoop's house his hazel eyes showed more than the red fog from the smoke in them, they held hurt and what looked like stress. I decided to proceed with caution.

"I don't feel comfortable with giving the exact figure but I will say it's been well over six figures for several years. If the world remains dependent on oil to keep running, that number shouldn't decrease." I smiled at the lost facial expression he wore on his face. "Oil, is as important or even more important than water and food. I invest in commodities and with the world dependent on them to fuel its motion, my dividends will increase even if the economy goes into deflation or hyperinflation."

The young man was high but I could tell it was starting to make sense to him. He looked me up down like he wasn't sure if he could trust me and then said, "How can

I get down?" I looked at him and he spoke up before I could shoot him down, "I know you can tell that I'm high and I look like a young bum but I'm an economics major and I know a lot. I've studied the stock market here and around the world. I'm about to try trading for the first time. I read those Robert T, Kiyosaki books and I've saved 10% of my income to invest. I have $2,800 and it's sitting in my bank account building crumbs in interest. I need a nigga like you…My bad, I mean a man with your knowledge to teach me the ins and outs and I'll be on my way. You don't look that old, you black, and you said you're born and raised in the M, you know it's hard out here, big bruh!"

"Wait, let me stop you. I'm not going to give you a chance based on you reciting my life to me and showing a little Memphis love. No, it's not that easy. You need to invest in a nice suit and tighten up your resume. When you're ready to get the hood out of the cracks of your eyes and see the money-making potential we have in Memphis, call my secretary, schedule an interview, and we'll take it from there.

A week later Edward met me at the riverfront dressed to impress. He had shaved the stubble off his face and had a Wall Street approved haircut.

"So, what's up? I got my suit, you've read my resume, so now can I get down with you?"

"You did what I asked of you but that was only to qualify for an interview with me. That doesn't mean…" my attention was stolen when I saw a fool jogging with Apple ear buds in his ear and I'm sure my iPod was in one of his pockets. Chauncey was running my way with a huge smile on his face...in my full workout attire, including the accessories.

"What's up, cuzzo?"

Edward let out an exasperated breath when Chauncey stuck his hand out to slap and dap mine. It didn't go unnoticed by Chauncey.

"Who's this little nigga in his funeral best? You must be hiring for a professional ass wiper, huh, cuzzo? I can look at the smoke stains on his lips and tell he ain't shit!" He laughed at his favorite choice of humor, his own, and then continued. "Where you find this baby boy at, the Orange Mound Boys and Girls Club? Ha! Look at him in his monkey suit, he looks like he receives welfare to work vouchers, don't he, cuzzo? Hey, little bruh, tell your mama I'm trying to buy some food stamps. I got fifty on a dollar, what's up?"

Chauncey pulled a $50 bill out of his pocket and I wondered if it was mine. He held it in front of Edward and waved it at him tauntingly. I know my cousin, he wanted Edward to shoot shots back at him so round two of his burning session could commence. While Chauncey watched him, Edward looked at me for the okay. I gave him a subtle nod of approval and Edward in return went in.

"I've never wiped ass but if the money was right, I've shined the hell out of a few shoes. I appreciate you sharing your profession with me though. Hey, Dwayne, he must be fresh out, huh? His jail house haircut says it all."

Edward now looked at Chauncey, "Look, big homie, we're over here talking dollars no cents so take your ass over there until real men finish talking, nigga."

Chauncey stepped up but I didn't think Edward noticed because his eyes were back on me. He must have seen the disgust on my face and decided to switch his approach up, quickly.

"Excuse my previous words, it was the testosterone talking. What I should have said in return was, how have you planned for your future since you have time to laugh, joke, and even jog?"

"Fuck you say, little nigga?" Chauncey shouted as a smile consumed my face.

I wanted to see where it would go with the monkey wrench Edward threw in there, so I hyped it up some by saying, "You heard the man, how have you planned for your future?"

"I make moves every day, youngin'. A nigga's future is bright, bruh. Don't let these workout clothes fool you, I'm caked. Call me Mr. Baker 'cause I get all the dough, boy." He chuckled and Edward dove in with his next question, shutting Chauncey back up.

"So, you invest? Do you have IRAs, CDs... No, you look like a bonds man. What's your non-working income? You know, your residual income? How much do you really have stashed away for a rainy day and are you prepaid if the rain turns into a flood?"

Chauncey caught wind of my smile and said, "Fuck both of y'all white boy ass niggas, I invest in my plug and in the safe arrival of the load. I'm gone!" He took off in the same direction from which he came.

"You've got the job but only if you can explain to me why you are on probation for petty theft?"

I watched his victory smile diminish just as fast as it had appeared.

"We got hungry and Mama didn't have any more magic tricks up her sleeve to feed us. So, I ran into Save-A-Lot with a bag and grabbed $20 worth of food with a note promising to pay them back but that shit doesn't work in movies so I don't know why I thought I'd get away with it without cameras rolling. The chick who was working the register went to school with me and told the cops everything she could about me and when they got me from under the pile of men who stopped me from running out before the police came, I went to jail. Messed up part about it is as soon as I got in my cell they fed me but I couldn't eat knowing my mama was still at home hungry."

"I understand but I don't! I've been there but I went to Save-A-Lot and asked 7 people to buy me one item in the store until I had what I needed for a nice sized meal. Look, I'm good friends with Marcus Campbell the attorney on the top floor of the federal building. In my opinion, he's the cream of the crop. I'm going to set you up with a meeting with him and see what he can do for you. If he can't help I don't think no one in Tennessee can. And Edward, rule of thumb, if you can't pay for it, DON'T

TOUCH IT!"

From that day forward Edward had become my loose cannon protege but the lessons went deeper than finance and now it was time for another.

"Edward, why didn't you tell me you were in the market to buy an Aston Martin? You know I have connections at different car lots and I never pay full price. I don't buy vehicles from retailers, I use auto brokers to get wholesale pricing. My partner, Chris, out there at the spot we went to in Atlanta also works for Harris Auto Brokers. I pay him $1,000 finder's fee to find the vehicle that I want, he goes on a hunt for it, and when he finds it he gets 10% of the price of the car. My Mercedes retails for a little over $200,000 and all I paid for it was $99,000."

"You got it for half the price?" Edward's eyes lit up the exact same way mine had when Chris called me and gave me the price on it.

"Exactly 50% of the retail price. You have got to learn to look at all of your purchases as investments. Look, I can drive my car for a year, sell it, and still make a profit from it. I'm not going to stunt like the car was brand new. It had 3,420 miles on it but coming from where we come from that is new…"

"Hell yeah, that's new!" Edward interrupted excitedly to agree.

"Go get me your paperwork and let me call Chris and see what I can do. If I fix this shit, we're switching cars for a week!"

Edward walked out of my office laughing to go retrieve the documents that proved he fucked up while I checked my calendar to see what days I could travel to Atlanta to properly stunt all over the city in his shit.

Nivea

The headboard repetitiously hitting the wall sounded like clapping inside an enclosed auditorium. It was the wooden sleigh bed's way of encouraging the beating Riko was putting on the fatty meat between my thighs. As if the sounds of my moans weren't enough the bed decided to compliment him, ain't that a bitch!

To be honest, I was impressed that he knew how to please every inch of my body without me giving him an instruction manual with pictures explaining step by step on how I liked to be fucked. Most men make me feel like I'm a damn stewardess going over safety procedures before takeoff to orgasm.

I had to give it Miya, Black Professional Meet Dot Love did prove itself worthy of helping to find the right connection and they were going to have a five-star review coming from me. I was enjoying my connection with the suspended paramedic from the Bronx.

We had chatted online for about two hours before Riko invited me to cuddle and watch movies with him. I wasn't comfortable with the condition of his brownstone seeing that I'm a neat freak and if a pillow was out of place I'd instantly get irritated, but I needed the dick knowing that it was the only way I'd ever get over Evol. My mom would disagree since she was comfortable with the cobwebs that kept her womb warm after my daddy left her but I'm sure there's a magazine or blog that agrees with me. It was pure logic to think it was easier to get over one man if you were riding and cumming all over a new one. So, the piles of dirty clothes covering his bedroom floor and the old take out boxes he stacked next to his overflowing trash can would be overlooked this time.

Neither one of us took his invite to cuddle and watch a movie seriously it seemed. Having no panties on under my pencil skirt is what told on me and the fact Riko had discovered I wasn't wearing any by rubbing on my booty at our introductory hug is what told on him.

"Damn you're beautiful, I see why you don't have a profile picture up. Those cats would be sweating you hard." He had a handful of my ass as he spoke. "Shit, you feel and smell beautiful too, come in and have a seat."

I guess he meant on his tongue. I barely had one arm out of my jacket before he fell to his knees and mouthed the peach under my skirt while I was still standing up.

"You taste so good."

I didn't know if I should thank him for the compliment or not so I decided to ride his tongue like it was a surfboard in calm waters. He licked, slurped, pulled, and nibbled on my slightly furry fruit for 30 minutes without coming up for air nor did he take a break. It was the neatest head I'd ever received on two feet due to his thirsty mouth not allowing a drop of my juices to go astray. My hands were too busy occupying my nipples to try to reach his pants and rub on him but the long grunt he let out was notification that he had popped his first shot from his birth given gun by the taste of me alone.

"Hell yeah!"

He said while came out of his clothes quickly and stood to his feet naked in front of me. He was panting, which made his gun move to the beat of his breath enticing me to touch it with whichever part of my body that I wanted to.

"You see this big ole dick, girl?"

My eyes liked his size but not enough to see if I put it in my mouth if it would grow some more so I stroked it for a while hoping I didn't accidentally pull his trigger prematurely. I didn't know how many rounds his gun held but I couldn't risk assuming he had more than two in him.

"Don't tease me with them lips, baby, give daddy's dick a kiss."

"Daddy who?" I asked and he laughed lifting his pelvis up so his big ole dick could move closer to my mouth and like I was uninterested I turned my head from that big ole thang. Riko was slow to catch on to my refusal to suck on him. I wouldn't be returning the oral favor and after making three attempts to bring it to my mouth by adding pressure to my shoulders to weigh me down while he stood on his tippy toes he caught on. Once he threw in the towel giving me the first victory, he took a condom out of his pants pocket and held out his hand to me.

"Let's go in my room beautiful."

I accepted his hand as he led me through his bedroom door.

"Lay there and let me look at you," he said now pulling on the head of his stiff meat. "You're so fucking bad. I already know the pussy is going to be so good." He jerked faster, put the condom on, and then made his way on top of me. The first 60 seconds were filled with slow shallow strokes, he was sticking his feet in to test my waters. When he felt confident he could handle my sea, he picked up the pace and found his rhythm.

"Oh, shit, girl, I knew this pussy was going to be good."

That was way too much talking for me so I pushed his head into my breasts to shut his ass up. Now that I had him pacified it was my turn to talk shit through whispers.

"Of course, this pussy is good and if you fuck me right it might be yours."

He hit me with some deep strokes at my words, a quick back paddle and then he swan dived deep inside of me causing the headboard to add sound to his movements for the next ten minutes.

"Yes, that's how I like to be fucked. Do you hear me Riko? Keep fucking me like that…yes… I'm cumming on that big ole dick. You like when I say that huh, when I say that you have a big ole dick?"

He didn't answer me; his mouth was full and 30 seconds later he began moving erratically like he was drowning when he couldn't go any deeper. Before I could tell him to slow down out of fear he'd hurt himself trying to feel all of me it was already too late. The condom was full, he was sweating profusely, and softly thanking God for me as he wore all the symptoms of being sleepy on his face.

"I want you to lay right there and don't move, we aren't done yet, beautiful."

"Thank goodness..." I mumbled.

"What did you say, baby?"

"Oh, I said...um...I can't wait!" I tried my best to sound excited. The dick was good but I needed more than 12 minutes of it with my greedy ass. I was trying to get over a man who fucked me until I lost track of time. I didn't want no minute man.

He rubbed my peach with one hand and his empty gun with the other. I was asleep before he could get it reloaded.

My dreams displayed how pathetic I was as I dreamed of being left at the altar not once but three times. I begged and pleaded with each man to stay while two of them walked away. The third groom managed to stay long enough so I could watch his face transform from Riko's to Evol's. He walked closer to me but left about five feet between us, pulled out a water hose, and sprayed me with it as his wife appeared by his side laughing at me like I was a clown in a circus. The warmth of the water felt so real that I wasn't surprised to open my eyes and see Riko peeing on me but moaning like we were still having sex.

"NIGGA!" I bellowed in disgust.

"What…what's wrong baby, what happened?"

I couldn't tell if he had been asleep or if he was pretending that he had been.

"You pissed on me!"

"Hell no, I ain't into that Kelz shit. I didn't pee on you!"

"Yes, you did, Mr. 12 Play, look!"

I pointed at my body, the puddle that formed from his urine in my belly button, and the wet yellowish-brown stain on the white sheets.

"Shit!" he said once my point had been proven. "I was asleep and dreaming that I was nutting all over you. I'm sorry, beautiful, get up."

"Sorry? What the fuck does the word sorry fix?"

Sorry held no weight in my books. In my opinion, it wasn't a real word being that it was an adjective of sorrow and there wasn't another way to express it. Sorry-ing, sorry-ed, or even sorry-getic couldn't be defined in the dictionary but apology, apologize, apologized, and apologetic could. I was well past the disgusted stage and so lost in thoughts of slapping him and then leaving that I hadn't noticed the bedroom door slowly opening nor did I see the frying pan of hot grease making its way across the threshold.

See, while Riko and I slept, his cousin, AJ, and the true owner of the brownstone, came home. He had a new cut across his face from his girlfriend cracking him across it with a broom. He had been caught cheating again and verbal abuse wasn't the only consequence he'd endure this go around. By the grace of God, he made it out of her wrath with only being hit twice and ran to the safety of his home.

He never gave Riko permission to invite me over nor to have sex in his bed but he allowed us to continue when he heard my moans seep from under his bedroom door. He didn't want to mess up his cousin's groove and decided to take the couch for the night now that he needed to clean his linen before he could get back in his bed.

The apology text and calls were coming in from his broom swinging baseball player and he knew he wasn't going to get any sleep. With nothing else to do besides repetitiously hit ignore on his cell, he decided to take a shower. As he bathed his girlfriend used the key he hid under his doormat for his cousin on drunk nights and crept her way in. She hoped her pop up visit would lead to a night filled with apology sex and his promise to never do it again. She stripped to her birthday suit but when she went to open his bedroom door the sound of two sets of snores stopped her from turning the nob. Peeking through the old fashioned key hole her eyes landed on the most perfectly shaped and prettiest breasts she'd seen in her life, mine and the murder music from scary movies came on in her head as she thought of a plan of surprise attack. She saw a broom and thought about beating us both with it but she wanted her attack to be more traumatizing for her soon to be ex-man than she had ever done to any of her ex-men. When her eyes saw the casket iron skillet hanging on the baker's rack she thought of Al Green and grits but the bottle of vegetable oil was in arm's reach plus the bitch didn't know how to cook grits.

She heard the shower and assumed it was AJ's cousin Riko. As the oil heated on high she dressed and then went to the bathroom door to make sure Riko wouldn't complete his shower before she could complete her act of revenge against his cousin and stop her. Hearing the water still running in the bathroom and smelling the hot grease feet away from her, it was time to bed fry her man and me, his slutty lover. With both of us standing around the bed naked the only decision she had left to make was which one of us would be her first victim.

"I HATE YOU, AJ, BURN IN HELL!"

She tossed the piping hot grease onto his backside. The oil landed on his lower neck, shoulders, back, butt, and his hamstrings. Riko yelped out in agony as he hopped around the room praying for relief.

"OH MY GOD!"

I yelled it as the empty pan came flying my way and I ducked but still, a very small amount of the grease managed to catch me on the back of my arm bringing me to tears.

"THAT'S MY MAN, BITCH!"

With my attention on my burning arm she charged

across the room, landed a blow with everything in her onto my left cheek bone, and then snatched me up by my neck. When she gripped it in her hand to her satisfaction she choked me down to the floor. I was out powered and out weighted as she used her 220lbs to control my 175lbs.

Riko continued to scream profane words and his cousin emerged wet with a towel tightly wrapped around his waist. He quickly surveyed the room and then tackled his girlfriend, knocking her off of me, pinning her down.

"What the fuck is wrong with you, Kalisha?"

Her boyfriend's words snapped her out of her trance as she realized while he spoke the screams of pain never stopped which meant he wasn't the victim. Turning to face her true victim, her crazy state began to fade away as guilt kicked in, but she wouldn't allow her newly found sanity to make her feel insane. To save face, she kept her rant going by slapping her man across his face.

"Fuck you, A.J! You ran from my house to come home and have a threesome with your cousin and this plastic tittie having bitch?"

I wanted to correct her and tell her they were saline not plastic, but she had her eyes locked on me again and cocked her fist back landing one on my nose, causing blood to flow after the collision. Riko couldn't help me although I looked to him for help. He was now lying on his stomach crying for someone to call 9-1-1.

A.J must have known that as long as I was there naked, Kalisha wasn't going to calm down, so he used more power to restrain her.

"Hey, put your fucking clothes on and get the fuck out!" he breathlessly demanded as he tightened the bear hug he had on the bull he was wrestling like he was hedging while trading. I wanted to do as I was told but a part of me felt guilty about leaving without trying to help Riko, although the nasty bastard did pee on me, he did have a little potential.

"What about Riko?" I asked sucking the blood back up my nose like snot.

"I got him and her; just take your ass on. Did he pay you already?"

"Pay me?"

"Look, bitch, this ain't the time for you to play dumb. I know he got fired from the Super 8 for buying pussy on the job. Did he pay you so you can get the fuck out?"

"I thought he was a suspended paramedic?"

Not that his employment matter in that moment. I was in awe that he had sized me up as being a paid ho but I nodded my head yes, dressed, and exited the brownstone running to the nearest subway station vowing not to stop until I got to the ticket booth.

I had a knot on my cheek bigger than my breast and the burn on my arm had already bubbled up to a quarter sized white head bump. The blood had stopped flowing and had dried around the rim of both nostrils but that wasn't the worst part of it all. My ego was shot to shit from being labeled and treated like a prostitute. That was the real reason why I cried the duration of the subway ride home. The words ho and prostitute were floating around me more than my plan noted and my interactions with the opposite sex were starting to leave a stain I didn't think bleach nor Shout would be able to get out. If I didn't slow down soon, that stain might become the true reason why I wouldn't be able to attract my king.

Miya was gone when I walked in the door at 4 in the morning which meant her online hook up had to have been more successful than mine. I showered and tried to fix my face so I could make it to work at 7. The IPO of my company was a week away and there was a lot in the office that I needed to do to ensure its success but the tittie on my face forced me to decide to work from home. I called the office at 7 instead and gave my daily motivational speech by phone and gave both of my personal assistants lists of things to do for the day.

There was still over an hour to go before the stock market opened so I spent it popping bee pollen by the handfuls and working out to speed up the natural weight loss that God's most perfect food in the form of an herb caused. Working out used to be a part of my daily regimen until I noticed the bee pollen caused me to shed pounds without it. I hate to give him credit but Evol put me on to them. He wasn't shit but he had a true understanding of the Bible that you'd never expect from a constant sinner like him, but hell, the devil knew the Bible too. I was struggling with a lot of health issues that I wasn't paying attention to but as Evol noticed them he started bringing me herbs in all forms to fix them. When I mentioned the inconsistency in my periods, he brought me red raspberry leaf tea and to my surprise, it did more than straighten my menstruation out, it tightened my cat up and turned her back into a youthful kitten. When I complained about my weight he gave me six trace mineral tablets and told me not to leave the house. I didn't understand why until I found myself glued to the toilet unable to get off it if I wanted to. It was the best colon cleansing I had ever undergone and once I made it out the bathroom he handed me a bottle of Alkaline water and some bee pollen. I started taking two pills of bee pollen a day and one trace mineral tablet to keep me regular but now I'm up to 12, sometimes more and I only take trace minerals once a week and its more out of habit than for regulation. I fell in love with bee pollen when I realized it was making me lose weight and curbing my hunger. It even tightened up the excess skin with all the true protein in it but not as quickly as lifting weights did. With taking my company public, I had become too busy to remember to take my herbs besides my daily cups of red raspberry leaf tea. In a months' time, I hadn't gained any weight but the flab and water I was retaining made me look as sloppy as I had looked before I had learned about the benefits of taking herbs. My weight was housed in all the right places now but I needed the boost physical exercise gave in smoothing and tightening up. I stayed on the elliptical until I mentally heard the opening bell at the New York Stock Exchange.

It never failed that when I readied myself to trade

from home that my cell phone always came to life.

"Nivea, are you coming home for Christmas? Everybody keeps asking about you especially since I posted the link to the Wall Street Journal article about you and your company on my Facebook page. Many of my friends don't even know what an Initial Public Offering is. Hell, I didn't know what an IPO was until you told me it meant people could buy shares of your company and you'd have a New York Stock Exchange ticker symbol like Mc Donald's and all the other big-time companies do. All they saw was that you made the newspaper and those money hungry bastards knew dollar signs would follow. I almost wished I hadn't shared it now that your auntie called saying she needed help paying her rent this month and if I didn't have it if could I ask you for it. Then your daddy had the nerve to reach out to me for your number. He said you've been coming to see him and staying in contact..." she got quiet and waited for my explanation for what I was sure she assumed was treason against her but I didn't say anything.

I had reached out to him years ago, to invite him to my college graduation but he didn't show due to his failing health. He was suffering from dementia and had given himself a new past. He now thought that he used to be a big-time pimp when he lived in California which was far-fetched for a retired sanitation worker who lived in Las Vegas from the time I was six years old. When his new wife told me he hadn't had any other children as the result of knowing that he'd failed at being a father to me, I forgave him for walking out on us. I soon realized the benefits of having a parent who wanted to spend the rest of his time on earth making things right with me and he was the owner of an address in a business tax-free state. Allowing him to smooth things over with me felt destined as I used his address and money to set up my first company so I could day trade while in grad school.

"Did you give it to him, Mama?"

"Now you know I wasn't going to give his ass shit. He has gone crazy in his golden days, calling me his first bottom bitch like he was some type of pimp. He wasn't pimping nothing but those burgers he flipped while we were together and he couldn't even do that right. But I take it you've been talking to him so you already knew all that, huh?"

Again, I didn't respond.

"Don't play deaf, I asked you a question!"

"Yes, Mama, I've been talking to my father."

"You mean your daddy, he was never a father. God was the only father you ever had and you ran away from him, it wasn't the other way around. After everything God and I have done for you what would make you start talking to him?"

"Well unlike you, God and I forgave him for leaving us and I needed his help with some things."

I could hear her choking on her words as they came out.

"You needed some help from him? Girl, I raised you not to need nobody but God, you don't even need me. You're going to have to break that all the way down because saying you need him is like saying you need a bullet in your leg!"

"You wouldn't understand, Mama."

"Try me and if I don't, make me understand."

I took a deep breath as I got my words together. I knew no matter what I said she'd say it wasn't a good enough reason.

"There's more to trading than picking a stock and becoming rich."

"And you needed him to help you trade? A deadbeat with no money that's damn near brain dead."

"Oh my God, Mama! What's the point of trying to tell you if you're not going to listen to me? It's funny that you never bashed my daddy to me as a child when he wasn't there but as soon as you get wind that he's in my life as an adult its fair game to shoot him down. I guess you're without sin so you can cast the first stone, huh?"

"Don't you dare act like I'm comparing sins. I know one sin doesn't out weigh the next and as a matter of fact, I'm the parent who made sure you knew that. I see he has you brainwashed like he used to have me so go on and tell me, I'm ready to listen."

I could see her rolling her eyes at me through the

phone all the way on the west coast. She tried to come off like she was pissed but I knew it's true value was hurt. I could have proceeded with caution in view of the fact her feelings were involved but we were talking my language now and I loved speaking Bowen-ology. If my daddy didn't bring prestige to his daddy's name, I sure in the hell would. Move the fuck over Wall Street and you tight-tie wearing business men assholes. There are a lot of bears and bulls in the market but there's only one educated rhino with last name Bowen and I was on the prowl. Mama or not, she'd get it like everyone else got it, that's the only way I knew how to serve it.

"Like I was saying, it's more to it than that. Every day that I trade and make a profit 50% of it is taken in capital gains expenses. If you have portfolio income it comes with a discharge that's extended to Nevada. Secondly, there's an obligation to satisfy day trading margin requirements specified accordingly by the SEC. So that's what I needed him for."

The goal was to rhino her over with unnecessary complicated jargon that only those in my world would understand. It was supposed to make her back off like most people do when I open my mouth. Unfortunately for me, my mama was what I like to call a smart dummy.

"Oh ok…well, you're right. I didn't understand shit you said first or secondly. Now that you've flaunted your Ivy league degree in my face, why don't you break it down to me using your roots words. You know, that street shit you use to talk before I helped pay to expand your vocabulary at Yale."

She mumbled something underneath her breath. I didn't catch the beginning words but it ended with her saying, "Yeah, she talks that bullshit real good."

It was hard but I managed to hold in my laugh and took her request seriously. I had picked on her enough.

"Ok, Mama, let me try it this way. My daddy lives in Nevada, Nevada is a tax-free state. Every time I make money off trading, I'm taxed." She parted her lips to talk but I didn't let her. "Wait, I can break it down further. When I buy into a stock and sell it, I'm taxed. Not by what I make or lose at the end of the day but by every trade I make in a day. So, if I make a $100,000 profit and sell my position and then buy into another one and lose $99,000 I still owe taxes on the $100,000 I no longer have. They also charge commission fees per trade I make. That's when I have to pay a service charge to the broker for trading by the trade. Are you with me so far?"

She took a second to digest my words, said, "Yes," and then I continued.

"If I trade in a state where there are taxes, I can lose more money in the markets than I'd ever see. I learned in college that if I incorporated a company in a tax-free state then I don't have to worry about paying any taxes which means all of my profits are mine besides the commission fees. When I hooked up with Daddy he helped me set up a company there and I used his home address for everything, including for my driver's license. Mama, if it wasn't for you I wouldn't have made it that far and I hate to have to say this to you but if it weren't for my daddy I'd be broke, homeless, or in jail for unpaid taxes on money I never even got the chance to touch."

"Well, you still didn't have to get all close and shit to him to use his address. I still don't understand why you would forgive him."

"Money."

"Money? He ain't got no money."

"He didn't but his wife did and after I brought up missed birthdays, child support, and all the sacrifices you made throughout my life he had her write me a check to pay for my incorporation and the day trading requirements under the law. In order for me to buy in and out of stocks whenever I want to I must have at least $25,000 in my brokerage account. She cut me a check for $40,000 just to be safe. When I started making money off it I started sending you money once a week to help replace everything you lost from the time he walked out on us and didn't provide one cent for me. Mama, you were and still are the strongest woman I know and not to blow my own horn but you did a helluva good job with me."

She didn't say another word about my daddy but began ranting about everything she could think of as I moved my attention over to trading and bought a position in an oil ETF I had previously researched. There wasn't anything flashy about the company's information that I found but with shares priced at $3.00 a pop I quickly bought a thousand of them. With my senior investment managers in the office pushing the same stock, the day should make for a good day of trading.

"Are you listening to me, Nivea?"

"Yes, Mama, I am. People are always asking you for money, you're tired of postage constantly going up and something about changing the color of the car I bought you due to, too many people in your neighborhood have the same car. Yes, I'm listening."

"Well…" she said taking a pull of her joint that she swore her doctor gave her for cataracts, "I know you send me $1,500 a week and I'm thankful for all that you do for me, baby, but if you're not coming home can you send me money as a Christmas present? If I have to be without you for the holiday, I'd rather be in Vegas until New Year's Day and Eddie said he has never been."

Seconds before she finished, I had logged into my work email account to give the messages my attention but the name Eddie froze me in place.

"Who's Eddie, Mama?" I asked with a smile on my lips.

"Oh, Eddie, he's just a friend who lives down the street that I've been helping while he mourns his wife's death. You know, I'm just trying to help him see that there is still life after the death."

"Umm hmm, sex does help heal wounds."

"You better watch how you're talking to me. We have never discussed my sex life and I don't care how old or rich you get, we won't. Don't you think since you're fucking everybody but the man that's going to be your husband and you're good buddies with your daddy and his new wife now, that we're open to discuss who I'm fucking, understand me, Nivea?"

"I do."

"These aren't vows you're taking!"

"Yes ma'am, I understand you!" was all I managed to say while turning my attention back to my unread messages. I read and replied to a few of them and forwarded employment opportunity inquiries to the HR department as my mama continued to fill me in on what was going on the west coast until a new email came in and stolen my attention. The subject read, "A meeting of great minds," and was sent from Dwayne Hollingswell, a name I wasn't familiar with.

"Mama, I'll call you tomorrow after I deposit $5,000 into your account for your trip. I apologize for disrespecting you and for not telling you I reconciled with my daddy years ago, but I have to get back to work. I love you, Mama, I really do. You'll always be my favorite girl!"

I hung up before she could return the closing and opened the email.

Good Morning Ms. Bowen,

I'm Dwayne Hollingswell, the CEO of Zion

TOXIN

Venture Capital located in Memphis, TN. We are a small, up and coming investment firm that manages five funds with three more funds on the horizon, making us the largest firm in Tennessee. I came across the article on you and Bowen Capital Management this morning and besides congratulating you on your success via email, I'd like to sit down with you over lunch and perhaps exchange knowledge...

I stopped reading there. I was tired of people reaching out to me for information they were too lazy to research on their own. If I had to work hard to achieve my position, why did others think they wouldn't have to do the same? And with the last name Hollingswell, he probably had a long line of finance gurus in his family. There was no way I'd waste my time entertaining nor helping a spoiled brat from Memphis who hadn't realized Memphis wasn't a growing market when it came to those looking to invest. I hit delete on his email and never gave it a second thought.

Dwayne

It was raining hard the morning of my flight to New York to meet the CEO of Bowen Capital Management like it hadn't been almost 90 degrees the day before. I had sent an email requesting a meeting with Nivea Bowen and had never received a response, so I took it upon myself to leave a message with her assistant with my travel itinerary and intent to meet with her. I waited for the overnight doorman who I also used part-time as a driver to return with my car under an awning and gave the woman lying on a cardboard box in front of my building a smile.

I didn't understand why neither of the two doormen never called the police on her for trespassing but I knew the reason why I hadn't. I didn't believe in kicking anyone while they were already down and the good book said if I did, I would one day be their footstool and I couldn't let that happen.

"Mr. Hollingswell, why do you always smile and greet me?"

The question itself seemed out of place but what riddled me the most was how the woman who was visibly down on her luck knew my name. With my curiosity at its peak through furrowed eyebrows that almost touched, I shrugged then said, "Why shouldn't I, you seem like a nice woman? You might have had a few hard times but you still seem pleasant enough to be around if you permitted me to."

She laughed in a very educated manner. "You're on

the banana boat, even if you permitted me to be in your space it would only be temporary seeing that people can't entertain you unless they can fluently speak all of your favorite languages like Wall Street jargon," she laughed.

I chuckled and then asked, "Banana boat, what's that?"

She tapped the empty milk crate that sat upside down, "Come have a seat in my office."

I checked the piece of sidewalk she claimed as her office twice. There was a suspicious puddle on the center of the box too far away from the rain to be confused with rain, as she read my thoughts.

"It's not urine, Mr. Hollingswell, and I don't bite... Well, not anymore, I had that little problem fixed," she giggled, "Can I also borrow your shiny gold expensive pen that you keep in your suit coat pocket, please?"

My eyebrows re-enacted their almost meeting point as I cautiously sat on the crate holding my breath. She was right, my pen was very expensive and one of a kind. If she thought she could steal it and out run me I was ready to show her my double-breasted suit wouldn't have any effect on my speed.

"Let's pretend that this is Yankee Stadium..." she said drawing a circle onto the oil stained portion of the box. "This is the parking lot around the stadium." She drew a square around the circle and filled it with lines then said, "and these lines divide the parking spaces."

She lost my attention when she thought the best method to teach me something was by using elementary artwork. I checked my watch preparing for her to waste my time.

"Don't worry, Mr. Hollingswell, I'll be done with my arts and crafts before the opening bell sounds." She finished with another wholesome smile and started drawing crescent moons to represent the boats. "All the extreme yet original thinkers that most call smart, fill the boats while the rest of the world files into the stadium. This is where my process of elimination begins." She gave me a full pearl white, perfectly straight, box of Tic-Tacs smile and then hit me with a Birdman style hand rub. I would have missed it if I had blinked.

"Listen, Dwayne, only the smart or geniuses will understand what I'm about to say to you. The reason being is that they qualify for the title and their genius is so grand that it invokes fear in others. The word smart gets changed to strange and genius becomes weird. Next, they are being prescribed medications for this condition of being smart and strange. If they accept the meds, then they also accept a ticket into the stadium of normal life. They get off the boat without looking back and their full intelligence will never come back." With hurt etched on her pale white and wrinkled face, she crossed off four boats.

"Next round of eliminations are for those who've heard they've had a mental condition for so long that they believe it but are smart enough not to take medications. They say things like, I've been diagnosed with ADHD that's why I can do this or they apologize for being smart like it's a disease. They get kicked off the boats for simply lacking a spine."

Five more boats received a capital X through them. She had my full attention and I felt the need to show her she had it by asking a question but the fear of her changing her mind about me being a banana boat rider made me keep my mouth closed so I wouldn't ask a dumb question. She started back up.

"Up next are the love birds. You know the type that will put being in love before all. They give up on their dreams and logical thinking which is the real common sense to make their hearts happy. They're on the never-ending journey in the pursuit of happiness and are so in love that they forget the definition of the word pursuit. Most of these people willingly leave the boat when they realize love is waiting for them inside the safety and normal feel of the stadium's walls."

Ten boats were eliminated leaving eleven.

"We're almost to the good part...the group that follows the love birds are the go getters. Those are the people who focus on meeting the goals they set out for and make it to the top. They've used their talents, gifts, education, or whatever fuels their genius to soar to the top. Once wealth is achieved from that one goal they set they willingly exit the banana boat to try to live a normal life." She crossed out all the boats but two.

"Here's where you are. You're on one of the last

boats in the parking lot and one that is permanently tailgating. You'll never worry about what life is like in the stadium, you're 100% sure it's tenfold on the banana boat. Who needs a stadium when you're in the best of company on the boat? You're with Bill Gates, Steve Jobs, Michael Moore, and men and women who are like them. They don't let anything or anyone stop them. They marry those who are like them or understand them, people who truly back their dreams while they bull doze their way to the top and the top is only the beginning. They make goal after goal and die trying to reach them all. Sure, they marry and have kids, it's a part of their plan. They want their hard work and money to be left to those who share their DNA. I'm not saying they are religious people although they do run across God during their research…"

She stopped her words to take a swallow of water she had in an orange juice jug and then she picked up where she left off.

"People like you are self-motivated and don't settle for anything being left unknown. Men like you don't need nor want relationships. You've convinced yourself that they are too time-consuming and being a man of Wall Street I'm sure you view time as the biggest commodity. I wouldn't be surprised if you didn't walk into Goldman Sachs and attempt to buy swaps on time." She shook her head while she floated from her words and I stood there shocked.

"That's who you are, Dwayne. A kind-hearted rider of the banana boat."

I didn't know what to say after that but I was certain

that I agreed with her analogy as my driver had finally pulled up. I took a twenty off my flight cash and tried to hand it to her but she declined with a shake of her head.

"I'm on the banana boat too. I'm sure you must have wondered why Jeffery doesn't call the police on me for blocking the entrance. Well, I not only own the building I also own 20% of downtown Memphis and a few other places around the globe. My condo is on the top floor and between the two of us..." she leaned in my direction like she was going to share some CIA/FBI top secret stamped in red on a manila envelope information, but instead said, "...between the two of us, I got some really nice shit up there." She laughed until she was forced to wipe the tears out of the corners of her eyes and then turned serious. "Do you know why I dress like this and sleep out here all day, Dwayne?"

I was too stuck in the disbelief of it all that I didn't try to make sense of it. I shook my head no. I tried to think of a good reason for a million or even billionaire to not want to bask in the glory of their wealth but a pliable notion wouldn't form.

"...I'm free! My wealth has granted me freedom from the restrictions this matrix we're stuck in calls laws. If I didn't own this building, I'd be committing a crime which could lock me away in a box and steal my freedom from me. I'm sure you understand how important freedom is."

The look on her face said she knew of my arrest and jail time and I was sure she did seeing she had to process my application to get the condo. My record was expunged but with the type of money she had, there was no such thing as closed doors or sealed information. I nodded in agreement and said, "Yes, I do!"

"As I assumed. So, I bought the building and earned the right to loiter legally. I'm not restricted to anything and my wealth ensures this!"

"Have any of the tenants ever called the police on you?" It was a weak question but it still warranted an answer.

"Oh, of course, all the time and when I find out who they are I pay them to move as far away from me as possible. I don't allow stadium people to dwell around me and you shouldn't either. Well, Mr. Hollingswell, it's been a pleasure but let's not keep Jeffery waiting on you. New York is calling and I'd hate to make you late answering its call."

She pulled out a bag of mixed nuts and began eating like she'd never said a word to me. I grabbed my pen off the box and got in the car.

"I see you've met Ms. Blakemore. Nice lady but a different breed altogether," Jeffery said as I approached the car.

"Very different indeed...take me to the airport, Jeffery, I don't want to leave my car."

"To the airport it is, sir."

*****

I made it to JFK International airport and went straight to Wall Street by subway. The stock exchange was open for another 2 ½ hours and I used the remaining hours of operation to trade at the Starbucks that sat at 14 Wall Street. It faced the New York Stock Exchange doors and was the closest I'd get to trading in the historical building without spending a million dollars for a seat on the floor. I'd never forgotten that Starbuck's address from previous visits. The gold engraved numbers caught my attention as all the other gold-plated addresses in the area had done. A little after 3:30 I made my way around the block to Bowen Capital Management on Exchange Street.

I'd scheduled a four o'clock meeting to give the office time to adjust from the close of the market which didn't seem to make a difference as I watched the people scurry around the office like hard working ants from the waiting area. I smiled as I made a game out of guessing what the employees were doing and guessing what their title with the company was. I saw a huddle of people with stacks of papers in hand and I could tell they were analyzing profit and loss statements. I would have kept the game going longer but the light bulb in my head finally came on as I noticed much of the office was female and I hadn't seen one black face since Ms. Bowen's assistant walked me to the waiting area. I couldn't wait to question Ms. Bowen; she was becoming more of a Wall Street cliché than I thought myself to be.

"I apologize for your wait, Mr. Hollingswell, but I checked, double checked, and checked for a third time but I couldn't locate a meeting scheduled for you with Ms. Bowen today. If you can give me your business card, I'll go speak with her to see if she can see you today since you've traveled all the way here from Tennessee."

I gave her my card and she walked down the hallway that was the length of the building vanishing into a large office at the end. I let her get a head start and then followed. If Ms. Bowen didn't give her a good explanation for declining to see me I would walk in and demand it myself.

"Ms. Bowen, there's a Dwayne Hollingswell here to see you. He claims he emailed you and spoke with Chrissy to schedule a meeting. Here's his card, he's here from Memphis, Tennessee."

"I didn't agree to meet with anyone. Schedule an appointment for next week, I'm way too busy for some fucking financial chitchat," I heard her say.

My hand shot up to the handle but her assistant's voice paused it from turning the knob.

"Ms. Bowen..." I could hear the pleading in her words. She had empathy for me traveling from Tennessee even though I had come uninvited. "He isn't local and will only be in town until Sunday. You have an opening tomorrow at 4:30..."

"I know my schedule, Karla. Here, give him this invitation to the IPO celebration and schedule our meeting for Monday. Is that better?"

"Yes, that's much better," she laughed.

"What's the geeky laugh about?"

"Is it okay to be frank with you?" Karla's voice changed into a whisper that almost sent me away from the door thinking she knew I was eavesdropping.

"Please do, I've always liked frank."

"Well…he's the finest man I've seen in real time. Daddy's wearing a suit but it doesn't conceal his muscles or the dreaminess of his face and, girl, he smells so freaking good. If I wasn't married, I'd grab and lick him to make sure all my senses agreed he was a perfect piece of chocolate. When I'm done, walk me out of your office, and sneak you a peek. You can't stay single forever and if he's a walking reflection of his bank account you need to cuff that!"

I made it back to the waiting room before she walked out of the office and after she gave me the news I'd already heard, I checked into my hotel and went to sleep.

New York was an hour ahead of Tennessee's time yet I still managed to wake up early enough to jog from my hotel in the financial district to Time Square in time to trade from my iPad outside of the NASDAQ. I didn't have time to trade aggressively. I bought 1000 shares of two of the companies that make up the 30 known as the Dow Jones and held both positions while I started the journey of finding something to wear to Bowen Capital Management's

IPO celebration. Out of habit, I went straight to Brooks Brothers but didn't care for the small selection of black tie items they had and it seemed like I already owned everything in the section. Macy's was a little better when it came to having a variety since it had multiple areas for big name fashion designers like Louis Vuitton and Gucci, so I grabbed my black-tie attire there.

I'd visited New York plenty of times but that didn't stop me from looking like a tourist as I dived back on the curb after almost being run over while flagging down a cab to get to Harlem. There was a barbershop on 125th near Amsterdam I wanted to try out and I must admit that the barber was getting me right. The way his skills complimented my waves you'd think I'd driven to the Atlantic Ocean and then swam north to New York. He used a razor to line me up and to clean the new growth stubble off my face. I didn't mind the jokes that he and the occupants of the shop made about my Memphis accent every time I spoke; the conversation we were having was one of intelligence which is becoming extinct.

"I'm not ever eating meat again and I'm dead ass about it. I did some heavy researching on all that shit and it does us no good. Peep, we already die a little every time we drink that fluoride laced water coming out of our pipes, I'm not about to let meat speed it up. My new shorty is up on that all-natural shit and it makes sense to me so I jumped on it too," Prynce, the barber whose chair I sat in and owner of the shop, said after one of his waiting customers offered him a slab of ribs that he was elated to have smoked himself.

"Then more for me, son. I know that brown sugar, cayenne pepper rub I put on them bitches is gon' have that pork tasting like premium cut Angus beef," the customer proclaimed with light laughter in his voice.

"Pork? Aw hell nah, I'm not eating that shit. Man, mind control is real." When Prynce said the Latin definition for government my mouth flew open.

"Yeah…they got us brainwashed with meat among other things. It's crazy, in slavery time they gave us parts of a pig to eat as scraps and 400 years later we still eat pig feet, chitterlings, and the snout like those aren't scraps. But, chicken and beef is no better. Then turkey on Thanksgiving, a food that was eaten for the murder of Native Americans but that's another story," I said.

"You ain't lying. Man, the shit so screwed up they're dipping bacon in chocolate and calling it dessert. That ain't shit but a sugar induced heart attack," the barber shouted out. I snatched the microphone back.

"The Bible says in Deuteronomy 14:8 basically, not to eat the meat of a pig but since there's no picture of a pig next to the scripture, people can't seem to decipher the words. Flip forward to Leviticus 11. It tells us not to eat bottom feeders but shrimp and lobster are always the highest shit on menu. We're paying top notch dollar for a speedy death or if we're lucky a disease that will buy some time as it kills us slowly."

"That's why I don't eat shit that comes out of shit water. That's where everything from the toilets goes. The only thing worth breaking bread over is a juicy ass steak and you get protein from it," the rib cook said and the voices in the barber shop went up in agreement.

I wasn't sure whose mouth it came out but some foolish soul said, "Men got to eat steak for the protein or our bones and muscles fuck up." I got back on stage.

"Who said that shit? Do you know that you can get more protein from two spoons of bee pollen than a 20-ounce steak? Yeah, they told us to eat steak for a good source of protein but steak has no protein when it's cooked. Real protein has to have 22 amino acids, and that steak ain't got it unless you eat it medium-well or rare to get closer to it, but again, it's a violation in the Bible to eat blood. We shouldn't be eating meat but we are foolish and always listening to what man says when there's a Bible with all the rules and laws to life written in it. I can't do it! I learned not to put my trust in man, I put it in true knowledge."

The young guy getting his haircut in the chair next to me that looked every part of a street hustler before I was forced to prejudge him turned and said, "Damn, nigga, who the fuck is you? I thought you were one of them Wall Street jerk ass niggas but now I don't know if you are a minister, doctor, drug dealer, or what!"

The barbershop went up in laughter and I joined in by laughing a lot louder than the rest but my barber didn't blink. He even wore a look that read, "That shit ain't funny." As I was about to respond to the ignorance, the same guy asked me, "What the hell are you laughing at, nigga? I'm serious! Who the fuck are you, the feds?"

I almost cried laughing but I could feel every set of eyes on the back of my head and the air was becoming thick enough to cut with one of the barber's straight razors so I decided to respond through a chuckle.

"Before naming anything, I'm a child of God first, I don't deal with doctors, I go to an herbalist. I don't push drugs, I push a profit every day like a drug dealer does but faster, easier, and legal. You think I'm the feds? Well, I don't do police and the system of slavery they are tied to, brother. Government means mind control and I'm not under anyone's control but God's. And if you want to think of me as a minister, I won't stop you, but I'm not ordained. I'm only a man living for the Lord and by his rules, any more questions?"

The silence in the shop remained which was always occurred after I'd spoken my piece on my beliefs. After it was obvious the man didn't have any more questions for me the barber broke the soundless peace by asking me, "What I really want to do is find me a plug for Alkaline water, are you on that too, brother?"

"Yes, sir, and I even keep strips in my wallet to check my alkalinity throughout the day." I dug in my wallet and handed him five of my strips before continuing, "I don't know who has it here in New York but in the meantime, I'll send up some cases of water to the shop from my connect back in Memphis."

"Nah, bro, if you're going to look out for me like

that I'll give you the vitals to the crib and this cut is on me."

He removed the cape from my neck, we shook hands, and then I locked his contact information in my cell phone. I was about to walk back out to the busy street but my alter ego, the cowboy known as Mr. Black Wall Street, wouldn't allow me to leave without asking, "You own this shop right…are you investing?"

It never fails, we ended up talking for two hours as we walked up and down 125th. We talked losses, profits, risk, commodities, and how he could receive residual income through dividends and he was all in. I told him to give me a call Monday and we could discuss scheduling a face to face meeting on my next visit. It would have been short and sweet but he went there about his theory of disease and how he thought there were really cures for all of them and I felt it was my duty to tell him the truth.

"You're right but let me tell you why you are right. You have to know that there's only two causes of disease. First, every disease is one and the same. Cancer, kidney failure, HIV, and so on. Remember all diseases are a malfunction of cells and there's only two reasons why your cells would malfunction. The first one would be a deficiency, meaning that the cells are lacking something like a mineral to function normally. The second is toxicity. Do you know who doctor Dr. Sebi is?"

"Doctor Sebi? Oh yeah, dude ol' girl from TLC used to visit before she died."

"Right!"

I walked over to a bench at the projects and sat down. Class was in session and since he didn't mind paying the tuition with his attention, I didn't mind sharing my pearls. I could tell he wasn't swine.

"Real food is organically produced, fresh, whole, and unprocessed. It's full of nutrients that Jehovah intended us to have and is free of man-made toxins like herbicides and pesticides. There are fake fruits and vegetables floating around called hybrids. They are made by man and Leviticus 19:19 tells us not to eat man-made foods. Dr. Sebi is known for talking about hybrids but his true claim to unwanted fame is that he healed people of every disease known to man."

"You had me until you said that, son. Come on now, if he cured everything why aren't we using his cures?"

"You want the raw truth?"

He nodded.

"There's an endless amount of money in sickness. Why would the powers that be let all the money that comes from healthcare get cut? I know you don't really believe that the preservation of life means more than money, don't be fooled. Can't preserve nothing on this earth without it."

"I'm not fooled but wouldn't there be a big buzz about him curing shit? A while ago I heard about another dude who said he cured something with apricot seeds and they threw his funky ass in jail. Why didn't they throw Dr. Sebi in jail if he was fucking with the church's money?"

I laughed.

"Yeah they tried to lock him up in '87 but he went in front of the Supreme Court and won. He had 72 witnesses that provided documentation showing his facility cured them of these diseases. There are other doctors who've cured disease too but the way information is hidden, you won't hear about them either."

He pulled out his phone and googled Dr. Sebi. Once he read the articles we spent another hour talking about the not so secret organizations and the only reason we cut our discussion short was that his next client was blowing his cell phone up from impatience after waiting for him to return.

*****

Thirty minutes before the main event started I strolled in and the entire room's eyes fell on me like I was wearing an optical magnet. I was accustomed to compliments from the opposite sex but hearing them from men wasn't something that happened that often in the South.

"Excuse me, that's a really nice tux you're wearing. Where did you get it from?" the extra tall white man asked with a smile deeply curved on his lips. Out of habit, my eyebrow raised. That happened every time the situation I was in felt suspect. I wanted to accept his compliment at face value but the heterosexual in me had to make sure I wasn't confusing a compliment with a flirt. With way more bass in my voice than usual I said, "It's from Macy's," and walked off as if he had the Bubonic plague.

I cased the room for familiar faces which was a waste of time with this crowd. Financial tycoons rarely showed their faces enough to be visually recognizable unless it's Warren Buffet, Jim Rogers, and Mike Maloney. Those three are a few of the crème de la crème of investing and the media loves to plaster their faces everywhere whenever the opportunity presented itself. What I needed was to be able to hear names, job titles, and what firms filled the room. I put a faint smile on my lips and tightened my jawline to give myself a business edge. There was something about a firm jawline that non-verbally said; no nonsense, determined, and rich. Once my facial expression was active I went on an introduction handshaking spree.

"I'm impressed, Mr. Hollingswell and I'd love to hear more of your prophecy on the market. Maybe later tonight if you're free?"

"Maybe…"

The beautiful investment banker from Goldman Sachs, I believed she said her name was Amy, but for some reason, I wanted to rename her Becky, was practically handing me access to what she held in her panties.

"If you're free after this, Dwayne, how about coming back to my place and let's talk deeper about your predictions for the market over drinks?"

"Good idea but wrong venue. How about you follow me to my hotel and we talk there?"

Taking a step closer to me she ran her hand down the length of my tie then said, "I'd love to but are you sure your wife won't mind?" while scanning my finger for a ring.

I heard her question but the hushed conversation behind us had my full attention. There were four people huddled up scared and almost on the verge of playing rock, paper, scissors to decide which one of them was going to tell their employer that they had dropped the ball when it came to her paperwork and her company would not be going public as the celebration suggested. I assumed one of them was her CPA, another her securities attorney, and the other had to be the underwriter or one of the other investment bankers who managed the IPO.

Them dropping the ball not only meant a loss of money and a negative buzz for Ms. Bowen and her company in the world of finance, it also meant the same for those she'd chosen to work with on her IPO, and the companies they represented. She'd sue them and win. More likely than not, they'd settle out of court and try to pay her not to black ball them in the industry but with the room filled with a representative from almost every financial media outlet there is, she wouldn't have to. They'd be blackballed as soon as her ticker symbol didn't surface. I was saved from having to answer Amy's question by the start of the ceremony.

After all the unnecessary bells and whistles we finally made it to the opening speech and to my surprise Ms. Bowen wasn't teary-eyed. She spoke with strength and was level-headed. Hearing her speak made me wonder exactly where she fit on the banana boat.

She concluded her speech and began making the rounds, shaking hands, and thanking all of those who congratulated her until she made her way to me. I extended my hand in preparation to introduce myself and she seductively bit down on her bottom lip, but there wasn't anything sexy about the words that came out of her mouth.

"Mr. Hollingswell? Yes, that's it! I'd never forget the name of an uninvited guest but I'm glad you could come out and celebrate my company with the rest of them. What was it that you thought we should talk about again?"

"I'm in the process of opening a firm here in New York and thought…"

"And thought what? That I'd take you in as a friend and teach you the ins and outs of fighting against the titans of Wall Street on the strength of a five-minute friendship? No, I don't work like that and friendships don't pay my bills. I will need a consultant fee which we can discuss on Monday as my secretary already informed you."

She was confident in her position and I'm sure it helped her effectively run her company but I wasn't one of her peon employees. I was the owner of Zion Venture Capital, so I spoke that boss shit right back to her ass.

"I'm leaving here Sunday and it would be foolish of me to think that, but I see your mind can manufacture foolish thoughts. I don't do friends, Ms. Bowen, and as a matter of fact, I don't do anything that ends in the letters e – n - d including having a girlfriend. If you get that close to me, we're family. I have some information about your IPO that I was going to share with you for free, but you're right, free doesn't pay my bills. And I think you'd prefer to hear it from your underwriter. Enjoy your party, beautiful. You might as well since your legal team will be paying for it anyway."

I bowed and then walked away making sure to dodge Amy as Nivea shot invisible bullets at me launched from her eyes. I wasn't in the mood to get stock tips from Jezebel. My flight in the morning couldn't come soon enough.

Nivea

I was upset at how Dwayne had strode into my office uninvited and smiled that sexy contagious smile at my office manager to get an invitation to my IPO party. Not to mention the fact that everything about him made all of me want him and it was sealed with a bite of my bottom lip. From the strong wave pattern in his hair to the shine on his Cole Haans that covered his feet, I wanted to suck his soul out of him and then hand it over to God on his behalf on judgment day.

He had forced me to crave him for who he was and hate him for what he wasn't in the same blink of my eyes. My mouth salivated as curiosity of the measurements in his pants made me hanker for the taste of his unborn children but in those same seconds, I had to fight the urge of letting the saliva build volume in my mouth and ejecting it forcibly onto his handsome face.

Mr. Hollingswell was cocky and there was something lingering in his southern accent that made me feel he was untrustworthy. I still didn't know how he found out my company wouldn't be going public before I did, but I was sure that I wouldn't be asking him. The shit was heartbreaking and I'd be lying if I didn't acknowledge that taking a knife to the wrist with a bottle of pain pills and bourbon felt like a sound option at that point. My plan for my life had failed because I failed to hire people who understood my dream. Their focus was on the paycheck they'd receive for services rendered and distant from the legacy I was building. They couldn't see the lights and flashing cameras that would make each of them look like polished trophies in the financial world because they all had reached their personal goals and were too comfortable to go out and obtain more. All that planning, research, and devoted time gone due to something as small as building a team with the wrong people. Anger only trumped the sadness because disappointment pointed the finger back at me. I refused to punish myself by asking an outsider how he could see my mistakes with magnified vision and there was no way I'd contribute to making Dwayne feel important…but why did he have to be so damn fine?

We had only spoke briefly yet the impression he left on me had me sitting at my computer desk staring at his business card. Out of curiosity I went to his website and was surprised to see that he managed a fund for the utility company in Memphis among offering many other services both personal and commercial. The site was easy to maneuver through but the color scheme was wrong. He needed to remove the green from his site's background, it didn't compliment the black and gold theme he had going. Before I knew it, I was filling out the contact us form on his site.

Your website is nice but remove the green! - Bowen Capital Management

Clicking on his photo gallery there was a picture of him wearing a suit minus the jacket with a bow tie and suspenders. He had his arms crossed in front of his chest B-boy style that broadcast his muscles like breaking news. It was obvious that the photo was old. His face was hairless, full of youth, and he had a wavy Mohawk on the picture that to my astonishment didn't take away from his professionalism. Fuck it, hands down Dwayne was fine. Gawking at him instantly coerced my panties to come to life like I had stolen Niagara Falls and had it hid in between my slightly less talkative lips. If he could get me this wet with his looks alone, I needed to get me a southern man. I didn't care what the situation was, there was no way in hell I'd be messing with his witty and arrogant ass!

I logged onto Black Professionals Meet Dot Love and changed my search location. I started with Georgia, South Carolina, and then eased my way over to Tennessee. Feeling defeated, I ran the cursor to the last page of my Nashville search results and a profile caught my attention. It read:

I Just Want Something Real!

Username: My last shot at this love stuff

Age: 37

Location: Nashville, TN

Occupation: Small business owner- Plumbing

Looking for: Relationship

Bio: I'm a plumber that's tired of dealing with shit...I mean when it comes to relationships. I just want that "real thing" everyone talks about and male R&B singers whine about in their songs. I've never been

married and I don't have kids but that doesn't mean I'm not open to them both. To the ladies who are already blessed with children, I apologize in advance. I wouldn't be a good stepfather and with me being honest and sharing this, I'd think less of you if you still reached out to me after reading it. Next, if you can't hold a conversation outside of sex or what's currently trending on social media pass me by too. I want brains and beauty..."

I enjoyed the little I had read, sent a quick message, and then went to see what Memphis had to offer. I didn't know if Mr. Hollingswell was born and raised in Memphis but if he was then judging by the men I was looking at he was one of a kind. There were so many with only half their hair cut with the other half plagued with non-manicured dreads and gold teeth to go through that I moved my search to Florida which was where I hit the jackpot. I would be visiting Miami real soon.

I tried touching myself to relieve some of the buildup but I couldn't get in the mood. My mind wouldn't let me forget that the stress I was feeling was caused by my failed attempt to IPO. It was hard to process the notion of firing and suing my legal team to replace them with people who weren't with me from the start but I knew I had to let them go. If they couldn't do something as simple as working together to file paperwork properly, what did I need them for?

I needed to rest so I'd be energized for all the looks and questions I'd be bamboozled with about not going public in morning.

*****

As I predicted, all eyes were on me like I was wearing a 'Rest in Peace Tupac' t-shirt at a Biggie memorial but the looks didn't bother me until Miya came running in my office screaming.

"I'm pregnant; I'm really pregnant this time!" She waved one of those pee-on sticks around as if it was air freshener. Instantly the stares I got made me feel pitiful and like my life was spinning out of my control.

"Excuse me!" I said to the group of my employees I had huddled together to explain the legal battle I would be facing and quickly ushered Miya into my office.

"I didn't think I could get pregnant with all the abortions I've had but bitch, I did and it's his!"

She was so excited but I didn't give a damn.

"Miya, this is a place of business, my place of business, and the air is thick in here right now. Even if it wasn't, don't you ever bring your ass in here as anything other than a professional or I'll have my security carry your ass out to the streets with the rest of the gutter rats, do you understand me?"

She nodded with a look on her face that reminded me of a child's after having their balloon popped by a bully. The friend in me decided to try to understand.

"Who are you pregnant by Miya?" I asked and like

magic, the sadness disappeared from her face and the excited look she had at her time of arrival returned.

"Man-Man, I didn't want to tell you but we started back creeping. The sex is so different now. He wants to be inside of me all the time and he doesn't even try to pull out anymore. He even says shit like, you gon' have my baby bitch, while he's nutting."

She was so elated about her sleazebag that I proceeded with caution.

"So…you do know you are having unprotected sex with a man that you know is a compulsive cheater, right?"

She rolled her eyes at me and let out an exasperated breath. "See, that's why I didn't want to tell you. You're always quick to point out my fuck ups. Why can't you just be a friend and be happy for me?"

"I didn't make you run in here with that bullshi… You know what? You're right. Congratulations, if you're happy, I'm happy for you," I managed to say through gritted teeth not knowing if I was truly happy for her or if I had seen this entire scene on the Lifetime channel and was reenacting it. "Will you be moving back in with him?" I had to ask.

"Well throw me out in the street barefoot and pregnant, why don't you! Yes, I'm getting out of your place, he's coming to get me and my stuff this weekend. You only have to put up with us for four more days." She rubbed her stomach in the manner a visibly pregnant woman would and then said, "You know what? I think he finally loves me too. Everything will be perfect when the baby comes, I just know it."

My ears refused to keep feeding my brain the dumb shit she was talking to digest. Since when was a baby a magical being that fixed already broken, no substance having relationships? I don't understand why some women think pregnancy is a ball and chain to keep a man with when the vows taken under God of marriage won't even keep a man nowadays. She'd be lucky if he didn't fuck off on her during the six weeks of healing she'd endure after having the baby and that's if he didn't break bad and leave her before then. But then again, what did I know? I didn't have nor want kids anytime soon and the shit I was watching her go through was the reason why I didn't.

"I have to get back to work; we will talk later." I opened my door and didn't see her out. Dwayne's concept on friends was making a lot more sense at that moment.

*****

The day seemed to move at a turtle's pace and with all the apologetic emails I received from the titans of Wall Street pretending to be grief ridden by my failure, I ran out of the office at 4 o'clock. I attempted to shower the embarrassment away but it wasn't working so I walked to the Jacuzzi dripping wet to soak my troubles away. I wanted to fill a cigar to its maximum capacity and smoke my troubles away but my weed supply was low and I had made a promise that I wouldn't make another purchase of it. I had read an article that listed a few non-THC having herbs that were also smoke-able to help with relaxing, and had promised to convert over to those.

The water did help my nerves relax some. I towel dried, cleaned up my trail of water from the shower to Jacuzzi, and put on my robe. I popped a handful of herbs for dinner and once they passed through my system, I planned to snack on fruit if hunger showed its masked face. If I wouldn't have realized hunger was a game played by hormones secreted from the stomach that makes its way to our brains that triggers the need to eat, I would still be fighting my battle with weight. It's sad to say but always wanting to eat or eating until you're about to bust out of your pants is all physiological. Hunger pangs are real but they are caused by the stomach emptying after the digestion of a meal. The walls of the stomach rub against each other but why does that mean we need to eat something packed with calories to get it to stop? How about drinking a cup of water first and seeing if the pangs go away? I guess that's why God made sure to make laws, rules, and commandments over food. He had to know that our minds wouldn't reveal what's best for us on its own. But like they say, whoever "they" are; with knowledge comes power and in some cases, so does good health.

It had been months since I had opened the drapes that covered my condo living room's picture windows and enjoyed the view I overpaid for and it felt like I needed to. I loved my apartment in Harlem but with the growth of my company and bank account I gave it up as my plan instructed me to. The goal was to live near my office in the financial district and when the money presented itself, I paid 1.5 million to be two blocks from my office on the left and to have the Statue of Liberty to my right, a blown kiss, and some water away from me.

It was breathtaking to watch Lady Liberty whenever the urge overtook me, especially when home for me was on the opposite coast. I didn't have to live in New York because of my career goals, I had to live in New York to add more value to my goals and to make it easy to keep my eye on the prize.

"What the fuck is that?"

There was a Starbucks cup with the name Jay written on it perched on the edge of the ledge outside my window. I'm on the 37th floor with no balcony which meant one of the raggedy ass window washers must have left it out there. I flew to my computer to get the property manager's number but my inbox on the dating site was lit up like Lady Liberty's torch and I couldn't close out the tab I left open from the night before without reading what the men I reached out to wrote me back.

The real estate agent I chatted with in Florida told me he had been in business for over ten years. If he had survived the crash in 2008, he had to know what he was doing and the light-bulb glowing in my head announced the possibility of an opportunity. I dropped the flower shop owner shit quickly and came at him with my CEO status pinned on me like a name badge at a Narcotics Anonymous meeting.

"I'm a hedge fund manager here in New York with a taste for real estate. When can we meet?"

While I tapped my fingers on the desk hoping he'd respond immediately a new message came in from the plumber in Nashville.

I usually don't respond to messages because there's nothing worth responding to but your words and your profile warranted it. I wish you had a picture uploaded but I understand the safety behind it, hence my own profile. You're in New York? That's quite some ways from here but I'll be heading your way more frequently. I'm thinking of battling some of the plumbing issues there. If this is a real person I'm responding to and you're not into P2P, I'd love to get a reply.

I began typing:

What's P2P? Seeing that I've never heard of it must be confirmation that I'm not into it. New York can always use more plumbers so allow me to be the first to welcome you here. I like to think I'm as real as real gets. Honestly, I don't think there's anyone realer... that was a joke, laugh. What's your name and what do you do for fun when you're not battling pipes?

There was a delay in his response. I used the opportunity to relieve myself. That's one of the things I loved about herbs, they kept me flushed and full of energy.

I checked, still no response so I threw on a sports bra and some yoga pants and hopped on the elliptical. I don't know what motivated me to but I turned on local news which I never watch. After five minutes of enough violence to make me move as far away from the Earth as possible, I turned on CNBC to check the pre-market company earnings reports. Thirty minutes in I received a message from him.

Thanks for the warm welcome, I'm Raymond but you my New York friend can call me Ray. When I'm not plumbing, I'm reading something. I try to read anything and everything I can get my hands on because I believe the truth is hidden in the word. I try not to let information pass me by and I research what I read. It doesn't sound like something a typical plumber would do but whose goals are typical anyway? I hope I didn't put you to sleep...laugh, that was a joke. Corny, but still a joke.

I wasn't bored, reading was my passion long before the stock market and not too many understood why. But, if it wasn't for reading everything my mama felt was too grown for me to touch, I would have never picked up the Forbes 400 magazine at the nail shop and read it. Most of the people named as the richest in the world had made their money from the stock market or a tie to it like an IPO. The magazine left a stain on my mind and I knew I wouldn't stop until I was featured in it. I quickly replied.

We share the same passion for knowledge or so it seems. Although I'm working in my floral shop all day,

I keep a book or two in front of me. There's nothing I enjoy more on this Earth than reading besides the sweet scent of my flowers.

I threw that bullshit line out there about the scent of flowers to keep my lie going and it worked. We continued to go back and forth non-stop for hours and we touched on so many things we had in common besides our love for reading. We both didn't eat pork, took herbs, and believed that small business owners should be investing. I pretended not to know that much about my investments seeing as he didn't seem to know much about his own. He said he had hired some guy to invest his money for him and every month he received a small check in the mail. I went with his flow agreeing that I had done the same.

Ray was easy to chat with, kept the conversation going, and most of all he was intelligent. After college he dived into the family business. He learned the hands-on part of plumbing from watching his father and grandfather and had learned the business side from the internet. My true identity wanted to tell him it was dangerous to build his company's foundation from articles found on the web but before I could, I saw Miya come strutting in with Evol's wife behind her. It didn't surprise me to see them together; I knew they were friends, that's why I never told Miya about my relationship with Evol. Miya was in their wedding, so was Man-Man, and the four of them were air space tight. I kept her in the dark; I wasn't sure where her loyalty would lie if she knew my truths.

"Hey, Nivea, this is my girl, Zamora."

When Miya said my name, Zamora looked at me quickly. She knew exactly who I was and the look on her face said she would make it known that she did.

"Wow, so we finally get to meet," Zamora said as she made her way to my couch and sat down like I had offered her a seat. "If I know who you are I'm more than sure you know who I am. Come on over here, you home wrecker, and sit down in your nice ass spot with me. I've waited years for us to be able to talk."

Zamora scanned the room and nodded her head like she was impressed with my place while Miya looked at us confused. She still hadn't put our connection together.

"So, what happened between you and my husband? The two of you haven't messed around in weeks. I almost miss the alone time I had while he was out committing adultery!"

That's when Miya connected the dots.

"Wait...what? Nivea, you've been creeping with Evol and didn't tell me? Hold up!" She turned her back to me and faced her friend. "And you didn't tell that you knew Evol was cheating on you? Damn, what kind of fucking friends are y'all? I thought y'all were my girls, I tell both of y'all bitches everything!"

I decided to deal with Miya later and the way Zamora looked at her I'd say she came to the same conclusion. I can't explain it but something in me was dying to answer her question. If she thought she could provoke fear in me because she sat her funky Puerto Rican ass on my couch she had me too fucked up. I'd beat that bitch down and then have her arrested for stalking and trespassing. I paid good money to live there and to keep the trash away.

"I ended it with your husband when I realized he'd never love me like he loves you and I don't settle for second place."

"You settled for second place for three years. What happened, your side chick membership expired?"

"No, it didn't expire. I called it quits for personal reasons that I don't have to share with you."

"You shouldn't have started it in the first damn place or you should have at least stopped when you found out about me!" she said scooting up on the edge of her seat like she needed the leeway to spring on me and I hoped she did. My fist yearned to bust her in her smart-ass mouth.

"You're right, I should have stopped it and I'm not trying to come off disrespectful but you know what it's like to be loved and made love to by your husband. Walking off wasn't that easy. Furthermore, if he didn't respect you and the marriage, why should I be forced to?"

The look on her face said she understood me and she didn't understand at the same time. I prepared for her to go throwback Rosa Perez on me but she didn't.

"You know, I could make this a nasty first-time face to face between us like I've dreamed about every night my husband didn't come home to lay up with you but I'm not. I can't 'cause what hurts me the most now is watching my husband sick over losing you." She shook her head, I assumed to do away with the image of her husband that crossed her mind at her last words. "Evol doesn't want to do shit anymore, not even hustle. He keeps saying he's going through something. He's lying saying the feds are watching him so he doesn't want to leave the house but I know the truth is that he's missing you..."

I stopped listening to her just to dissect the toxins and strength in her last words. My mind couldn't imagine what it felt like to be married and in love with a man who you know is in love with someone else too. The strength that she had to muster to accept it and the strength it took for her to tell me it, gave me a hint of what Evol saw in her but his toxins were making her use that power she had wastefully. If she continued to use it for battling the toxins in her marriage, she'd lose it. Most importantly, she'd lose herself in her love for him and that was the same situation that was happening to me. I was losing myself in her husband's fantasy fuck-world of love. His toxins were taking over my mind, body, and actions and I couldn't think clearly from inhaling his deadly fumes. I could feel his poisons consuming me as I sat back stupidly yearning for more of it. That's why I called it quits with him but unlike her, I didn't have the strength to tell my truths to the other bitch I knew he loved, his wife.

"I'm not a Sam-Sasha head chick, blinded by my love for my dog but I do know that my dog-ass nigga loves me and he keeps me and our daughter first. He strays for bones, easy to access snacks, and fast food that pleases his flesh but not his soul like your nothing ass but he always comes home for his real meals. He doesn't stray long, he already knows that nobody will love him like his owner. Did you hear me bitch? NOBODY!"

Zamora stood to her feet, unzipped her Ivory soap white First Down bubble jacket enough to flaunt the handle of her pistol and once she saw that it had my attention as well as she, she walked to my door victoriously.

"I'm going to help my husband get over you this time, but escucha..." she told me to listen in Spanish like its meaning was more powerful in her native tongue or as if she thought it would help her venture of provoking fear in me succeed and then said, "If I hear your name associated with my husband ever again I'm going to squash your homewrecking ass like the bug you are, Jezebel. It's never taken anyone three years to kill a roach and the fact that I let you continue to breath ain't shit but a sample of God's grace. Be careful of what you do from this point, puta. I gave your sins to God!"

She clicked her shoes together like Dorothy from the *Wizard of Oz* to shake the dust off her feet as she exited my home. Once she was no longer inside of my unit she said, "I promise you it will be more bearable for Sodom and Gomorrah on judgment day than for you. You can try me or the Lord if you want to. This is the calm before the storm, appreciate the warning!"

I didn't catch it at first but she hit me with the book of Matthew chapter 10, verses 14 and 15 from the Bible and while Miya started raving over the encounter between us, all I could do was pray, that bitch had me scared!

Dwayne

It was hard to get to sleep; my thoughts were of Nivea and I wasn't feeling the consumption. She was an earthquake that had hit my mind from the moment I read her name in the paper and like a Californian, I was more terrified by the aftershocks her beauty left. She had to be toxic, this I was sure of. If she was my type of sexy something had to be toxic about her. Bold, beautiful, caramel complexion with a sweet swirl in her round cinnamon roll as she walked. Thick, but if I had to sum up her body in one word I'd have to say solid. Not that I was staring but she had nice sized breasts that made sure to introduce themselves and left you questioning their authenticity. She wore a nice amount makeup that only enhanced the tightness in her eyes and the fullness of her lips. I couldn't tell her hair length but it was definitely all hers, another plus in my book.

Her toxins floated silently and moved deadly as she unknowingly attempted to control a part me I had already tamed, my dick. I wasn't a little boy who couldn't rule over the sleeping giant in my pants but she managed to be an alarm clock that he couldn't ignore as the seductive nibble she placed on her bottom lip woke him up. Honestly, her drive for success alone turned me on. I'd never met a woman whose goals were identical to mine and the thought of wearing matching outfits of success in finance was intriguing, but her mouth wouldn't let me get lost in her toxins. She needed a filtering system for her words and her ego wouldn't afford her one. I didn't care if your looks were a 10 in my book, what you let come out of your mouth could drop you down to a zero with no problem and she was already ranking in the negative digits.

Like I always say you can upgrade the body like ass and tits, but you can't fix the IQ of a lower-class lady. Nothing from nothing leaves nothing and I didn't want to think about a nothing so I got up and went to the computer to find me an S.T.D, something to do. I cruised my company's emails and a new one from Bowen Capital Management came in with the subject line: Website. The email was short and to the point. I debated on responding and decided to wait until I got to work. I logged out of my emails and logged on to the dating site. I had received a few profile likes and one message. Curious about the women Raymond had caught the attention of, I went through the likes and then responded to the message. The account owner didn't have a picture displayed but the headline caught my attention. It read:

If you're looking for anything other than real love, DO NOT APPLY!

I ran through the profile information and found out she owned a flower shop in New York. That was more than enough information to spark some interest. Maybe if it worked out, I'd have a home away from home in the Big Apple. I sent a message and within seconds she had responded back. We went back and forth for a while and then she disappeared. I didn't know much about her but something screamed different and not just the fact that she owned her own business. She took herbs, could listen just as good as she talked, but what really won me over was the fact that she was intelligent enough to work for herself and wise enough to invest her profits. Robert T. Kiyosaki had come up with something called the cash flow quadrant. It was a cross shaped graph. The left side of it represented the employees and self-employed but the right side was where the rich and the financially free dwelt which were the business owners and investors. Brenda, if that was really her name, was embedded on the right side. I just wished she knew more about the stocks, bonds, or IRAs her money was tied up in. I questioned her as far as I could without looking suspicious but she didn't have a clue about what her broker had her set up in besides that she received a dividend check quarterly. After gazing over our words for a little while longer thinking, *She has to be too good to be true,* and hoping she'd return, I was able to get some sleep.

I walked to work in the morning but I still took the parking lot ramp up to the office to see what Chris had worked out for Edward over the weekend. The 2016 Aston Martin had been replaced with a Knight Rider black, 2011 version of the car and in my visual opinion, a better buy.

"Good morning, Heather, send Edward into my office in thirty minutes and I'd like you to call the website guy and have him take that ugly green off it and replace it with gold. Call me when it's done."

"Yes, sir, and your new shipment of Robusta coffee came in. I told the girls to go ahead and grind it up for you."

"Great, have them bring me a cup when it's brewed."

"It's already brewing in your office. The girls and I got you a gift to show our appreciation," she said with a smile of gold that only showed a peek of the gold she had in her heart.

"You ladies didn't have to do that but I know you so I'll say thank you and walk away before you tear into me."

"Smart move, Mr. Hollingswell!"

The smell of the coffee brewing in my office would have shut Starbucks down if I wanted to go into that business. Robusta was the only style of coffee I'd drink besides Arabica and that was only as an emergency backup. I had popped herb after herb ducking and dodging coffee to get the pick me up that I needed. I wanted energy that wouldn't crash and found it hunting through herbs. I ran across a story about some donkeys eating a bean that filled them up with so much energy that it caused them to jump. I had to have that bean so you know I was surprised when I learned it was coffee. I guess that is why coffee is always the number one or number two commodity that investors invest in. Without the sugar and the creamer, coffee had become the edge to give me my superpower.

Pouring myself a cup I thought I'd check my messages on the dating site before truly starting my day. The conversation was getting too good for her to have walked away from it like she did and I wanted to see if she had ever returned, sadly she hadn't. Slightly feeling concerned I sent a message that said,

You ran away from the ball at midnight Cinderella and I found your glass slipper. I hope you'll allow me to give it back to you by picking up where we left off...

It was weak and I knew it. I didn't have any game but being Raymond and not Dwayne I felt comfortable in giving it a shot. I had a message from a model whose pictures made her seem more like a social media model but what was the difference between the two now days anyways? It read:

Hello,

I came across your profile and you seem cool. I'd really like to get to know you especially if you're a man who ain't fucked up about paying to play. I sent you some pictures, hope you like them.

Your boo,

The Head Hunter

Pussy, wet pussy, and big titties with rock hard nipples are all I saw. I wouldn't pay to play and now that she'd told me her goods had a price on them, I wouldn't try to hit but I would enjoy the pictures she sent. It's funny but I'd never fancied a strip club but every now and then I'd glance at an X-rated picture. Hell, being single was a lonely status and if I didn't have the real thing sleeping next to me every night, what did it hurt for me to look? I repented daily for my sins and some days lust made that list. I clicked on one of her pictures where she was on her knees with her lower lips spread underneath the two camel humps that made her ass and my office door flew opened.

"Damn, I forgot to knock," Edward said closing my door back. I took one last look as my growing meat deflated, logged off the site, cleared my browsing history, and said Psalms 51, the prayer of repentance before telling him to come in.

"Did you see my whip? Chris hooked me all the way up. That baby is mine and I don't have a note so what do I owe you? I know that isn't a $40,000 car I got. How much did you add to it?"

"Another $40,000 or so and I see you know me. Go home and pack and then get to the airport. Your plane tickets will be there waiting for you."

He sat down in front of my desk. "Where are you sending me this time Dubai or Singapore and for how long?"

"Singapore of course."

"Yo D,' that's a 16-hour flight and you know they are going to have a layover, make it 28."

"Which makes it worth the $45,000 I paid to fix your shit. Go home and pack you'll be there until Thursday. That's when you'll sell the position I tell you to buy Wednesday since they haven't released the ban on day trading. And Edward, I'm going to drop you off at the airport so I can hold on to those keys. I might upgrade the system in it and put those 26s I got in storage on it. You'll hear about me smashing through the city bumping *Purple Heart* by Sevin in it when you get back from handling my business. If you're questioned about anything on your trip..."

"I already know," he said cutting me off. "I love roulette and the best tables are in China."

"I taught you well."

He mumbled something that sounded like a whole lot of shit talking about me bumping Christian rap in his new ho-mobile underneath his breath. I decided not to question him about it as he left my office.

There was a beat played on the wall. I got up and went to my makeshift walkie-talkie, which was plastic tubing that ran from my senior investment manager's office to mine.

"What's up?"

"Hey, D, the shit is happening," Elliott whispered into the tube sounding louder than he would have speaking normally. I wasn't paranoid, I had it installed as an extra protection. Precaution had run out years ago.

Elliott was one of the few people who understood what loyalty meant. I met him due to a fuck up, it was avoidable but the truth was, I had fucked up.

The arrest from my ex- Cynthia felt like a spiritual

battle, like good vs. evil. There were times where I thought I was stuck in a video game or a Wall Street version of the show *Punk'd*. No one around me saw it the same so I should have known the law wouldn't recognize it as a fight against a demon. So, in 2015, days away from the termination of my probation and getting a chunk of freedom back, I got fly. I was back investing; my parents had every dime that they ever lost and I felt good. It was one of those days where nothing in your closet is right and I needed a new gray suit. I spent bread, something I said I'd never do after taking a sip out of Broke's cup. Every dime counted after that but biblically I came up with excuses for my spending. You know, when you find a scripture that fits your situation and you don't read all the others surrounding it to get the parables in your situation? You can call it spiritual suicide. That's exactly what I had committed as I pretended not to have read the scripture about doing it for the world. I walked out of some specialty store with a $3,000 handwoven scarf. Like I said, I got fly, even my nuts smelled like they were expensive and brand new. I put the top back on the Lambo I had bought seconds earlier and I hit the ground like a cheetah mixed with a greyhound on Noz, I was gone. I hit places that I used to fancy when I couldn't afford them just for the solitude in them. They had become my upgraded library and place to study. I had to revisit them now that I had my money. I was feeling myself, chin up, and if I would have taken a second to look down, every venue I had hit was filled with people who already had envy for me. Even with my empty pockets, people had managed to still find something to envy. In their eyes, my history trips were more of a, "I'm still shit'n on you expo." Like I said, I got fly.

I didn't realize I was tempting them like a T-bone over a lion until it was already too late. They tried to rob me heading to my car, pulled out heats on me, and in the moment, I thanked God he'd allowed me the money to have hired bodyguards. I don't really know what's happening with the case so I can't really speak on what happened but what I can say is, that both of my bodyguards told me to smash off and they had it covered. I smashed off, got maybe three blocks away, and was being pulled over for speeding. All three of us went to jail and had to wait 12 hours before we could make bail. I had to sleep the wine off and my bodyguards had a few holds on them.

The joke in all of it was that I had been in that jail so many times over that girl all the sheriffs knew me and how could they ever forget me, I was always GQ.

"No, Dwayne, what are you doing here? It's been almost a year, I thought she had finally left you alone!" Mrs. Davidson said as she took my fingerprints. "Damn, boy, whatever that cologne is you're wearing it smells good." I laughed. "Well I hate to see you but it's good to see you still doing and looking good but I think this other guy has you beat tonight. I think he said something about investing too. I hope I don't need to start sending all my daughters to visiting hours just so they can get a good man and they leave y'all out there in the street or in your situation Wall Street." She laughed and patted my hand.

I don't know what it's called but when Elliott and I looked at each other we had already spoken volumes to one another, I walked straight to him.

"SEC got me. What did you do? And I'm Elliott by the way."

"I'm Dwa-"

"Dwayne or Mr. Hollingswell, yeah, every sheriff who sees me says I'm another version of you. Why are you here?"

I was listening to him but three other dudes in our holding tank were listening to us and making commentary as we spoke.

"The SEC? I guess them niggas got something to do with college basketball, blood," the shortest and stockiest of the three said.

"Yeah, they probably coaches who got caught taking bribes for throwing the game. On bloods, them niggas clean though. My daddy had a suit like the nigga in the gray when he was pimping them bitches behind Beal Street," the oldest and roughest of the three said as I answered Elliott's question.

"Going 120 over the speed limit as I ran for my life but the cops weren't trying to hear that part. I'm not going to worry about it, my money won't let me stay here long. When my alcohol level goes down, I'm out."

"Fuck that weak ass nigga and his church boy suit. His ho ass just said he's in here for running from some niggas like a straight bitch. I bet he was in White Haven and my blood niggas were about to rob his ass. He better be lucky I wasn't out there or I would have put the pistol to his bitch ass," the last of them and deadliest looking one said. He had enough tear drops tatted under his eye to cry anyone a river but I didn't fear man and Justin Timberlake was from Memphis too. Before I could address the nonsense, Elliott was back talking.

"That's bullshit and you know it, D, let that ego you woke up ready to pet, go. You're letting whatever you drank do the talking. Are you on papers?"

"Yeah, but I get off in two weeks."

"You heard that?" the shortest one said, "that nigga said he's on papers."

"Yeah, for jacking his dick at the river front or littering outside the Fed Ex forum. That nigga ain't do no real time and probably crying on his mugshot," Teary-eyed said and the others laughed but my attention was on Elliott's next words.

"Not after tonight, you don't, if you let them keep you in here while they search for other shit. That's a for sure violation of your probation. You got money and Memphis wants every dime of it. Keeping you on papers mean they get paid. What do you do in finance, you smell like Wall Street?"

"Nah, that's that One Million cologne you're smelling," I laughed before continuing, "I've been moving solo through a private fund trading ETFs and commodities but the true goal is to monopolize the global markets through a multinational hedge fund. My mentor lives in China and he told me that the smart money is leaving the stock market and heading into physical commodities, agriculture, and preparation for war. I researched his findings and I'm in agreement. In other words, I'm thinking it's time for me to open up my own firm."

He looked up at the ceiling and said, "Thank you, Jehovah. At one-point, Dwayne, I was a very, very rich man but about three hours ago the SEC just raped me for everything. They charged my firm with misconduct, insider trading, and the manipulation of stocks through our funds. My firm is going to have to settle by paying fines, 100 million dollars plus, which will go back to the investors and we will have to shut down but I'm going to have to fight my crimes against the SEC. I'll win against the money hungry scavengers, but I'll probably end up serving jail time and that's the easy part. The hard part will be listening to the SEC ban me from it all. Trading is my air, how do you live life when you can't breathe, D?"

The oldest of the three was listening to us and his mouth dropped when he heard Elliott say he was rich. He immediately cut off the conversation his boys were having without him and made them focus their attention back on us.

"That's on Peaboy, rest in peace, that nigga in the Gucci just said he was rich from the SEC and worked as a manipulator for the Jehovah Witness. The one in the suit like my daddy's said something about having one million and smelling like money. He fucks with some emperor in

China named hedgehog like Sonic and they are opening their own firm called Smart Money Law. I bet they can hook us up with a lawyer so we can get off this bullshit."

"Stop dick riding, on bloods, you sound like a gold digging bitch. We ain't asking them faggot ass niggas for shit and if the one in the gray suit looks this way again, I'm going to beat his Jehovah Witness ass for always leaving them magazines in my door." His words made the stocky one laugh. I kept my eye on him since he was the quietest and then spoke to Elliott.

"I don't trust nobody off the knuckle but I know a Witness when I see one. We're family, if you can help me fix mine, we will work together to fix yours. You'll work for me and get whatever money they take from you back plus interest. We'll hire the best attorney to look over your ban. I'm sure there will be a crack and if there isn't, there are always other countries. I need to get out of here like you said!" I told him.

"Say no more, give me your date of birth," he said walking over to the payphones. On his way there, the oldest Blood grabbed him by his suit coat.

"Aye blood, can you help us get out too? We don't have no bread but I'm willing to work off any debt."

"Didn't I tell you not to ask them ho ass niggas for help? Keep walking nigga before I…"

"Before you what?"

I was standing behind him ready to flex him the

second he said something to Elliott. He looked at me from over his shoulder and didn't say a word. I stood behind him until Elliott had made the calls he needed to just in case I needed to beat Justin and N'snyc's ass for messing with my new ace. I was out in 45 minutes and the old blood dude was walking out with me thanks to Elliott being the solid dude that he was. After he served his 3 months in jail, I'd kept my word, and he'd been my right-hand man ever since.

"As I knew it would. Tell everyone to start buying as many shares as they can of UVXY."

"What about floor caps? You have a lot of them maxing out at five hundred thousand. How about we bump that up to 1 mill?"

"Better make it 1.5 and send in Sunday's best, I'm going to church."

"Church, right now?"

"Yeah, why not?" Elliott never questioned me unless he came up with a way to out execute my killer instincts.

"Smart move, bad play. Do you really want to stop them from buying right now?"

"No, you're right. Send them to me first thing in the morning."

My office phone rang abruptly ending my private meeting with Elliott. It was Heather calling.

"Mr. Hollingswell, the website has been updated is there anything else I can do for you?"

I pulled up the website before responding and removing the green was the exact touch it needed.

"Yes, one more thing. I need you to have six dozen red roses sent to Bowen Capital Management, the address is in the Rolodex." The other end of the call fell silent. "Heather, are you there?"

"Yes, sir, I'm here. I apologize, it caught me off guard to hear that you were dating. Congratula..."

"I'm not dating," I interrupted her to say. "What made you assume that?"

"Oh, the choice of flowers. Red roses mean love or I love you so six dozen of them..."

"Seems like I'm proposing. Okay, let's scratch that then. Send a mass amount of whatever color roses mean thank you and include a card. I'll email you what it needs to say."

Heather laughed and then said, "Yes, sir," before ending the call.

I should have told her to send whatever flowers meant sorry since her company did indeed fail to go public but if she was anything like me it would feel like salt in an open wound. I guessed asking Heather to send flowers for me felt like salt too but that wound should have been closed years ago.

Nivea

The Starbucks locations in the financial district were always at the maximum capacity set by the International Building Codes so I rarely participated in the morning rush myself. Whenever I wanted or needed a caffeinated fix I'd wait until I made it to the office to send one of my assistants to deal with the headache. After having the shit scared out of me last night and sleeping with one eye open, I fended for my Joe myself.

"Let me have a Venti white chocolate mocha, heavy cream, and one of those muffins over there that doesn't have any nuts on it."

"Would you like anything else?" the twenty-something-year-old lady behind the register asked as she gave me the total and grabbed a cup.

"No, that will be all, thank you."

"And your name please?"

"Nivea, N- I- V-..."

"Nivea? Nivea Bowen?"

A strong professional voice called out from the end of the line. The sound of my name felt familiar in the tone it was spoken in but I couldn't place a person to the familiarity. I looked back and it seemed like everyone behind me was wearing a smile on their face. It was possible that everyone could have been having a good morning but I doubted it. Too many of their eyes were locked on me. We were in the financial district with the New York Stock Exchange sitting in front of Starbucks' doors. I knew why everyone was smiling at me after hearing my name and it had nothing to do with them liking the uniqueness of it. I'll admit my mom used all the style she had left over from her youth of the '70s when she named me Nivea. My name was different yet it wasn't a common name floating around the world of finance until now. You see, now every broker, agent, analyst, and quants, who are better known as the rocket scientists of Wall Street, knew my name now that everyone knew Nivea was the name of the chick who's firm recently publicized their move to IPO in every financial news outlet and had failed to. With all eyes on me, I raised my head high enough to where my chin would rest comfortably on the tops of their heads and pretended to be unbeatable by their stares. I turned around to face the front with confidence that I had borrowed from the lie and a few seconds later, I felt a slight tap on my shoulder.

"Well look at what the cat drug in, a thingamajigger and it's still the prettiest unnamable thing that I've ever laid eyes on."

A thingamajigger is something you know how to use or how it's used but you don't know the name for it. There was only one person who called me that and I confirmed it was him by the smell that tickled my nose when he walked up.

"Ananias, Ananias always smelling good, Levi.

How are you doing, sir?"

"I'm alive and in the flesh, so I guess that means I'm good, right?" he said pulling me into his embrace and I took this forced show of his affection to get a deep whiff of his skin. No one's natural body scent smelled as good as his when it blended with Jean Paul Gaultier. I inhaled deeper causing my kitty to jump as he continued, "It's so good seeing you, baby girl, especially with your head up high. I saw the bullshit articles about the IPO crap. I knew you were too strong to go into hiding like most of them suggested you would."

There were a few soft snickers from the line behind us at his last words but I pretended like they went unheard. Seeing my old Israeli study and fuck buddy with no ties attached, trumped any Donald Duck bullshit that came quacking out of their lips.

"Of course, I wouldn't hide. Why would I when I'll be suing everyone involved for millions after these so-called professionals dropped the ball? When you hire the best, Ananias, and they fuck up, knowing how grand the compensation will be for their mistakes will put a smile on your face. Why would I hide?" I laughed and the line went up in multiple whispers giving me a chance to speak with him with less listening ears.

"Why don't you grab your coffee and let's play catch up. My condo isn't too far away."

"We'd love too but unlike yours, my husband's firm is doing exceptionally well. We have a high success rate and a team that's the cream of the crop that we handpicked ourselves. You see, we didn't have any problems when it came to taking our company public so I'm sorry, he can't play with you right now, music video slut."

I knew that voice, it belonged to the only bitch that could make Ananias switch up on me, Sapphira. Running my mouth to prove how well rounded I was is how I fucked around and introduced my college dick to his soul mate. I'd never forgotten the day. We were all in study hall doing more chatting than studying and then all of a sudden, the small knowledge I had of the stories in the Bible had come to me.

"Hey, Ananias, do you see that Indonesian girl over there in the red sweater?" I asked cheesing like the Cheetos cat.

"With the long black hair? Yeah, I've seen her around. She's in a couple of our classes but she's taking computer science or something like that. I think I heard someone say that her career goal was to be a quantitative software engineer for a big firm like her dad. I heard he created the software Goldman solely uses and his salary is something like $270,000 a year but some reporter asshole publicized his W2 and box number one was well over 1.1 million so you already know they're rich, but why'd you ask?"

"Because her name is Sapphira," I blurted out unable to control my excited laugh and after forty seconds or so I realized he had no clue to why that tickled me. "You know, the story of Ananias and Sapphira in the Bible?"

"Unfortunately, I don't. Why don't you tell it to me?"

"I'm no raconteur, but they were husband and wife. Ananias sold some land, over charged the buyer, and then lied about what he made off it. When one of the Holy Spirits' apostles asked him about it, he lied and suddenly died at his feet. Hours later his wife Sapphira was questioned about the price and lied, she died suddenly too. Anyways, they are famously known as the couple who died after lying to the Holy Spirit about money. Isn't that funny that both of you have a hankering for finance?"

It was funny; however, the last laugh was on me. As soon as I finished telling him the story, he made it his business to share it with her. Not only did they hook up, he cut me off from his dick, and they married while we were still in school.

"Sapphira, how are you? I see that you're still as bland, flat assed, and chubby as I remembered you. Do you still prefer your dick in the rear rather than in your fat ass mouth?"

"Oh wow, I didn't think you'd be able to talk with all the different broker's dicks that I've heard you've had in your mouth since graduation. I guess sucking and swallowing the nut from your whole legal team didn't work out for you this time, did it, Nivea? Is that why you're ready to suck on my husband's? Sorry to tell you, sweetie, but Ananias no longer feeds the homeless."

The line broke out in laughter and I noticed a few of

the so called upscale professionals of Wall Street were using their phones to record our encounter, but I still had to have the bitch.

"Sounds like you're still hurt about me taking your husband's virginity but I understand. How does anyone expect you to get over the fact that he showed up late to your wedding after he begged me to fuck him one last time before settling for bear meat? You should be happy I did, Yogi, or you could have ended up being one of those starving bears I heard they had to rescue from that Indonesian zoo."

The crowd cheered us on, back and forth, like we were having a verbal boxing match until Ananias had enough of the beating I was giving his wife. He quickly began ushering her out the building but not before sliding me his business card with a wink. I held it up to the camera phones that were recording me, memorized his number just in case I ever needed a late-night snack, and then ripped it up.

"When you messy fuckers post that video on World Star and whatever other social media outlets you plan to share it to make sure you include the fact that he still slid me his number." I laughed and then rushed to my office so I could pray that the couple had the same fate as the couple they were named after in the Bible.

*****

I haven't owned a Bible in physical form in years which I'm sure made my grandmother somersault in her grave. I had to look up the meaning to the footwork Evol's holier than thou wife put on me at the door online. My first thought was right, it was from Matthew chapter 10 verses 14-15. I read it out loud from the New International Version to make it sink in, "If anyone will not welcome you or listen to your words, leave that home or town and shake the dust off your feet. Truly I tell you, it will be more bearable for Sodom and Gomorrah on the day of judgment than for that town."

I wasn't a Bible thumper but I knew there was more to the meaning of the scriptures than what I was reading. Even a dummy could tell that those words were a part of instructions, my question was, instructions to what? I used the mouse to take me to the first verse in chapter 10 and my office door flew open without warning.

"Ms. Bowen, you have to come out and see this shit for yourself!" Karla said and then disappeared as fast as she had arrived. She hadn't given me time to redirect her for not knocking but I was glad she hurried off. Something in me didn't want her to catch me reading the Bible. I didn't know why I hit the red X on the tab when the door flew open like it was porn, but I did. It was small shit like that, that confirmed, I was too gone into the ways of the world.

"What shit did you want me to see for myself…"

I didn't get around to finishing my question by ending it with her name because my eyes sent my jaw dropping. From my personal office door, down the long hallway, and leading to the entrance to my offices' suite the floors were covered in at least 100 glass vases each filled with three dozen pink roses. It looked like I had gotten trapped in the middle of a rose garden. If it wasn't for the small walkway Karla created to come get me, I would have been stuck in the potpourri.

"Karla?"

"Yes, Ms. Bowen."

"Who sent these, is there a card?"

"Yes, the delivery guys have it and are in the hallway waiting for you to sign for them. Who do you think they are from, Ms. Bowen?"

I ignored Karla's question. My mind had already hoped that they were from Evol and I wanted them to be. I know I promised myself that I'd leave him alone no matter what he did but if this was the way he'd beg for me to come back, I'd listen. Hell, three dozen pink roses were $71.00 and the only reason I knew that was thanks to my fake online persona, Brenda, who had researched the price of roses just in case Raymond asked. If there were 100 vases or more flooding my office, then he had spent $7,100 just to get my attention. Knowing that he was a small-time street hustler and that was probably a month's income for him, I'd give him a chance to beg.

"Sign here please."

The delivery man holding the clipboard looked beyond tired which I understood seeing that my office was located on Exchange Street and vehicles weren't permitted to park in front of it, not even for loading and unloading.

Not to mention the fact my office was located on the 21st floor and the service elevator was out. Although the gentleman didn't have to take the stairs up because the regular elevators were working, I'm sure there were multiple trips made to deliver the roses. I signed, thanked them for their trouble, and then ripped open the card. To my surprise, it was from Mr. Hollingswell.

Ms. Bowen,

Please accept these roses as compensation for your consultant fee. Seeing that I don't believe in fiat currency I hope they suffice. I'm hoping you check your schedule and can arrange an appointment to meet with me soon since you have been paid in full.

Thank you for your prompt response,

Mr. Dwayne Hollingswell

P.S We updated the website. I hope it's to your liking!

I can't lie, I was a little disappointed that they weren't from Evol, nonetheless they made for a nice surprise.

"Ms. Bowen, I need your approval to exceed the buying limit on the floor to take advantage on a huge short position that will be very lucrative in a short amount of time..."

I probably should have been listening to my analyst,

Kishi, as she gave me the details on the short position she wanted all the traders to buy into heavily but Dwayne's gesture of apology and attempt for a do over had my attention. I trusted Kishi's decision's and it wasn't due to stupid stereotypes regarding Asian's educations. She was the best analyst and momentum trader in the United States, hands down.

"I trust you, Kishi. Raise everyone's limits to half a million for today only. Is that good enough?"

"Yes, that's perfect," she nervously replied at my lackadaisical response. "Are you okay, Ms. Bowen? You granted permission without hearing every detail. I don't mean to question your decision but I know you are strict about following protocol."

"I made the protocol. Would you like me to say no instead?"

"No, ma'am!"

Kishi ran off and I ran to Karla's desk to get on her computer. I typed in Dwayne's company website and the green was gone. He had it replaced what was supposed to be 24k gold. I was hoping he'd pick more of a 14k color since that's what the world was used to seeing the most but following what the world thought was best is what had me embarrassed of being caught reading the Bible.

"Karla, I need you to call Mr. Hollingswell and schedule an appointment for him with me for whenever he is available. If his availability doesn't match mine, move my appointments around..." I could feel her looking at me like I had lost my mind so I sped up my dictation, "Also, thank him for the roses and tell him the website looks a lot better." I started playing hopscotch through the roses to get back to my office. When I arrived, Karla was calling me on the phone.

"Ms. Bowen, you have a call from an unwanted caller on line five. I told him you weren't here and he threatened to come see for himself. I told him I'd go double check your whereabouts."

"Didn't I tell you not to answer his calls when you see it on the caller ID?"

"He isn't calling from his number, per the information on the caller ID, I think he's calling from jail. You know, that one free call they give you at the precinct?"

I inhaled until I felt lightheaded before speaking again.

"Transfer him over, Karla, and I know the flowers caught you off guard but I need you to refrain from moving off personal feelings. Make sure you always knock on my office door no matter what the circumstances are. You interrupted me reading the Bible."

It instantly became a priority to tell her that I was in the process of building a relationship with the Lord especially after she announced that the devil had called to temp me.

"This is Nivea Bowen; how may I help you?"

"Cut the fake shit, you know I already know your assistant told you it was me calling."

"You're absolutely right, let's cut the fake shit. If you told her who you were why didn't you tell her what you wanted with me? I'm busy!"

"Oh, now you're too busy for me?!"

"I've been too busy for you for almost two months now but your wife has time for you, she made sure that I knew she did."

"Fuck her, I didn't call you to talk about her."

"Then what do you want to talk about. I'm too busy for chitchat and judging by the number you're calling me from, your time on the phone is limited," I giggled while hoping I was shooting off enough attitude to send him running.

"Nah, I actually can stay on the phone for another four hours. I don't get off work until 6."

"Um, so the hustler has become the hustled. From being snitched on to becoming the snitch, I guess you call that the circle of life." I don't know why that bullshit felt theological coming out my mouth but it did and it felt good.

"Shut that shit up. Do you miss me?"

"Is that what you called me for? You decided to use the State of New York's taxpayer's money to sneak on the phone at a job you haven't even worked 90 days on to ask me a dumb ass question? Hell no, I don't miss you and to be honest if Karla wouldn't have told me that it was you, I wouldn't have recognized your voice."

"You trying too hard, Nivea, you know daddy knows when his baby is spitting fraud. So, if you missed me why haven't you come to see me? You know where I be at."

"Exactly, which means I don't miss you like I told your wife last night. As a matter of fact, is that why you're calling me? Did the Mrs. tell you about our little face to face powwow and you wanted to see if I had on my big girl panties? Well let me tell you like I told your owner, you dog ass nigga, I no longer want you and I sure in the hell don't miss you. You called me and..."

He cut me off to say the truest words I think I had ever heard come off his lying tongue in the three years I'd known him, "Then why haven't you hung up the phone on me yet? You don't owe me an explanation or a breakdown of what happened between you and my wife. Tell the truth, Nivea, you want to argue and talk shit to me. It's the only way you can fill that void of not having me around. Yeah you miss me but you want to act like you're the shit and full of pride now, that's cool. Baby, you can stunt all you want but I've never been impressed by your acting. I miss you, I love you, and that's real. So real that my wife knows. I'm sure it's fucked up to be in love with a married man but like I told you when I met you, I'm in love with both of y'all and I can't live without you both. Now tell me you don't love me like you mean the shit and I'll never reach out to you again, that's my word."

Evol's words in my ear were replaced with the steady rhythm of the dial tone. For a second there I thought he hung up on me for not responding and then I pretended that I mustered up the strength to hang up on him but when I looked at the cradle to my phone, Karla's freshly manicured index finger nail was what ended the call.

I hadn't noticed the steady flow of tears streaming down my face until she carelessly tossed a box of tissues my way.

"Like you told me when I came to work crying over my ex-husband, wipe your face. Tears ain't never fixed a motherfucking thing; there's money to be made!"

As I wiped and blew the loose fluids from my nose she pulled up Black Professionals Meet Love from my browsing history and opened my new messages. I was waiting for her to say a few personal words like some woman to woman advice, instead she said, "Is there anything else I can help you with Ms. Bowen?"

I smiled as the last sniff confirmed my nose had already dried and thought for a second, "Yes, make sure you and the girls put as many of those roses in my car that will fit, put a vase on every table in the break room, in the conference room, and the lobby. After that, make sure every member of the staff gets a vase to take home with them."

"Okay, and what should I do with all the rest of the

roses?" she followed with a laugh.

"Fill your car up with as many as you can carry home and then call the nearest battered women's center and have them pick up and pass them out."

"Good idea, boss, and I promise that's the last time I walk in without knocking on your door." Karla softly rubbed my hand and gave me a wink. I allowed enough time for her to make it back to her desk and then I replied to Raymond.

Of course, we can pick up where we left off and you can keep the glass slipper as a keepsake. That way you'll always have something to remember me with.

Dwayne

The usual warmth of the parking garage had transformed into the cold chill of a graveyard at 2am on Halloween morning. If death approaching had a warning feel to it, then I was certain that, that feeling was all around me. I couldn't tell if I was surrounded by ghosts, at least not by sight. The only thing my eyes could see was motionless vehicles parked in designated spaces. I had never been to the office nor the parking lot connected to it at 5am and after the eerie feel of things, I would never go that early again.

Throughout my childhood I could remember thinking there was something spooky in the soil of Memphis and I didn't mean the paranormal activity horrors dream up but the true terror we find in the reality of life. It frightened me to see so many people content with not having accomplished anything, the daily killings, and slim to none growth opportunities. All jokes aside, I remember crying myself to sleep while clutching a Bible throughout the night when I learned at 15 that the average household income in Memphis was $37, 099 a year. That meant between two parents neither one of them made $20,000 a year and the $18,549.50 it divided to was proof that each parent was only making $9.66 an hour. Who needs to fear Jason chopping off your head with a bloody knife and wearing a hockey mask when the future of the majority of people around you equated to providing for their family at the cost of a value meal per hour? Thinking of growing up there had become a living nightmare.

I hurriedly got out of the car and popped my trunk. The plan was to snatch and dash. I'd snatch up the folders I needed and then make a dash to the elevators. I didn't fear man, but everything else earned the right to me raising my eyebrow to it and although I wore the full body armor of Christ, I wasn't in the mood to fight a demon, it was too early.

It's funny how shit becomes obvious that you normally overlook when you become uncomfortable. I parked in this garage every day and hadn't noticed a thing. There I was alone and now everything had caught my attention. From the shortage in one of the lights to the sound the trees made scraping the walls whenever the wind blew. My engrossment in the flaws turned my imagination on, I'll admit but not enough to cause false evidence to appear real. You know that feeling you get when you're not alone in a space, it usually meant you weren't and as soon as I reached into my trunk, the sound of a twig snapping behind me confirmed that I wasn't. I closed my eye and prayed.

"Glad you could meet us this early, D," a squeaky high-pitched male's voice said and then an almost identical but softer voice said, "We brought a celebration breakfast!"

I took a deep breath and opened my eyes. The familiar sound of their voices meant it was time for church.

"Good morning, fellas, I'm definitely in the mood for a celebration breakfast. Can one of you grab these folders for me? We can go ahead inside," I said showing no signs that seconds ago one of them was about to feel the heat of the ungodly but prayed over weapon I kept in my trunk.

I turned around to face two brick wall shaped, identical in every way expect their accessories, human beings that I nicknamed the church. Jacob and Esau Halley were melanin diamonds. Standing at 6'0" and weighting 225lbs their structures reminded me of Terry Crews but their features favored Omari Hardwick. Both having firm jawbones and nicely trimmed thin goatees the only way I could tell the identical twins apart was by knowing that Jacob, the oldest twin by three minutes had a squeaky voice and wore one-inch full rim square framed glasses and Esau, besides wearing no frame glasses, had a mouth full of braces covering his pearly white teeth. I didn't see a need for the train tracks on his teeth but I'm sure they weren't his perception of mouth jewelry.

In my opinion, the twins were the creme de la creme however, brilliant, was the best singular word that described them. Their personalities were fueled by their hearts and reflected the love of the father. I don't mean their physical dad, I'm speaking of our father in heaven whose multi-strain DNA structure proved that we were brothers by birthright. Like myself, Jacob and Esau didn't take the absence of their biological father as a void. It was unnecessary since both boys' faith lied in the father they had up above.

We met when we were kids at the Boys and Girls

Club book drive. All three of us were hungry for a way to become successful to make our exit from Memphis. With my family not understanding my interest in finance I went to the book drive in search of free books on the subject so I could stop begging my parents for them and coming up empty handed. There were hundreds of books covering the tables yet there was only three of us interested in going through them. It was the first time I had ever seen those in the community I lived in turn down anything free but as the old expression goes, if you want to hide something from black people put it in a book. Good thing I've always thought of myself as of a man of melanin verses a lightless color that the dictionary defines as dirty, soiled, thoroughly sinister, and evil and that's only a few fuck yous thrown at my people.

"I think we should become doctors," I heard the squeaky voiced twin say as he held up a biology book to his brother.

"Biology majors? That's so limited. We can go deeper than that, how about some complicated form of scientist? That way we'll get more diversity than living organisms. Don't forget brother, we can do all things through Christ who strengthens us."

"You're right, Esau, you are indeed your brother's keeper."

The boys did some secret hand shake and returned to sorting through the books. I thought I was watching a movie or somewhere far away from Memphis as I heard the twins reciting Bible scriptures. They were shooting the

170

word at each other like pastors filled with the holy ghost as the organ player gassed them up by playing a few quick keys to keep them going. They had the spirit in them and their futures on their mind. Seeing that I didn't have any friends and never wanted any there had to be something special about the twins because I wanted to be an honorary triplet.

"Jacob, we're going to be the richest identical twins in history. Smart, handsome, God fearing, and filthy rich!"

"You can't serve both God and money," I said softly. I wanted my words to come off as a whisper, like I was sharing a secret among friends. I hopped that it was enough to spark a conversation between the three of us.

"We don't want to serve nor love money," Jacob snapped and his brother spoke up.

"Yeah, the love of money is the root of all evil. We already know that! We can have a lot of money without loving it." Uncertainty crossed his face and then he looked at his brother and said, "Right, Jacob, God wants us to be rich?"

"Yes, brother. You're right. It's what we do with the money and how we get it that's matters to God," Jacob replied with his chest out.

"You're both right, I only spoke up after hearing your first choice was a doctor and then a scientist. Great career choices that make a lot of money but both seem like careers that force you to play God. That's all I was trying to say."

I had finally found a book on finance in the pile. It was *Buffettology* written by Mary Buffett and I couldn't retain my excitement. It was one of the books I had begged my parents for and there it was laying under a stack of useless books for free. Esau saw the look on my face and quickly snatched the book out of my hands.

"What's this, smart guy?" he asked taking a once over of the book as Jacob joined him flipping the book over to read the synopsis.

"Finance and you talk to us about serving money?" the squeaky voice demanded.

"You say it like it's a sin. Money is the second most talked about subject in the Bible. It's only second to the kingdom of God and I want to be an investor. If I keep studying hard and learn the markets, one day I'll become a day trader."

"An investor has to love money, that's all they do. Matthew 6:21 says, 'For where your treasure is, there your heart will be also.' If investing is your treasure than your heart is filled with money," Esau said adjusting his glasses before they slid off the bridge of his nose.

"The Bible tells us to save for a rainy day, leave an inheritance to our children's children, and speaks on debt, lending, and interest but I won't argue with you about our father's words. I was enjoying hearing you speak them like it was its own language. I'm Dwayne by the way."

I stuck out my hand and both boys introduced

themselves and the three of us became inseparable. After spending hours reading finance books with me they decided to join me in the field. We had plans of graduating, getting our degrees, and opening a firm together but reality set in once we reached the second semester of 12th grade. They were accepted to private universities and Ivy League schools. They were geniuses, two Albert Einsteins, and me, well... let's just say that I'm thankful that C's are passing grades.

The twins moved up North for school and I never heard from them again until I opened my firm and their applications came across my desk. I couldn't believe it but what God puts together no man can separate. Their mother had fallen ill and they had moved back to Memphis. Jacob saw the ad for the position on an online career site and told his brother, they had no idea they were applying to work for me. Even if their resumes weren't as impressive as they were, and if they both hadn't graduated from Harvard with all those achievements in finance, I still would have hired them. I knew they were the best of the best before puberty kicked in and with their devotion for the father, I nicknamed them The Church.

"Okay, fellas, you got me up early and said we needed to talk before the markets opened today. You said you weren't mistaken about the move to buy up UXYZ yesterday so what did you want to talk about?"

The twins looked from one to another, this was a move that they pulled on me a lot so I knew it would eventually lead to Jacob taking the mic first.

"We'll get to that in a minute, D. We'd actually like to know why you asked to meet with us since all we did was request an earlier meeting time with you to discuss a few things. Maybe our reasons for meeting will be one and the same."

They were my brothers but a part of me still wanted to remind them that I was the boss. After debating for a while with both of them staring at me I chose to put my power card up for a more useful time.

"Well, the market isn't open yet but I would like to know how you two geniuses came up with the move months ago and knew the precise day that we should execute it?"

"That was easy," Esau, the freer spirited and sometimes cocky or should I say overly confident, twin began saying. "We'd learned the importance of watching the futures from the time they open Sunday evening until they close Friday, before we graduated high school and have been watching them ever since. UXYZ isn't the only VIX short term future we short but it is the one that seems to always demand our attention."

It was like watching a wrestling match but instead of him tagging Jacob in with a touch of his hand, Esau nodded and his brother took over.

"As you know when the Dow Jones goes down, the VIX goes up and that's exactly what has been happening. In 2011, we watched it drop from 12.1 Million to 5.1 Million in a day and there were a few other times that has

174

occurred since then."

Jacob nodded and they switched.

"To sum it up like our professor at Harvard taught us in our Human Capital Strategies class, the abnormal rises and falls of the Dow Jones index can be caused by the news, economical catalyst, and many other things that would probably get me killed if I shared them..."

"The point Esau is trying to make," Jacob said cutting him off before he slipped and told their latest conspiracy theory. "...is that the stock market is covered in human fingerprints and although we know the Dow is made up of 30 major individual American companies, the rises and falls of the index are based on each company's supply and demand. When investors are buying more than selling, the price of the index rises."

"And with the election coming we knew the Dow would rise judging by who the American people elected. So..." Esau nodded so Jacob could conclude.

"We started buying positions long term months ago."

"Wait, so when the Dow Jones broke a record and reached $21,000 a share that means you lost money, my money!" I snapped and they both nodded but neither spoke up. "Oh, this is when one of you needs to start talking and I mean now!"

I pushed the celebration off my desk and into the trash as the church continued to sit there in silence giving each other looks that seemed to speak volumes between the two. After I cleared my throat to snap them out of it, Jacob spoke up.

"Well, D, that's what we wanted to talk to you about. We've been sticking millions in the UXYZ since June 2016 and I must honestly report that we lost the company millions of dollars due to our premature decision."

"Millions of dollars!" I yelled, "Exactly how many million?"

I could feel my stomach churning and tightening into knots. I took a deep breath to brace for the impact of Jacob's next words.

"Around 77 million dollars and then we margined it for another 77million." He closed his eyes and I could feel my heartbeat slowing down as I knew his next words were going to kill me. "And then we called the primary broker and he three times our original 77 million bringing the total to 308 million dollars to be exact, which caused the company to show red in the fourth quarter among other things."

"What the fuck! That's impossible, I looked over the numbers myself and my CPA didn't mention it to me."

"Truthfully, we actually kept that report when it arrived and switched the date on the one from last year," Esau declared with his chest out like he was telling me something good.

"Don't forget that you are a man of God first, D, our triplet second, and that money is the root of all evil," Jacob announced and I had a little announcement I needed to make myself.

"It's the love of money, and being a child of God and your brother won't stop me from firing you or putting my hands on both of y'all if y'all don't make this shit right. You had me raise the floor limit yesterday when I should have been filing bankruptcy!"

"Ye of no faith!" Esau blurted out and then shook his head. "The move we made yesterday will not only recover all the loses we made but break the company's record for one-day profit earned. When the stock market opens we will all be rich, even the secretaries."

The boys embraced each other and then did their stupid little handshake that suddenly irritated the shit out of me. I didn't know what to else to do but the urge to shit took the words from me as I rushed to my private restroom.

My thoughts wouldn't organize as the toilet filled up after each courtesy flush that I did. I loved the boys, that was unmistakable, but that priceless feeling I normally held inside of me for them had finally totaled a number. 308 million dollars was only the beginning of the debt I'd be facing. There was interest, fees, and my mind was too cloudy to think of all the rest. If I had ever wished I was dreaming, it was that moment.

I pulled my iPhone out of my pocket and began looking at all the positions we bought the day before and the ones they had bought prior. It took me until 8:30 my time, 9:30 New York's, to figure it all out and the conclusion I came up with was it equaled broke. Not lint in the pockets broke but the type of broke that would have me being sued by our clients, black balled, and banned permanently while I begged for change outside of a liquor store in the hood.

Exiting the restroom, I was hit with both homicidal and suicidal thoughts at once. I saw myself standing over the handmade twin graves that the twins occupied with a pistol pointed at my temple. I hoped they weren't in my office when I returned but I knew they would be.

"Where did you go, D? The show is about to begin," Esau said popping open a bottle of non-alcoholic wine as Jacob held three champagne flutes in his hands. "It's almost celebration time."

The LED stock ticker display that traced the top of my wall in my office was in motion and the 24 multi-monitor display on my wall had 12 displaying the Dow Jones Index in different indicators, oscillators, and moving averages and the other 12 displayed the UXYZ ETF in the same function. I couldn't watch either with the scary movie killing music playing in my head as the twins acted as if nothing was wrong.

I couldn't help but ask, "Do we really have 2.2 billion invested in this move?"

"No!" Jacob responded like I had insulted him, "We weren't that crazy. We have 4.4 billion invested; we margin called it."

That was when I knew I'd died and landed in the financial district of hell. The torture was on auto pilot and the boys were the watch tower that called it in. I couldn't move hear or feel for at least another hour. When I could move I didn't know if it was too late to pray and repent for my sins in money but I had to give it a try. I fell to my knees and placed my elbows in the seat of my chair and before I could say my last prayer on March 17, 2017 the Dow Jones dropped a little over 200 points in the first hour and a half. In thirty minutes not only did the church recover the 308 million dollars they lost my firm but we made a 432-million-dollar profit. I wanted them to sell our position but they begged me to wait until the end of the day and I'm glad I did. Although if the 740 million would have gotten anywhere near 500 million I would have sold the shit myself I held off and we ended our day at 1.6 billion dollars. Not only did it feel good to break a record as a firm knowing that 25% of the money made was ours, we had made every client in the fund a millionaire. Now I could celebrate but not in Memphis, I'd do it once I made it to New York.

"Heather?"

"Yes, Mr. Hollingswell?"

"I'll be leaving shortly for New York on business. I'll return the day after tomorrow. Edward is still away for a few more days and Elliott called out sick again. If anyone needs anything please send them to Jacob and Esau. They will be in charge until I return."

"No problem and you asked me when you hired me to let you know everything that's going on big or small. Is that still a desire of yours?" she asked with an unsteady voice.

"Of course, it is. If the mail man changes his pattern or delivery time I want to know."

"I thought you'd say that," she said with a giggle. "Well, we are experiencing a heavy volume of hang up calls and voice messages with someone breathing heavy but no words are said. It's been going on since Monday and I would have told you then but I didn't want to come to a tentative conclusion. There's a brewing problem, its unmistakable."

"I'm assured. Keep a count of these calls and if they don't stop I will look into it when I return."

"Yes, sir, and safe travels."

I left my car in the parking lot and jumped in Edward's. Seeing that I hadn't cranked the engine since I dropped him off at the airport it was overdue. I had my bag packed and waiting for me by my condo's door. I doubled parked to run up and grab it but I couldn't believe my eyes. Ms. Blakemore was sitting on her cardboard box turning up a bottle of the cheapest vodka known to man and smoking a blunt stuffed with weed like it was legal.

"Ms. Blakemore, are you alright?"

"Today is not a good day, Mr. Hollingswell. I don't mean to be rude but you and that handsome smile can kiss my white ass," she gulped down the remaining fluid in the bottle.

"I'm sorry, but did I do something to you? I don't see the need for the aggression."

"Nope you didn't do shit but on the days when your smile is at its brightest my eyes are wet and my middle finger is nice and erect." She pointed her middle finger at me and before I could respond she said, "Fuck you and the smart pricks you have working for you too."

"Hold on, is this about the market dropping today?"

"Damn right it is!"

"I take it you invest in the Dow on the upside?"

"Nope, never invested in that piece of shit extra controlled index until it hit $21,000 a share. My dumb ass broker who I fired earlier today said with the new president it would keep rising so I bought 3000 shares of it."

"Oh no, Ms. Blakemore, I would have advised you against doing that. That's 63 million dollars down the drain."

"Say the shit the right way, that's 63 million of my fucking dollars down the drain. You invest other people's money in a fund, I'm my own fucking fund!" She pulled on the blunt long and hard, coughed softly like she hadn't, and then said, "If it wasn't for smiling while you were crying in 2008 I'd be a dead bitch lying in front of this building."

"I'm lost?"

"I see you left your brain back at the office. When you lost everything in the crash of 2008 I was one of the 20 or so who increased their net worth. Today's hit didn't cripple me but who do you know with money that likes losing it? I think you better go handle whatever it is you stopped by here for before you mess around and miss your flight. I'll apologize to you when I truly mean it."

I didn't know what else to say so I did as I was told. On my way out, I handed her my card and said, "When I get back let's talk about what we need to do so we can start smiling together."

"I like the sound of that!" She snatched the card and I jumped back in the car.

My phone went off as soon as I made it to the security check-in and the TSA officer gave me a look that read, *You better not answer it,* as I put my belongings in the bin on the x-ray belt.

"Sir, we need you to step to the side for further inspection of your bag."

It never failed that I get stopped for having bottles of herbs in my backpack. I wouldn't go through that if I checked my bag but after the airline temporarily lost my Louis Vuitton travel bag and it looked as if they ran it through an industrial size paper shredder when they called me to pick it up, I had vowed to travel with a carry-on only.

I watched as they performed a swab test. They claimed the purpose of the test was to check for chemicals that could be used by terrorists for bombs but at the moment it felt like a stunt to have me miss my flight. I had to run to the gate and if I would have stopped for a second to catch my breath I would have missed my flight. I boarded the plane, threw my bag in the overhead compartment, and powered off my phone without checking who the missed call was from.

I wasn't scheduled to meet Nivea until the next day but I had plans to meet Prynce, the barber, to sign his limited partnership and confidentiality agreement, collect the money he wanted to invest, a few disclosures regarding the money he was investing, and to give him his welcome package. Once business was done we followed it with enjoying a principal meal and small talk about the lies in the world. He had received the investment fund prospectus and the private placement memorandum I had sent him next day mail when I made it home. When his lawyer read over it and gave it the thumbs up he called me ready to move forward and I was more than happy to invest the $75,000 he'd worked hard for years to save up.

My business with him was done and I was in the mood to celebrate. I didn't know why I did it but I called the cell phone number listed on the card and Nivea answered on the first ring.

"How much will you charge me to point me in the direction of a hearty meal, Ms. Bowen or does the consultation fee I paid cover it?"

"No, it doesn't cover it," she sassed sounding the way I felt about the profit we made today. "Information on a hearty meal will cost you paying for mine if you'd like some company. I was getting ready to grab something myself, I might as well let you pay for it."

"Text me the address to the place and be on your way now. If I have to wait over an hour for you, you're paying."

"That's a deal and Mr. Hollingswell, I'm in no mode to give you your consultation tonight or even talk about the markets. Save it for tomorrow, okay?"

"That's a deal!"

She must have cried on days I smiled like Ms. Blakemore too, I'd give her break.

Nivea

There was no need to try and contest it, Chinese was hands down, my favorite food. It forced my taste buds to dance and no matter how much I ate of it in one sitting, it never made me feel like I was being fat. If I grabbed a ten piece and a gallon of punch, it made me feel like I was being fat. I was a thighs and legs girl. I liked the moisture in the dark meat but let's be truthful, the softer the meat, the easier it was to eat. Don't get me wrong, I'd eat a breast every now and then but that dry meat took too long to chew and I normally ended up smothering them in or dipping them in ranch dressing. I even experienced a need to keep a bottle of hot sauce just in case I ran across them. My mouth would be wrapped around a leg, about halfway through, and my free hand would be wandering through the chicken box on a voyage to my next piece. I felt to the left and ended up scavenging to the right as my fingers surf through the crispy crumbs. It didn't take me long to realize when I was down to my last piece. I'd get two different questions that would rattle my brain at the same time. The first was, did your big ass eat that entire box by yourself? And the other was, are you still hungry, should I run out and get some more?

With Chinese food, I didn't have to question myself like that, I already knew two things. One, I could eat as many Chinese vegetables until I got full without feeling guilty on days when I added a little meat. And secondly, it would only keep me full for two hours and it didn't matter how much I ate of it, my body would still react the same. The herbs did help me to lose the weight but I couldn't say that eating the right foods and changing my eating habits didn't do their part in my transformation. Whenever I had the choice of picking the restaurant it was my first choice, that's why I had Dwayne meet me at Mr. Kim Wang's in Chinatown.

Chinatown was blessed with some of the best Chinese food prepared on this Earth and I say this after eating many meals in China. Classy to trashy if you told me your dinner budget I could point you to the best of it within your price range. It might be the Cali girl in me or the humbleness from hustling my way through college, but in my opinion the least expensive or the ones people loosely call cheap tend to be the best. Mr. Wang sold one-dollar Chinese food. You'd get one full serving of whatever you wanted, each priced at a buck. It was definitely in my budget after putting all of my money into my company after college.

I had graduated in top 10% of my class, had taken almost every class the New York Institution of Finance offered and I was making a nice amount of money at that time day trading for myself. I went for a pop and filled this penny stock for an oil company with all of it. I'm talking everything, the rent and monthly food money was included, and not to mention my dad's new wife's trust fund seeing they both wanted to prove that they believed in me. That crappy stock did 260% in one day. With all the money I had pulled in, I couldn't wait for my date with compound interest.

TOXIN

In two and a half days of catching pops, we were rich. To top it off my dad and stepmom told me to keep their winnings as back child support. I took all of the winnings and put half into my condo and the other half into my business. I paid bigger salaries to keep my all female staff and I was smart enough to prepare for the pettiness that came with only working with women. I bought the entire 21st floor of the building so I could knock out walls for bigger offices with large spaces between them. Every office had a window with its own beautiful New York view and everything else was constructed in the middle like the restroom, conference, and break rooms. We didn't have secretaries, I made sure that everyone knew that the ladies at the front desk were my personal assistants. It's sad but titles are important to a lot of people so if it makes you think of yourself in a better way while you're working for me then everyone is getting a great title. No two titles were the same but they all were prefixed with, "Director of..." to make sure they knew everyone had the same line of power under me. I wasn't power struck, let's not forget that it was my company. My name, my time, my blood, my tears, and all the rest of my money went into it, I wasn't leaving anything to chance.

From spa type restrooms to me paying for a dry cleaners, daycare, gym, salon, and nail bar to move into the building for our convenience. By setting up my office like that I had already made history by being the first CEO to pay to fully accommodate their staff by buying the whole building and the first to offer every service a woman would need so she could work and still be a wife and mother all in one building, at their fingertips.

I spent every last dime; my closet full of penny loafers would soon be providing meals for me. You'd think those simple moves would make you rich but there were too many toxins around me to let me see any money. I was called sexist being that I wouldn't let men work for me even if they were gay so it didn't surprise me when I saw that I was being sued because some said that I had something against gay men. Being a woman knocked me down in the world of finance by a notch even with the manly numbers I was making and yep you guessed it, I was labeled a color and someone believed it. Not a color that made the eyes smile, I was labeled black. The only part of the coloring book you're not supposed to color. I was supposed to believe that I was created to only trace the lines in the book but I couldn't. I've never seen my people as only capable of tracing the lines someone else already created, nah that couldn't be right. We were innovators judging from my research so it was my belief to only expect answering to the color group, black is when you are being honored for using your black to draw and create your own damn lines. If you remove those lines from the coloring book pages you're left with a blank canvas. I'll never forget that America needs their lines.

In other words, I needed money and since I was following the steps in my plan, I had to IPO my company in the first 5 years at the latest, this was year five. I had a lot of my bills put off until my 8th year in operation and that time was approaching. I had planned it out so I knew I'd be broke but I never wrote down how being broke would feel and I slightly messed up on the math. I thought I'd least have value meal money until the profits we would make would come in but there weren't any. With one too many toxins floating around everybody had a different reason why they wouldn't invest with us. The only thing keeping my company's doors open was the small client base which made the saying Quality over Quantity factual. Our clients were rich and only gave us a chance with a small percentage of their money, only to save face and be privileged to say that they were a part of the movement for women rights.

Going public that year was mandatory and if I didn't, I needed a pop the size of a stock market crash. My everything was into the IPO and I never thought that I'd have to focus and research to go for a pop again. The IPO had fallen through and I hadn't planned my next moves. Lucky for me I had hired the best woman around for the job and Kishi stayed on top of everything. When the IPO crumbed before my eyes, Kishi had pulled a Phoenix and began reconstructing something new from the ashes. The irony in that was I couldn't have lost it all putting all my faith in someone else hands. I was sad how consumed I was with discovering who sent the roses. I even gave Kishi a hard time about it when she brought it to my attention that I was breaking rules that I had implemented.

The 200 million we made was exactly what we needed, hell, it was exactly what I needed so I could breathe and have fun money is coming next. When I'm done suing my legal team and the companies they are umbrella-ed with, I might invest in my own Chinese restaurant and sell herbs in the gift shop.

"Ten more minutes and you would have been paying for my meal," Dwayne said as he opened the door for me.

"That's not true, you were ten minutes away from washing dishes because I would have refused to pay for our meals."

"You look like you've dined and dashed."

"And you think because you can hang a suit and fancy the barbershop once a week you don't look like it too? That's why I still eat here to ensure I won't forget what it felt like when I had to dash."

"Understood, there's this burger spot in Memphis that will always get my money. It doesn't make sense to switch it now, I already like the food." Dwayne smiled and I was covered in a strange warm feeling. It was almost as if he had turned on an internal heater. "And by far, Chinese is my favorite food."

We went through the buffet style line picking out a variety of dollar Chinese foods. We sat down in a ripped up red vinyl booth. Almost simultaneously, we both pulled out our travel packs of herbs. I knew those weren't prescription medications and I could tell a bee pollen capsule anywhere. I was going to question him but he beat me to the punch.

"How long have you been taking herbs?"

Like clockwork I was going to tell him that Evol had put me on them three years ago but I still couldn't formulate my lips to call him my ex. I mean, I don't think you can claim a married man.

"The answer is another off-limit subject for tonight, if you don't mind?"

"I don't. Sounds like you had a rough day."

"No...well, I guess you can call it rough. It made me look differently at a lot of stuff and I haven't quite accepted the adjustment."

"You accepted the adjustment when you realized what you were looking at. Don't make excuses to move in slow motion now. Let it go or what you're supposed to get next will never come. Whatever it is, a person, career move, or an item, you must remember that you'll always spend more time thinking about it than it will spend thinking about you. That sounds like time poorly invested." He looked at the reason behind the shadow suddenly covering me and then asked, "Is there something we can help you with?"

The way he squinted his face let me know he could get rough but something in his eyes said that he didn't like to.

"Hey, man, I don't mean harm or want to interrupt. I just wanted to come say hi to an old friend." He walked to the outside center of the table where he could be seen by us both and then said, "How have you been doing, beautiful? I've been trying to reach you since I got out the burn unit."

Riko, now known to me as cooking grease, was standing over me covered in light pink patches that looked like they should have been concealed. His eyes were the only feature left you could use to recognize him without fingerprinting him.

"Hey, Riko, now isn't the time to play catch up. I'm actually working right now."

"Damn, you really are a prostitute? I saw my cousin pay you for fucking me but I didn't think…"

I couldn't hear anything after Riko said the word prostitute because the water that flew out of Dwayne's mouth at the word had landed on me. I probably should have wiped it off my face but I needed to straighten Riko's blunder first.

"Hell no, I'm not a prostitute,"

"I'll step outside while the two of you talk things out." Dwayne said, standing to his feet.

"No, you don't have to go anywhere. Riko, I witnessed you get your pissy little fish fried by your roommate's girlfriend. There was no way I was going to disagree with anything those crazy people said after watching you get cooked without batter. I'm not a…"

Dwayne was outside slowly walking back forth. I'm sure he was thinking of hailing a cab and getting as far away from me as he could so I sped up straightening out Riko and then ran through the door after paying for our waters.

"Maybe we should just call it a night and meet

tomorrow," he suggested after checking his watch three times within the same minute for the same time.

"That's your call. I still haven't eaten yet and one walking man, lotioned with hot Crisco, won't be ruining my appetite. Are you telling me I'll be dining and dashing the rest of the night alone?"

"No, I can't let you eat alone. I'd feel bad if I left you out here alone after meeting hot fish and grits, but this time, it's my pick."

He flagged down a cab and had him drop us off at the first by the slice pizzeria we saw. We ate slices of cheese pizza while we walked to the subway station after deciding to go to a bar near Time Square. I noticed after eating he popped more herbs.

"You must have diary allergies?" I asked

"Badly. My mucus membranes get backed up quickly that's how I learned about the benefits of taking herbs. I was researching how to get rid of the mucus instead of giving up on my poisoner." He followed it with a laugh.

The pizza hadn't filled me up but that wouldn't stop me from having a drink or two... okay, four or five. I was secretly depressed over Evol and after what the markets did that day, I had a reason to celebrate. By some fucked up twist in psychology, alcohol had been used for them both. People drink when they are depressed and people celebrate with a drink. I drank for both reasons.

"Let me have another Jack on the rocks."

"No, she won't, can she have a glass of ice water please." He turned from the bartender and looked at me, "I'm going to give you some trace minerals, they will help you stay on guard with all that liquor you drank."

"I have my own supply," I said pulling them out my purse while a familiar face walked through the door.

"Excuse me, Nivea, I need to step away to the restroom. Are you going to be okay?"

"Yes, go ahead."

I wanted Dwayne to leave in a hurry as I watched the face making its way over to me and I couldn't let Dwayne see me in another altercation with a man I'd slept with.

"Nivea, beautiful, is that you? I'd was hoping to run into you when the order of restraint was up."

Out of all the people I would put on a list not to run into, Isaac Britton's name was on the top and the restraining order he had placed on me had only been expired for a month. I walked right past him and hid in the lady's room until I was sure he was gone and surprisingly Dwayne was returning to seat at the same time.

"I enjoyed myself a little too much, Mr. Hollingswell and think I should call it a night."

"I was thinking the same." He stood up from his bar stool, dropped some cash on his plate, and then took my hand. "I think you should let me help you out."

I would have rejected his hand if I wouldn't have stumbled after taking one step. The liquor had crept on me and I hadn't taken the minerals. Once he saw my drunk attempt to play the stumble off as an offbeat two step, he wrapped one arm around my shoulder and the other around my waist. He held me in his arms and we gave off that new couple scent as everyone we passed gave us a loving smile.

"Does your driver's license have your current address on it?"

"Yes."

"Can you get it out your purse so I can tell the driver where to take you?"

"Yes."

"Can you please do it now, Ms. Bowen?"

I couldn't do shit, not failing to mention answering his question. Evol had his arm wrapped around some shorty from around the way's shoulder, Brooklyn style. The liquor made me introduce myself.

"How are you doing, Evol, is this your replacement piece?"

"Talk that shit somewhere else, remember, you don't miss me and as you can see, I ain't missing you."

The Jack I drank gave me the boldness needed to take off my thousand-dollar heels and send them flying towards his head. I would have tried to attack him but I could feel my feet dangling in the air. Dwayne had picked me up and he was forcing me into the back of a taxi.

"Aye, son, your bitch is crazy," Evol said shaking his head at Dwayne. Dwayne must have seen the wedding ring on Evol's finger.

"Hey, man, why don't you take your wife and just get out here."

"This ain't my wife, she at home. This is my new girlfriend," he said kissing the bitch on the cheek. The look of confusion on Dwayne's face spoke volumes and I was glad the taxi was pulling off as Evol finished, "Nivea my bitch too!"

*****

I don't recall how I got home but I woke up around 2pm with a text message from Dwayne that had come in around 5 that morning, it read:

"Sorry, I have to reschedule our meeting. I'll be in touch with you soon."

He wasn't sorry that he canceled and why would he be after my personal business took over the night.

"Nivea, unlock the bedroom door!"

I told the doorman to stop letting Evol in after he refused to give me back my door keys and I paid money I

196

didn't have to change the locks.

"Get out of my condo, Evol!"

"Unlock the door or I'm kicking it in!" I jumped up and unlocked it. "Who was that you were with last night?"

I could have died from how hard I was laughing.

"You sneak your way into my condo so you can question me about who I was with last night, Mr. Married Man? And don't forget that you had another chick wrapped in your arms when you saw me."

"We're not talking about who I was with, don't try to flip shit."

"Oh, my goodness, who do you think you are, Evol? The world doesn't revolve around you, I'm done letting you have your cake and eat it too. Who I spend my time with isn't any of your business. Save the snooping around for your wife."

Dwayne was the right man for being accused of dating. He has handsome and visibly rich. Why shouldn't I let Evol's imagination run wild?

"My wife knows better than to try and step out on me, it's you that's in need of taming."

"Taming? You said that like I'm your dog. How am I supposed to be your bitch, Evol, when you're a bitch yourself? Zamora is your owner, you can't own me!"

He flew across the room and grabbed me by my

face. "You are my bitch; do you hear me?"

"I've never been your bitch. You've been in a relationship since I met you."

He tightened his grip on my face and pressed his lips against mine forcing me into a kiss. I pounded on his chest trying to get him to let me go.

"That smart mouth of yours is going to get you in trouble."

"Don't talk to me like you're my daddy!"

"I wasn't; I'm talking to you like your man." He squeezed my cheeks together until I had duck lips. "Do you hear me? Like your man!"

Evol stole another kiss and I gave up the fight. I let him kiss me however he wanted to and when he noticed that I had surrendered, I kneed him in his nuts the first few seconds after he loosened his grip. I snatched my phone off the coffee table, went through my contacts, and then called his wife on speakerphone.

"Hello?"

I put the call on mute.

"Get the fuck out, before I tell her that you're here," I threatened.

"Go ahead and tell her, shit, she probably already knows I am."

"Hello?" Zamora said again into the phone.

"Are you really that coldblooded to keep hurting the mother of your child? Why don't you tell her that you don't want to stay true to your wedding vows? Why do you continue to feel like she deserves to keep being treated like this by you?"

"If someone's there, I can't hear you. You'll have to hang up and call me back."

"Even if you left your wife I would never be with you. I'm not stupid to believe that you wouldn't treat me the same way you're treating her. Now leave before I have to break her heart some more."

He stood in front of me and stared into my eyes for awhile. I didn't know what he was looking for within them but after seeing the disappointed expression grow on his face, I knew he hadn't found it. He headed out the door and I threw on my clothes to have a word with the doorman once I was sure that Evol had exited the building. Once I was assured that Evol wouldn't be allowed in the building without my consent I climbed back in my bed and went to back to sleep.

What are you still doing up, isn't it 3 in the morning in New York?

I had woken up at a little after 2am to raid my refrigerator. My growling stomach had woken me up and I logged on the dating site as I waited for my microwavable dinner to heat up. I saw the icon that said Raymond was online and then sent him a message to see if he was in the mood to talk. Our instant message conversation went like this:

Brenda: Yes, I took a nap earlier and I'm finally getting up. How was your day?

Raymond: Weird and unbelievably long. I'm actually glad that it is over and yours?

Brenda: I would say the same if I didn't sleep through most of mine. Do you want to talk about your day?

Raymond: I normally would say no but maybe I could get some sleep if I can talk this stuff off my mind.

Brenda: Go ahead Ray, I'm all ears.

I don't know why I volunteered to be a listening ear and if I would have known where the conversation was headed I wouldn't have.

My mom called me the night before last to tell me that there had been a very bad car accident that my God aunt and her son were involved in, down in Georgia. She told me I needed to get to Atlanta immediately so I took a red eye out.

I wanted to ask him if she was his mother's close friend why hadn't his mother flown out to be by her side but his next message came in while I was still typing.

That wasn't all she told me. What she called and said was that I needed to get to the hospital in Atlanta

fast because my Auntie V's son wasn't going to make it if he didn't get a blood transfusion. She told me I was the last chance at them finding a perfect match.

I hit the backspace button to erase what I had started typing to start over by telling him it was a blessing that he was a perfect match but again, his message came through first.

I hoped that I wasn't a match the entire flight there.

I finally beat him and was able to ask,

Why? Why wouldn't you want to help your god cousin? Am I missing something?"

There was a long delay. I didn't know if he had fallen asleep or if he stepped away. When I was going to give up waiting his next message came through.

Because, if I was able to help that meant my auntie V was telling my mom the truth when she told her that I was her son's father which meant I had finally failed as a son in the mission of not breaking my mom's heart. I know this will sound crazy but I lost my virginity at 16 to my mom's 36-year-old best friend.

How do you ask a man if he was molested without making him feel like you're taking stripes away from his manhood? It was a good thing his following message ensured that I didn't have to.

Hold on, let me clear something up. I wasn't

raped and to be honest I think I took advantage of her more than she took advantage of me. She did come on to me first but I decided to use that in my favor. I made her do somethings I had to be 18 to do and to get her to keep doing it for me, I kept having sex with her. It's sad but at 16 I remember wanting to wear a condom with her because AIDS was going around, I never thought about the possibilities of us making a baby.

His messages were better than a daytime soap opera and like a faithful watcher of them, I wanted to know more.

Sounds like the truth and I wouldn't judge you anyways. We all have a past. Did you find out if he was yours?

There was another delay in his response and it was longer than the first. The length of the message was the reason for it.

When I got there her husband was pissed and wanted fight me like I hadn't called him uncle for years. He was her off and on boyfriend at the time I was sleeping with her and apparently his only reason for marrying her was because he thought the baby was his. He even signed the birth certificate giving the baby his full name without asking for a DNA test. I wanted to tell him that I didn't want the boy to be mine and I'd pay him to continue to take over my responsibilities but they rushed me back for a DNA to see if I was a match.

I took it upon myself to ask because it seemed like he was skipping parts.

Did your aunt say anything to you?

He responded,

Yeah, she told me she was sorry and she always had a feeling he was mine but didn't want to trouble me with him. I stopped myself from asking her, then why would you choose to trouble me with him now? I'm not heartless but look at how I received the life changing news. Who wants to find out they have a 19-year-old son when the child is on his deathbed? The fucked-up part about it is that I didn't want him nor would I accept that he was mine until I saw him hooked up on all those machines dying. When I saw how bad he looked a strange feeling came over me. The next thing I knew I was on my knees praying to God that my son would pull through. I even tried to make God a promise to do right by my son if he let him pull through.

Tears were falling out my eyes and covering my keyboard like rain drops. I had to know.

Did your son pull through?

He didn't respond so I asked again.

Raymond, did your son make it?

He didn't make me ask him the question a third time.

No, he didn't make it and it wouldn't have mattered to me if he had since the DNA test results stated that there was no way that he could be my son.

My aunt or whatever I'm supposed to call her after all of this had confessed to sleeping with so many men back then that her son died not knowing that the man who raised him, wasn't the man that helped birth him. I don't know if that was his blessing or the curse his mother passed on to him with her sins. After going through all this I did make up my mind about one thing, when I have kids I'm never going to let them leave my side!

I tried to think of the perfect words to say but I couldn't find any. Everything that I wanted to say would come off judgmental and that wasn't what he needed right then. I decided to respond to whatever his next message said but fortunately another message didn't come through as I watched his online status switch to offline.

Dwayne

The extra trip to Georgia wasn't expected but it lined my day up perfectly. I was scheduled to pick Edward up from the airport at 9:30am and my flight landed at 9:10. I met him at the baggage claim.

"How was your trip?"

"Successful like usual and I even got some pussy from a chick I met playing roulette. How's my car? I hope you don't have the city thinking it belongs to a pastor with all that Christian hip hop you've been playing."

"Nah, they think it belongs to a minister. I put a decal on your back window that says, Jesus Saves, ask me how!" I laughed before he could take me seriously.

"It's cool, I think it's time to switch shit up anyways. Even my choice in women. Shorty I met in China raised the bar high and it's a lot of shit I'm done settling for like fucking with bitches. I didn't understand the differences between the two before but now I do."

"Is that right? Then hit me with a little Edward theology," I said as we threw our bags in the backseat of his car.

"Ok, so peep. There are two classes of females, women and bitches. Don't let the world trick you into believe there are more, D, I had two 16-hour flights to do the research on it. I'm not mistaken."

"Not mistaken, huh? I'm assured, keep going," I said trying to egg him on.

"A bitch is everything a woman is not which includes; a ho, a bad mother, a non-nurturer, confrontational, and a complainer,"

"Hold on Edward, you had me going for a minute there but I have to disagree. The Bible speaks on nagging women. How do you explain that one?"

"Easy, if a female is structured in her womanhood by the Bible, she is a woman unless she turns away from God. Nagging women can be fixed with the love of a God fearing and loving man but a bitch, is tainted and the toxins brewing inside of her can't be fixed without her having a mental crisis. Women change with love and bitches have to be broken from the lack of it, to truly change."

"So, if you believe that then you must believe the same has to be said for men and niggas?"

"Hell yeah, I'm still a nigga. I just have manly ways. If my life keeps heading the way it is over these bitches I'll go through my crisis soon. I'm ready to see myself as man."

"I'm glad that you are," I chuckled and then said, "drop me off at the office and you head home to sleep off your flight. You might want to call and thank The Church for the move they pulled while you were gone. With the bonuses, all of you have coming, you might decide to upgrade your car."

"For real? I need the money now too. After all those years working as a secretary at that bogus ass warehouse they let my moms go. I've been paying all her bills and keeping up with her cigarette supply. It would be nice to straighten her all the way out. Can't believe my mom is about to turn 40. She's getting old."

"Hey, watch your mouth, I'll be 38 in December. Old is a state of mind."

"Well, my mom had me at 14 so I know her state of mind must be telling her she's old as dinosaur spit if I'm turning 26 and fully providing for her."

All I could do was shake my head while thinking of what his mother might have gone through becoming a parent at such a young age.

Edward got me to the office in less than thirty minutes. He dropped me off at our street entrance and took off for his appointment with sleep. My fingers went numb like they used to do when something bad was coming my way. It was like an old person saying, 'my bones ache it must be about to rain.' I had a spiritual connection through my hands. I can't explain and I knew better than to question it. The first sign of the weather changing showed itself as I entered my office.

"Good morning, Heather, any updates?"

"Your newspapers are over there, memos and messages right there, and since it's Friday, I'm leaving early."

"Are you asking me if you can leave early or are you telling me?"

She shrugged her shoulders and gave me eye contact for the first time since I walked in which was far from usual and then said, "A combination of them both, did you enjoy your time with Ms. Bowen? I see she has you flying back and forth to New York and I think Bowen Capital Management is the first firm that you've ever had me send flowers to. Never mind, don't answer the question. I wasn't asking it from the friend zone you put me in."

"Do we need to discuss this outside of my office building, this sounds real personal? I have never made money while stuck in my feelings so if I'm standing in my building it's for one purpose only. If we need to go on a walk we can but keep your toxins out my office."

Her job was to do what I asked, when I asked, and for that service I paid a price. Heather was more than a secretary. She was my office translator and my personal concierge, she was the heartbeat to everything when it came to my business.

I met her one day in Whole Foods with her four sons and visibly pregnant with a least one more. She called the number on the back of her EBT card on speaker to check her balance. The recorded voice said, "Your snap balance is $982.93."

She ended the call and I hadn't yet seen her face, but at the sound of her voice, I knew everything about her would be different.

"Boys, it's time to play a game. I'm going to give each of you your own color. I don't want you to say it out loud but I want you to think about all the different languages you know how to say that color in. The one who knows the most gets to pick out the cereal we eat all month and with what type of milk. When I say time is up, it's up even if I don't call on you first. Ready, set, GO!"

It was like watching a genius magic show. The boys went from the loudest objects in the next three cities to silent, like ants sleeping. I looked at all of their faces and could see that all three were deep in thought. I leaned up to try to see her face and she turned to talk to the butcher.

"Can I please have $100 of..."

The butcher cut her off. "$100 of lamb and $100 of ox. I know your order by now, beautiful. Do you want the fish and turkey slices for lunch meat, too?"

Beautiful was titling her looks lightly, she was a passion fruit. Full lips, wide but slanted eyes, and with a skin tone powdered in gold. Instantly, I wanted her. I knew she was a rare fruit but I wasn't sure if her rareness was made for me so I decided to play it cool and give it some time. If she was indeed meant and made for me, it would line up perfectly but I still rushed to introduce myself.

"Hey, I'm Dwayne and I'm in shock. How did you just do that with the boys?"

"It's like I tell everyone, if you teach them to love it and make it the normal, when they see the error in the rules of the world they'll be intelligent enough to not fall for them. Excuse me for a second," She walked with this cute little pregnant waddle over to the biggest boy in the bunch and said, "Dwight, how many languages did you come up with? And you're 16 please know that I'm not judging your answers against your brothers."

"Why not, Mama?" he questioned as another voice spoke up.

"Excuse me for speaking out of turn, Mama, but I want you to, I know he's 16 but I'll beat him," the high pitched cracked voice said.

"Dwayne Ray, I know you can but it's bad enough that I'm setting y'all up to have a sword fight against each other and I'm your mama. At least let me line you up in the right battle."

"Yes, ma'am."

The one she called Dwayne stepped up beside her. Everything about him made me think of me at his age. The boy couldn't be still. I watched him juke his way to his mother and then gangsta walk once he had arrived. He had the bug, that same bug I had that landed me a spot in a world-famous dance group. His lips hadn't stopped moving from the time he walked up to his mother. I assumed he was singing his favorite song until I saw his mother shaking her head and her oldest nodding his head and quietly jumping up and down. When I realized the boy was naming his color in different languages, he was finishing up.

"I didn't tell you to name them, Dwayne!"

At her protest, the oldest son shouted out, "Hands down he killed me. What was that, D, like 50 of them thangs?"

The boys started shaking hands and their mother said, "I guess it's unanimous, Dwayne wins. Go pick the cereal baby."

Dwayne took off through the store like lightening. He wasn't running but he had perfected the definition of a fast-paced walk.

"I see what you mean, Mama, I would have done 115 with my eyes closed," the oldest said giving her a kiss on her cheek."

"I thought you would have done 150 of them easily, baby. Dwan and D.W, y'all both get to tell us how many the two of you came up with on the ride home and I'll make sure to drive real slow." The two remaining boys smiled like they had hit the lottery. She walked back over to me and said, "It's a pleasure to meet you, Dwayne."

"So, what are y'all, I can't judge your race?" I'm sure I sounded crazy but something about her energy made me feel nervous. There wasn't a ring on her finger and no signs that there had ever been one.

"I don't know what race we belong to but does anyone really know anymore? I prefer to say that we are exceptionally smart with a hell of a lot of melanin, my daddy makes you look pale skin, he was as dark as they come. If this is for some genealogy mapping or census information then we identify as Americans whose ancestors were stolen from Africa if that helps. Please select other, I've never cared for the word black."

I can't explain how I knew it but I was certain that I was staring at my wife. Even with four kids and something cooking in her tummy she radiated innocence and I'd hold her to it until proven guilty. I would never play daddy. Knowing that I wouldn't meant I'd take it slow with her until I was sure she earned the title wife and I was ready to master the role of father. I decided to take a different approach with her and pull a Napoleon Hill. I wanted to see if sexual transmutation was real.

"I'm looking for a secretary, how many languages do you speak and what other magic can you preform?"

"I don't do magic, that isn't of God. I'm only raising my kids with less educational hurdles than we had. Why have kids if you don't raise them to stay undefeated?"

"I don't know; I don't have any. If you can type at least 65 words per minute and can follow directions well, I'll start you out at..." I looked at her stomach and then said, "$100,000 a year plus bonuses but you won't be just any old secretary, you'll be a secretary on acid tabs. I'm going to work you on overdrive and you'll be the closet to me on the journey up."

"That sounds like an excellent opportunity and I would have said the same even if you didn't try to sell it to me. Give me the address and name and I'll look into it. I'll reach out when I make a decision." She gave me a twisted lip look, grabbed the meat, and got ready to take off.

I had to speak up, "It shouldn't be that hard to see the opportunity I'm offering you. No offense, but I want you to give the government back their assistance."

"Please believe I want to give it back, I just need to make sure I'm not cutting off a small demon to pick up the devil." She gave me a sexy smile.

What's crazy was that everything in me told me that Heather was the one but I had to see what she would do working that closely at my side as a preview. If she was to become my wife, that's how we would be until I sold the firm, and then even closer thereafter. Working and playing together makes it easier to build the unbreakable. She called me two weeks later and she'd been my right hand ever since. The fucked up apart was that before this situation, I'm talking a day or two before, I thought about telling her how I really felt but that would require that I fire her first just in case I was wrong about what we had. Now she was checking me in my office.

"No, sir, we don't need to go on a walk. I apologize, let me say it again. Is it ok with you if I leave early? It's a slow Friday and it's my son Dwayne's birthday. He was promised a fishing trip this morning and since that person failed to keep their word, I would like to make it up to him, if that's ok?"

"Oh shit, I'm sorry, Heather. I forgot."

The truth flew out of my mouth and I wished I could have taken it back. Heather told me when I first began my relationship with her boys that if I couldn't keep my word to them, keep my words to myself. I hadn't forgotten a birthday in the four years I'd been blessed to have them in my life and with me stopping by to check on them daily the boys didn't let me. I intentionally withheld information from her. Truth is, I didn't tell her the truth but I wasn't lying when I told her I was spending time with the boys as their mentor so they could have a steady man in their lives since their fathers broke bad on her. I only failed to mention that I was trying parenting on to make sure it was my size and that after spending six months with the boys, all five became mine. I didn't accept the key to pop up whenever I wanted to like she suggested, I took the key to the house because what man doesn't have access to his family?

"Don't apologize to me, you can tell Dwayne Ray when you come home...I mean, stop by tonight. I think I'm finally realizing what I thought we had was really nothing but fear. It's only False Evidence Appearing Real." She brushed by me towards the break room as the security guard walked in.

"Hollingswell, your vehicle was vandalized overnight and we need you to come to the parking lot with us so we can make a report."

"Who is us? Why do you always say us when you're clearly by yourself?" Heather asked returning to her desk.

"Did you already look at the footage from the garage?"

"We tried to but someone had turned the cameras off by your car when they left at 5:30 yesterday."

"Who the fuck is we? I've been in this office for four years and the only we I've ever seen is you. Not plural, singular. Why do all protective services say we? It can be one cop at your house but he'll say we. Did y'all get sworn in and take the oath in French?"

"Heather, that's enough!" I said looking back at her. She was pissed at me and I wouldn't let her take it out on the next person. I straightened her out before turning my attention back to the security guard. "So, this is an inside job? Are the police out there waiting on me?"

At the word police, the elevators doors opened and in came the FBI lead by the Securities Exchange Commission. I knew the asshole in the front seeing that he was on a mission to make my life a living hell. I met the prick at the door.

"Mr. Hollingswell, we're not here for you this time. I have to clean the gutters in order to catch the rat. I'll catch you later!" He handed me the warrant and then he pushed past me and I looked back at Heather. Again, she was wearing a look I had never seen on her face.

I glanced a second longer and then said, "Take the rest of the day off to help him pack. Tell my fishing buddy I'll see him shortly to take him birthday shopping for the fishing gear." She rolled her eyes but I got a small peek at the smile she worked hard to keep off her face. After she grabbed her purse and left I followed the crowd to Elliott's office. Two agents stormed into his office and the asshole stood in the hallway with me.

"What's all of this about, Spencer?" I asked

"This is what happens when you think you can outsmart the federal government and get away with it. Once a thief always thief and now he's stealing from you while you pay him that astronomical salary. All that money you give him on and off the books you'd think it would have bought some loyalty." He nodded his head while I watched Elliott get handcuffed. "He's going to prison for a long time this time but don't you worry, when we are done with our investigation we'll make sure that you're cellmates. Insider trading won't get you commodities in there."

"Insider trade these nuts! I'm not worried about the investigation or those bullshit lies you're putting together about money on and off the books. You just make sure that your dumb federal employed for crumbs ass and those astronomically broke agents you brought with you, book y'all asses out my office, I need to call my lawyer!" I made sure my middle finger bid them ado on my way to my office.

I called my attorney Marcus Campbell, but he was in court and I had to leave a message with his secretary to contact me after he checked on Elliott. I refused to let Spencer and the SEC see me weak so I kept a poker face while the feds took every document they could find in his office. Those assholes had the audacity to take pictures throughout the office and snapped one too many pictures of the talking-tube that ran from his office to mine.

Spencer didn't have to tell me that they would be back; I knew they would be. He's wanted to shut my office down from the time I hired Elliott against his warnings about me employing a criminal. The two of them had a super hero verses villain relationship and depending on the perception of the person judging, either could be looked upon as the good or bad guy. I inherited Elliot's beef with Spencer and the SEC when I prevented Elliott from hitting rock bottom like Spencer worked hard to ensure. I didn't mind the United States Securities and Exchange Commission or any other federal government agency that was responsible for protecting investors looking over my shoulders full time to make sure I was following the regulations in my field. What I did mind was having a prick that had taken his job personally and held a personal vendetta against one of my employees keeping an eye over my shoulder. It wasn't a fair fight. I told myself there was nothing to worry about. I did everything on the up and up but righteousness was hard to achieve while trapped in the devil's den. No matter what I did right, there was a twist on it that made it wrong. I had paid more fees and fines to the SEC than cell phone companies could charge roaming charges in no services areas.

"Excuse me, Mr. Hollingswell, but we really need you to come take a look at your car. It's our job to get to the bottom of this."

The security guard was at the door still speaking French. With everything going on at once I had temporarily forgotten I had other shit to deal with at the time. I didn't say anything to him as I stood to my feet. We, the guard and I, had taken less than ten steps down the hallway and were met by two uniformed policemen.

"Mr. Hollingswell, there was an incident in the parking garage that we need to speak with you about, can you please come with us, sir?" the light skinned cop asked me and the security guard spoke up.

"Thanks for your help, officers, we were going to call you after we took a statement from Mr. Hollingswell. You're more than welcome to join us at the scene of the crime if you'd like to. The parking lot is this way."

They looked at him as if he was invisible standing in front of me.

"Was your car vandalized here, too?" the darker and visibly younger officer asked.

"What do you mean here too?" I questioned and the older officer answered.

"The fleet of vehicles you own that are parked in the mid-central parking garage were all vandalized this morning. From flat tires to broken windows." He dug in his pocket and pulled out his cell phone. "Do the words or the handwriting look familiar to you?" He enlarged the picture of the words, "Friend Zone," spray painted on the hood on all of my cars. I couldn't focus on the handwriting, the shattered glass from my windows screamed for my attention. I couldn't see the wheels on any of my vehicles but I knew all of them were on flat by how low they all sat on the ground.

TOXIN

I shook my head no and then said, "I believe my car in the parking lot here, suffered the same damage."

Nivea

Raymond was beginning to grow on me and I longed for our daily chats but he had a lot of unusual personal stuff going on. My life was full of drama too but for a man, he could run his own daytime soap opera.

We hadn't spoken for three weeks. Our last conversation was about his almost son by his mom's best friend passing. When he reached out to me he opened with small talk but I soon realized that he had even more drama to report.

I had to fire my secretary today after four years of grade A service. She was more like my COO but somehow shit went sideways. I'll try to keep what happened short. When I got home from Georgia I found out my company trucks had been vandalized and the words spray painted on them I heard come out of her mouth many times. I didn't let the police get involved when I realized she had done it. I wanted to see if I could get her to confess and it took three weeks before she did.

I responded,

Oh wow, Ray! Why did she say she did it? You should have at least gotten a police report so you could file a claim with your insurance company or are you making her reimburse you for the damage?

Knowing it would take him a few minutes to

respond I booked my flight for Memphis in the morning. Dwayne said he really wanted to meet with me but had a lot going on in his office at the time. Assuming he was nicely turning me down due to the incident with the men he witnessed while he was here, I called his bluff by telling him I'd make the trip and he took me up on my offer. Memphis wasn't on my places to visit list but it was far enough away from home to play a little bit. I hadn't had any dick in months and I didn't recall taking a vow of celibacy. I was sure that I wouldn't be sleeping with anyone else in the state of New York but the 49 other states, the one federal district, and the five territories that make up the United States were free range.

No, she doesn't have to reimburse me and she's technically suspended indefinitely with pay. She has five boys and no daddy claiming them. I volunteered to be their mentor. I guess I failed to mention that she didn't physically do the damage herself but... wait, I'll just tell you what happened. We were getting hang up calls that she made me aware of and I told her I'd look into them. While I was away the cause for the calls walked her crazy ass into my office and befriended my secretary for information on me by playing on the feelings I didn't realize she had for me. You see, I was in one of those thin line between love and hate relationships that kept me in jail or in the hospital. My ex finally stopped with the police games but promised to make my life a living hell. It's been five years since she's done anything. I wasn't sure if it was her at first because she spray-painted my secretary's catch phrase on the trucks but

when I brought it to my secretary's attention she told me about the extra friendly guest and described her. I suspended my secretary for leaking my business with ease to someone pretending to be a friend of the family.

I would have fired the bitch on the spot for telling my business but I didn't want to tell him that. He was beginning to seem weak to me but I wouldn't tell him that either, instead I typed,

Sounds like a lifelong stalker. Maybe I should get my gun license since I've taken an interest in you. I'd hate to not be prepared just in case she comes after me for liking you. I'm allergic to crazy chicks.

The last-minute flight was $550. I definitely would be getting some if I was going to spend that much to fly somewhere I didn't want to go. I searched the Memphis area on the dating site again for potentials while Raymond responded to my message.

You won't have to do any of that because if we ever take this off the internet I'd protect you from everything. That's the real reason I suspended my secretary. She disclosed having feelings for me to the craziest bitch on two legs that the world had ever seen and I couldn't risk her becoming collateral damage because of it. I didn't tell my secretary that was the reason because I knew she'd play the tough role. I ended up hiring one of my employee's mother to do the job. She had recently gotten fired from a secretary position and needed the money. Instead of giving it to him as a hand out to help his mother out, I let her earn

it instead.

Raymond was a good guy, I could tell by his words and if I would have known him a little longer I would have flown into Nashville instead, fucked him until all his problems were off his mind, and then driven to Memphis to meet with Dwayne, but it was too soon. I hadn't decided if anything could come from our meeting yet and I only had one shot at a first impression. I continue to scroll until a profile caught my eye. I didn't respond back to Raymond because I needed to get to know my new friend.

Memphis airport's air smelled weird to me. I had become accustomed to the sewage smell that reeked through New York and the smell of combustion in the smog of Los Angeles. The country air was turning my stomach and I hadn't walked out into it yet. Dwayne sent a car and driver to pick me up from the airport Friday night. Once I was in the car the driver informed me that he had been hired to stay by my side until I departed Sunday morning and that he would be taking me to my hotel first to change for dinner. An hour later we were driving down the riverfront to meet Dwayne at the docks. He had arranged a dinner for us on one of the beautiful Mississippi river boats.

"I hope you don't mind the solitude but after all the interruptions in New York, I thought it would be best if we enjoyed a meal and a few drinks alone," he said reaching for my hand to escort me onto the boat. Instantly, I felt over dressed as I took in an eyeful of him. He was wearing a form fitting V-neck t-shirt, dark blue jeans, and brown Louis Vuitton loafers. He wasn't under dressed but in comparison to my ankle length white satin dress and pumps, I looked ready to say I do, and he looked ready for a plate of bar-b-q at a family reunion.

"No, I don't mind and I apologize for that. The first guy was a one-time mistake and the one I was ready to catch a case over was ex, or something like that."

"Yeah, something like that," he mumbled and I caught it.

"What is that supposed to mean?"

"Nothing, I'm not privileged to judge," he said waving his hands in surrender.

"I know you're not, Mr. Hollingswell, but I'd like to hear your thoughts anyway."

"No, ma'am! You called me by my last name after we've been comfortable using first names. That is a sign that I am walking on thin ice and I've never mastered the art of ice skating. I'll keep my thoughts on your rendezvous with married men to myself but I will ask, are you currently seeing someone? If so, I hope this meeting of minds was accepted by him."

I wanted to clear up whatever Evol told him when the taxi pulled off but Dwayne was right. He was on thin ice.

"You don't do things that end with the word end like friend and I don't do anything that sails away like ships. No relationships and when I get married it will be to a man I dated, not one that I was in a relationship with."

"Well you over explained that shit," he started laughing and shook his head. "Look, if you're going to be in your feelings all night about the past I'll just get with you tomorrow at our business meeting. I didn't want to share my five-star meal with you anyways."

Dwayne clapped his hands and the waiters appeared with serving trays.

"Show the lady what's on the menu tonight, please."

The first waiter revealed his tray and I almost bellowed out laughter when I saw the stack of hot dogs but I was able to keep my composure until the second waiter revealed his and there was a variety of off name brand potato chips.

"I apologize, I wouldn't want to miss this meal for the anything in the world."

"I knew you wouldn't," he said as he showed off that sexy smile that I was secretly hoping to see. We ate by candlelight with the best R&B songs of the '90s playing softly on his cell phone. The dinner was perfect, the conversation was priceless but the most memorial part of the night happened once the boat docked and we exited. We were heading to our individual rides to call it a night. There was an old school Chevy on big rims parked nearby blasting music. I had never heard the song before and assumed it was a local hit. I turned to question Dwayne about it and my eyes almost popped out of their sockets. He was doing some fancy foot work with this aggressive popping, sliding and slight jumping. His hands were moving on the same beat but they were as fancy as the foot work. When he saw me looking he froze in his stance.

"My apologies, that 90 days by Project Pat always consumes me. I couldn't stay still when I hear it if I wanted to."

"It's ok but what kind of dancing is that?"

"That's called Gangster Walking. It's as Memphis as Bar-B-Q, Elvis and the Loraine Motel where Dr. King Jr. was killed. I was famous for it as a kid."

"Wow, don't stop for the sake of me. Keep dancing, I'm really enjoying it."

He looked at me with curiosity in his eyes and then picked up where he left off. The driver of the old school must have seen him dancing considering he not only turned the music up, he played two more songs that must have been famously known as song Gangster walkers liked to dance to. When he stopped now sweaty and out of breath I refused to bite my tongue.

"I'm not ready to call it a night. I haven't enjoyed myself like this in years. If you're not busy how about playing tour guide and showing me Memphis through your eyes?"

"My eyes are boring Nivea. I haven't really done much in Memphis. The only reason I got good at Gangster

Walking was so my parents would ease up on me for spending all my time studying finance. It even shocked me that I was good at it."

"You're more than good at it and why didn't they want you to study finance? Did they not want you to follow their footsteps?"

"Their footsteps were imprinted in other fields. I'm the first to dive into finance in my family. It must be dominant in your DNA?" he said popping his truck and removing a sports jacket. He placed it over my bare shoulders and grabbed my hand. We walked around the riverfront talking and holding hands for an hour and then we walked across the street to have a cup of coffee at his condo. We were walking in the middle of the street as a car approached.

"Hold on, let's wait for it to go by," he said with our hands still entwined. The car picked up speed but we weren't in danger because we hadn't crossed the solid line that separated the directions in the street. I looked down for a second and next thing I know Dwayne is pulling me out of danger. The car accelerated and the driver attempted to run us over. Once it passed us we ran to the side walk in front of his condo.

"Are you, ok?"

"Yes, I'm fine. My heart is beating fast but I'm alive."

His phone rang as I spoke and the look that came on

his face after he said hello was horrifying. He hung up after a few seconds of listening to the caller's words and then said, "Something vital came up and I have to deal with it right now. The driver will take you back to your hotel, I apologize."

"I understand, is there anything I can do to help?"

His body language suggested that he hadn't heard my question. He was looking up and to the left which meant he was remembering a visual. I rarely got to use the excess knowledge I deemed unusable often so when a chance presented itself I took advantage of it. I had taken a course in my Human Capital class on the Eye's body language as an extra. I can't remember everything the professor taught but I did walk away with key points. Looking up and to the left meant remembering a visual, up and to the right meant constructing a visual and straight ahead, somewhat unfocused meant processing any visual. Audio worked the same besides the eyes were held straight to the left or to the right. Down and to the right meant a person was accessing their feelings and down to the left meant they are talking to themselves. Dwayne was thinking about the audio from the car, he was visualizing a memory connected to the call. Without acknowledging my question, he stepped off the curb and waved his hand. A little over a minute later my car and driver were pulling up.

"Here's a thousand dollars," he said handing the money to me. "Take her on Beale Street and stay close by her side. Ms. Bowen likes getting lost in the bottom of a bottle." He kissed me on my cheek and walked off without telling me good bye.

On the ride to Beale Street I called my new friend from the dating site and asked if he could meet me there but he said he wouldn't be free for a few hours. I was upset seeing that I told him I'd be in town but he made it up to me once we hung the phone. I sent a text message with my hotel information and he sent one back,

I'll be through after I catch this last bite. Do you smoke?

I responded as we parked near our destination. I wasn't happy about the walk to the overcrowded street but it was worth it. There were clubs, restaurants, and bars everywhere and enough people walking the street to put all of them at maximum capacity. With all the liquor being consumed out in the open I thought I landed on Bourbon Street during Mardi Gras but people were wearing too much clothing for that to be true.

Come meet me outside of the Rock N' Roll place on the corner

The text came in from my new friend and I sent my driver packing after getting his number so I can call when I was ready to be picked up. Big Cee was ten times sexier than the pictures on his profile and obviously had more money than he portrayed. His Black Professionals Meet dot love profile said that he was a retired policeman due to being injured on the job but his body shunned down the information. After having a few drinks, he danced me out of my shoes and then out of my clothes. It was a one-night stand that would be jotted down in my record books as the best.

Waking up to the sounds of taps on my hotel door would normally make me uneasy but when you get fucked as good as I had, I walked to the door with a smile.

"I'm sorry to pop up on you like this but I had to change our plans up for today and decided to stop by and tell you instead of sending a text. Is it okay if I come in for a second?"

Dwayne was wearing a gray suit with the hoody covering his head and had a back pack on his back. He Looked as if he had jogged from his condo to my hotel which wasn't that far of a distance. I wanted to tell him no. My pussy was still tingling from the beating put on it the night before and I wasn't ready to have to put on clothes.

"Give me a second to put some clothes on. I'll come get you from the lobby."

"No, I'll be sitting in the stairwell when you're done. I wouldn't want to run into any of my clients looking like this. You know they think we sleep in business suits now that we manage their money."

He laughed but it was shaky and forced. He was uneasy about something and trying hard to play it off.

"Okay, I'll be out to grab you in a second."

I ran to the bathroom and took a three-minute shower which was enough time to devout thirty seconds on my arms and the rest in the attempt of properly cleaning my puss and surrounding area. I dried off in forty-five seconds and through my sundress on with the other fifteen seconds. I put on a bra but no panties and was at the stairwell in less than five minutes.

"That was fast," he said taking a seat on the couch in my suite. "I thought we should have our meeting here. There's a five-star restaurant downstairs that delivers to your room and I brought a bottle of wine with me already chilled but we can fill the ice bucket if you want it colder. I think the more we can relax the easier I'll soak in the information I need." He took the hood off his head and pulled the hoody off. His muscle shirt rolled up to his chest and I got a good view of the washboard under his pecks. I bit my lip.

"Sounds like a plan to me. Let me grab my things. I brought you a handmade leather satchel full of goodies."

"You can keep the satchel. I know a cover up name for man purse when I hear it but I'll take the contains."

His lips curled up into a smirk and I fantasized of what they would feel like kissing my pearl.

"Soft pillows…"

"Soft pillows? What does that mean?"

"Oh, I was asking if you wanted a soft pillow from the bed to put behind your back since we were relaxing." *thank goodness for the ability to lie fast on my feet,* I thought at the blunder I made letting my thoughts seep out my mouth.

"Yes, a soft pillow would be nice. Thank you."

I snatched the pillow off the bed and could feel Dwayne breathing down my bare neck. His warm breath felt like the perfect temperature blanket on a frosty day and the scent of it was wild flower sweet. His energy hovered around me and gave the feeling of being swallowed whole in the shadow of a giant. The hairs on my arms stood like the needles on a porcupine and yearned to be stroked by his touch. I wanted to move to show him that he was welcome to do whatever he pleased but I didn't want to ruin the anxiety he was building. If I was lucky he'd push me over with force, roll my dress up like a window blind and ram me bull style from the back. I inhaled.

"Hey, I need to use the restroom if you don't mind."

Dwayne was standing in the door frame at least 15 to 20 feet away from me. *Was I losing my mind,* I thought as I nodded my head in the direction of the bathroom. It felt so real and my growing wetness agreed. When he got out of the bathroom I followed him back into the living area with a sweltering jungle in between my thighs.

"Let's talk shop!" he said.

Dwayne was shooting off questions so fast that I felt rushed to answer them. My thought process felt delayed and foggy. I couldn't put my finger on it but there was something wrong me. I wasn't sure until I embarrassed the both of us.

"That's a lot of sticking and moving." Dwayne interrupted me to say.

"It is but it's necessary and completely worth it."

"I'll take your word for it but if I find it as a waste of time, you'll have to make it up to me." He followed with a chuckle.

"I wouldn't waste your time or your money but if for some odd reason your execution is poor how would you like me to make it up to you?" I asked before turning up my glass until it was empty and pouring myself another. I was waiting on his response and when a minute went by without one I looked in his direction. He had his sweatpants and boxers pulled down to his knees while he remained seated stroking his meat. No, fuck that. It was the whole bull and the way his hand stroked it, I knew he was a deadly matador.

"If you're wrong, I'm shoving all this dick down your throat and I'm not pulling it out until you gag and cry with it in your mouth."

He stroked slower and the bull's head enlarged in size. I could see the wetness crest at the bull's eye in the middle and I wanted to taste its tear.

"Maybe I should assume you're wrong now and put it in your mouth. You look like you want to taste it."

"I do."

"Then beg me to slap your lips with it and fuck your

throat."

"Please spank my mouth with that fat ass dick and rub that big head all over my lips."

"If I give you what you want what I are you going to do in exchange?" he asked making his dick fight gravity while he balanced it in the air.

"I'm going to swallow every drop!"

"Then come over here and drain me."

The freak in me wanted to attack him. I had lust built up from wanting to feel his lips and sip from the fluids his tongue was submerged in. I let my sundress drop to the floor, straddled his lap, and kissed his lips. Our tongues began to waltz in his mouth as I grind my hips on his meat. His dick was too much for all this pussy to handle and in seconds, I had passed out.

Dwayne

When Nivea came to the door naked I knew something wasn't right. She didn't attempt to cover her nudity. Her words were slurring too but I assumed it was due to me waking her out of her sleep. The way she drank, she might have hit every bar on Beale Street last night and was still drunk. I felt bad about waking her up with a pop up visit but when my ex Cynthia called and said, "Make the bitch in the white disappear or I will. I didn't run y'all over on purpose but next time I aim, it will be to kill. Till death do us part, Dwayne, are you ready to die? Send her home now!" I knew I had to switch all of my plans up.

Cynthia wasn't the ordinary crazy. She was the kind of crazy that sent people to jail, hell or living on the streets from spending everything on bail. Filthy rich, amazingly beautiful, and powerful was a bad combination to mix with crazy and to make it worst, she was an atheist with pride in her disbelief. I didn't know that she didn't believe in God until our first argument a few days before she put me in jail for the first time. I tried to take our problems to Jehovah in prayer. I was fifteen seconds into it with my head bowed and eyes closed.

"What in the fuck do you think that shit is going to do? How do you think that somebody you can't even see is supposedly going to fix me? You're better off praying to the dog for help, he's more real to me than your God."

I kept praying and tried to convince myself that she

was shooting off obscene words because she was mad. Cynthia stood there in silence until I was finished and then said, "If you have a problem with me, you fix it with me. Don't bring your beliefs in shit that can't be proven around me. I'm atheist!"

She stormed off and I Googled the word for the definition. I needed to make sure it didn't mean she believed in the devil. Although Webster' dictionary said there was a difference between the two, her actions from that point on, confirmed she rolled with the devil.

Having Cynthia back around put everyone close to me in harm's way; that's why I suspended Heather indefinitely. She didn't partner up with Cynthia, she was tricked. Cynthia pretended like we were childhood friends and threw the question out, "I remember before he had all of this he used to say, when I get my money I'm buying me a flock of Benz. I'm going to own at least one of every model they come in and I'm putting blessed and what number it is in my flock on the plate. Did he ever do it?"

When Heather answered, "Yes." that was all the information she needed to track me down. Adam ate that fruit thanks to Eve thinking the wrong person was her friend and Heather had unknowingly done the same to me. I wouldn't punish her for not seeing the serpent in Cynthia but I would keep her far way until it died. It was one thing for Heather to confess having feelings for me to the snake and it was another for Cynthia to see that I had those same or stronger feelings for her, back. I told Heather she'd stay on the payroll but she was banned from the office until further notice. I cut all personal ties with her too. If she was my soul mate I didn't have to worry about us not spending our lives together. I looked at this like we were taking a small break. I knew the boys wouldn't understand my absence while I handled Cynthia so I sent them to summer camp in Georgia. Even her four-year-old Dwade made the trip which on the bright side gave Heather a much-needed break. Protecting my family was priority number one and now that Cynthia had almost hit Nivea, her safety became a priority while she was here.

I woke up, showered, and went on my morning jog. On most days, my jog did force me to pass the hotel I had put Nivea in for the weekend and today I made sure it did. I didn't know where Cynthia was or if she was watching so I kept to my daily schedule besides requesting that the alley entrance of the hotel Nivea was at door was open. I called the front desk agent from the phone at the doorman's desk in my building and promised a $2,500 bonus if she did so. Hearing the desire for the money in her voice assured that she would do it and she did.

"Hey, you're not about to doing anything crazy, are you?" the agent said coming up the stair case while I waited for Nivea to get dressed.

"No, of course not. I'm famous and I didn't want the paparazzi to snap pictures of me visiting my friends."

The young Hispanic girl didn't look moved. That's why her next words didn't surprise me.

"You don't have to lie about sneaking in for a booty

call. I saw the woman naked in the doorway but if your wife catches you and gets all crazy I'm calling the police on y'all. I promise you that I'll act like I don't know how you got in. We cool?"

"Yeah, we're cool but if my crazy wife does come up here causing trouble. If you call the police on her and not me, I'll double your money. Is that cool?"

"Hell yeah, but if you make it $10,000 I'll tell the police whatever you want me to. I'll even show up at court to testify against your wife."

The decency in me found it foul that the girl would be willing to mess someone's life up for only $10,000 but watching Cynthia go to jail after all the bullshit she did to me felt like her reaping and sowing. Now I hoped she would find me and show her ass.

"You look like a damn burglar sitting in the emergency exit. Get up off those stairs and bring your sexy ass in the room with me." Nivea said, now wearing a sundress.

We chitchatted for a few and I gave her the falsified reason for switching our meeting. I handed her a bottle of wine I had brought and my fingers went numb as soon as she popped the cork.

"Are you okay?" I asked.

"Yes, I'm good and feeling even better. I had a really nice time last night."

"What did you end up doing?"

Her face went from a grin into a smile and her eyes rolled back in her head as if she was reliving it. She said,

"I really don't recall what I did."

I was familiar with the look of satisfaction so I knew better than to believe her.

She shuffled off into the bedroom and I followed in need to use the restroom that was inconveniently built inside her bedroom. Nivea made it to the closet dragging her feet and threw a bag on the bed. I assumed it held the satchel with the information inside of it that she said she brought for me. I was going to ask to use the restroom but I don't think she heard me follow her. She was standing stiff as a strongly rooted tree playing with her nipples. I watched them go from invisible behind her bra to out in the open for the world to see. Her nipples grew with each twist she gave them. They were beauties and I wanted to see how they fit in my mouth so I snapped us both out of it by asking to use the restroom. She turned and faced me then nodded to the bathroom door. My wood was stiff before the urine made its way out of it.

"I knew you'd have the biggest dick I've ever saw."

Nivea was standing at the door with her breast still out and her eyes locked on my dick.

"Um, can I have a little privacy please?"

"No, you may not but thanks for asking. I don't

swallow nut from financiers any more but that big ol' thing is too pretty for me not to look."

I shook it, wiped the tip, put him away and walked out the bathroom with Nivea on my heels. Something was definitely wrong and instead of trying to figure it out I jumped straight into the purpose of our meeting. There was something off with Nivea but I could tell her heart was in finance, more so trading. To every question I asked she gave a detailed answer I was sure I could bank on. I was impressed and sad to say, hearing her speak my language had turned me on. I decided to wrap up our meeting before there was a need to keep a pillow over my lap but Nivea lost it. She started talking about sucking my dick and telling me how she really felt about me.

"I'm scared of you, Dwayne. You're the type of man that I need and I knew it the first day we met. How you showed up in New York uninvited and then put me in place at my IPO party, I knew you were the man that could tame me. You're a king, even in that sweat suit you reek of power and demand respect. I know I could be a queen but it's going to take a real man to crown me one. Will you crown me, Dwayne?"

She bowed her head until her face was down in my lap. I couldn't see what she was doing but I could hear kissing sounds.

"Hey, Nivea, sweetheart, I think you're still drunk form last night. Let me help you into the room to sleep it off."

TOXIN

I slid from under her face and went into the bedroom to get the bed ready for her to lay in. I grabbed the trash can from the bathroom and sat it next to the bed just in case she had to vomit. I wouldn't leave her alone but I needed her to think I was gone so she could keep her hormones in line. Once I got the pillows stacked and walked back into the living room to get her, she had gotten worse.

"Fuck me harder, I know your dick is bigger that!" she moaned into the couch as she went up and down on the neck of the wine bottom. Her eyes were low and rolling in the back of her head. When I grabbed her to get her to stop, her skin felt hot, and after looking me in my eyes, Nivea blacked out.

*****

"We're waiting on her test results but we've stabilized her and once we get a cause for what happened we'll let you back to see her. She's lucky you were there!" the doctor squeezed my shoulder before walking away.

If alcohol was the sole reason behind the black out, she'd never drink more than water around me.

"I told you to get rid of her, I never said to try and kill her."

Cynthia's breath crawled up my neck while her hand scooped a handful of my dick. I wanted to elbow her teeth out of her mouth but I convinced myself to still treat her like a woman.

243

"Keep your hands off me and if I ever decided to kill a woman, it wouldn't be her."

"Cute threat but next time put more bass in your voice if you want to instill fear. How are you doing, long lost husband of mine?"

"I'm not your husband you crazy ass bi…" I wanted to call her one so badly but if I did, she'd see the power she had over me. I couldn't let her know that she still had the power to make me mad.

"Yes, you are!" she screamed out and everyone sitting in the waiting room gave her their attention. "We took those vows under God, you said we didn't need man's approval. Now keep your word!"

"Fuck those words. I know it's hard for that malfunctioning mind of yours to register what's real, but I lied. I would have said anything to get you to drop the charges you put on me and you're an atheist, you don't believe in my God."

"No! I gave you five years to realize that you messed up and to miss me. I let you build your little company and get you some chump change of your own in the bank. Time's up, Dwayne. It's like I told you, if you walk out of my life, I'll make sure your life is a living hell." She kissed my lips and I mushed her in the face as the doctor returned.

"We found gamma-hydroxybutyric acid also known as liquid ecstasy in her blood…"

"So, you drugged her like you did me?" Cynthia's voice was convincing but her acting was impeccable. The tears cut on like sprinklers in the summer and I looked at the doctor to see if he believed the show. I caught him in the process of nodding his head at the security guards for assistance. When he saw me looking at him he said, "It's a date rape drug so we performed a sexual assault kit on her and we found semen."

"Drug 'em and rape 'em. I really thought you had changed, Dwayne. All that therapy for nothing." She hung her head like a wilting flower to add drama to her performance. She took the microphone and turned it into a Shakespeare style tragedy. "I knew you should have stayed on your medication, but stupid me. I asked you to stop taking them so your erections could last longer than forty seconds. All I wanted was for you to get help so we could be a family. A happy family with a baby we'd shower in love. I thought, if only we could have a baby the sexual predator that's in you would die... I can't believe you raped her, she trusted you!" Cynthia hit the floor crying and I was snatched up by security while they told dispatch to call the police.

I couldn't hear much while I was being carried away but I was certain that I heard her say, "I'm his wife, we've been separated since the last time he hospitalized me."

Security skipped the lab and I was placed in the inmate holding cell at the hospital. Nivea was drowsy and couldn't undergo questioning yet. I wasn't making a move until the results from the rape kit came back or Nivea woke up to tell them the truth. Until one of those happened, I was going to be imprisoned again, and again it was thanks to Cynthia.

"Your wife would like to speak to you before she leaves," one of the security guards that had roughed me up the entire trip to the cell came walking into the room with the devil at his heels.

"Do you mind if I speak to my husband alone?"

"I can't let you and if I could, I wouldn't. I wouldn't leave any woman around a man like him."

She did this quick, circular wave across his chest and upper abdomen while looking at me. I don't know how the guard missed the darkness in her eyes, they were black. Once our eyes met she told him, "He's not going to do anything to me while you're standing right here. He's a punk. I only want to whisper something to him. I want your protection." She cut her eyes at the guard and gave him a smile. It was like watching the devil get some practice in before tempting Jesus on that mountain. She had him floating in her toxins.

"I'm right here for you, beautiful. Do what you need to do."

Cynthia took a few steps my way.

"I don't want any visits...I'm refusing my visit," I spoke out.

"Shut up, nigga," the guard mumbled under his breath. I don't think he would have had a problem saying it aloud, but he was occupied with the process of turning his back to pretend he didn't hear me. My hands and feet were cuffed to the rails and she had me trapped. The crazy bitch locked her nails in the sides of my face and twisted my neck back.

She stuck her tongue in my ear, nasty wet Willie style filling my ear with spit, and then said, "I want to play roulette with you before we eat dinner, Friday night. Will you meet me at the casino or should I make sure that the semen found inside of her belongs to you?"

"I'll see you Friday."

I'd told myself I'd never conform for her ever again and when the opportunity popped up I confidently did the opposite. I was rich and could buy my way out of the traps she was setting up for me now. I realized most people who do a lot of time in jail do so for two reasons. No money for the top lawyers and for having melanin in your skin, or in America, being black as they like to call us. There was nothing I could do about the skin and I take pride in that but I had the money. I'd made that type of money that demanded respect, you'll never see it beg for it. I would play it her way so I could show her that justice does keep a change purse tucked in her bra. Depending on the change you drop in it, her scales may weigh in your favor. I'm not saying that the more money you drop the less the melanin shows. Hell nah, that's not the way true acceptance starts and there's no way around being black. Rich or poor, if you're black you are black. Look at the situation with Tiger's arrest or listen to what Lebron dropped when he spoke out about being robbed. I'm saying, they may not respect you but they will respect the small volts of power that comes with money as long as they can see a way to control it, hence, the SEC. She wanted to talk Friday, I didn't see any harm in talking.

It took seven hours for them to come and tell me my sperm wasn't a match. Those were seven hours I spent chained up and treated like a dog. I think they let me pee twice before they chained me back up. Those seven hours of my life, I could never get back.

Nivea had progressed and was in a position to tell the officers what happened her. It must have been a rough story to tell because she asked them not to tell me and she seemed like she was blaming herself, she held a guilty expression on her face as she spoke.

"Dwayne, I am so sorry. I don't know why all of these toxic altercations keep arising. It's like everything started happening at once. All of my dirty laundry is spread out but the universe is only showing you my dirty panties. There isn't that many of them but when you put them in a pile, it still looks like a lot. I'm not sex driven and I don't…"

I covered her mouth with my hand. We were watching the market news on a local channel I didn't know existed until I saw Nivea's secretary and staff being escorted out of her office by the FBI. The camera had the company's name in every shot although the report made sure not to say its name. I pointed up to the screen and she read it out loud.

"The SEC freezes a trio of brokerage accounts behind rumored insider trading. Wait… what the fuck? Dwayne, reach me my…"

"Two steps ahead of you," I cut her off to say and called in three first class flights on the first early bird that said fuck the watching fox, I'm getting my worm in the morning. She was ordered to stay in the hospital a few days which she needed to but I'd get her a nurse practitioner to stay by her side for a few days and there was no way I was leaving her alone. I couldn't, not until I knew she healed from this.

The rest of the night she kept her head glued to her cell phone and her eyes locked on her Mac book screen once I grabbed her stuff from the hotel room. I wanted to swing by the house and grab a bag but I didn't know if Cynthia had a command post setup to keep an eye on me. I took a cab to her hotel and then called for an Uber to swing me by my condo on the way back to hospital. Mrs. Blakemoore's makeshift patio was still in its place. It was 11 o'clock at night, I hoped I wouldn't see her sitting out and was relieved the pallet on the patio was empty. I could see man doorman adjusting his tie by reflection in the sliding glass doors and when I looked at my picture window I saw my maid naked bent over with her entire left side pressed against the glass and Chauncey beating her down in my bathrobe.

"Stop the car!" I yelled. I can't recall if I was in or almost out the SUV when I said it. My doorman saw me on the camera and had the elevator ready for me to go up.

"I didn't let him in this time," he said after stepping inside the lift with me and pushing the respective number to my floor. When the doors were closed, I tucked in my lips and looked down so the cameras wouldn't see me and said,

"I know, I'm going to handle this."

You could hear Larry Dodson's voice of Bar-Kays blasting from my condo before we arrived on the floor. I unlocked the door and swung it open. I wanted to holler out his name but the music was blasting. I handled that first and both eyes fell on me.

"Guess I know why my windows ain't never clean. Drop the keys, I'm not calling the police, count that blessing as your last paycheck and cuzzo, you got 60 seconds to get off Riverside drive for the rest of your life or we gon' have our first real problem." Chauncey immediately started snatching up his things but I wasn't done, "You can keep that robe too and go ahead and dust your feet at my door. You remember what Meme taught us?"

At the mentioning of my grandmother's name, Chauncey froze up.

"The way you're talking cuzzo sounds like we have a problem either way and you didn't have to put Meme all in it. The bitch invited me to fuck and I thought who better to get caught fucking in your place than me? I only crept up in here once, it gotta make you wonder who else she's invited." Chauncey nodded her way and she dropped her head low. I wanted to hear her voice, instead he started back up, "I wasn't going to come but I had to tell you about Tom Lee."

"Tom Lee, who the hell is that?" I asked while my ex-employee wouldn't let our eyes meet.

"Tom Lee is the bitch who sucked my dick and let me fuck her in the park by that Tom Lee memorial. You know I had to tell you about that, that's history!"

My ears cut off because I knew Chauncey wouldn't get serious with and audience watching. I took a step closer to her.

"Aye, how many people have you let in my Condo? I don't want to stress that you only get one shot at telling the truth."

"...She was like, read it to me again, read what the statue says again. So, I pushed her face down into the concrete underneath the statue of the boat. I stroked that thang and read it to her one more time." Chauncey continued telling his story.

"He was the only man I had sex with in your house?" she cried out.

"Why?" I said stepping up and Chauncey assumed that I was asking the question to him.

"Because I don't think the bitch could read it herself. You know I don't mind putting in volunteer hours for the less fortunate and after the way she sucked on my..." I cut him off to get her full attention.

"Why did you assume I asked how many people you've fucked in my house? That wasn't the question. Take a second and think about it. I'd hate for you to fuck up after you thought you stole yourself a chance. Nah, that one was on me."

She looked at Chauncey who was still telling his story and back at the hardwood floors that she did actually clean. I could see our reflections through the mop and shine she used.

"Only him and this girl I met, that's it."

"It's crazy how people fuck you over and then act like a bitch when you find out. You're doing right for firing her ass cousin. I'm thinking about uppercutting her ass right now for that garbage bag pussy she's passing out. She better be glad Meme raised us not to hit hos or I'd jab her ass for trying to poison my di..."

"What girl?" I asked stealing the audio from Chauncey.

"Some chick I met about a month ago when I was taking your trash out. She was flirting but it wasn't working. When she realized I wasn't interested she straight out offered me $10,000 to let her walk around your place and she promised she wouldn't touch or take nothing. I took the money and stayed by her the entire time."

"What was her name, what did she look like?"

"Like she was rich too and real pretty. I think she said he name was Le'trice or something like that."

"That ho is lying, we don't know no flips name Le'trice." Chauncey snapped.

"Did anything stand out about her?"

"Yes, she had the biggest diamond I had ever seen in my life on her finger and her eyes were spooky. It's like her pupil had swallowed all the color around it and only a line of hazel was left."

I would have described her eyes the same exact way. It was her, my fake wife that had her ex-husband by her a $20,000 wedding ring as her parting gift for the divorce. I didn't buy the shit nor did I place it on her finger but you couldn't tell the crazy bitch that it wasn't from me. If you did, she wouldn't believe it.

"Cynthia Annette…" I shook my head as soon as I said her name.

"Cynthia? Now that shit sounds vaguely familiar. I don't think I've fucked a Cynthia… wait… Cynthia? Not the bitch who kept you in jail. That crazy bitch is back?"

Nivea

My company, my fucking baby, got shut down and it was top financial news. No IPO by year five and now, the SEC froze my shit behind rumored insider trading?! Hold on, I need a minute…

Dwayne

Nivea woke up at the opening of the door and she cut her eyes as I walked in her room. Dealing with Chauncey took longer than I expected. I banned him from my place as his consequence. I understood the opportunity but not the lack of respect. He could have bust her on the floor, he knew I hadn't bent anybody over yet to the outside view. I wasn't in the mood to deal with her attitude and I didn't have to, she went back to sleep. The nurse practitioner arrived at 4 am, we boarded our flight to New York at 5:50.

The flight was quiet as expected. While we were riding to the airport Nivea had already spoke her piece.

"I appreciate what you've been doing for me and there's really no nice way to say this, umm…if you plan on being around through this, don't ask me shit about it. I'll tell you when I'm ready."

"No problem, I'd want the same but I wouldn't have let you make this trip. It would have been mandatory to go through this alone."

"Scared to show your feelings?" she questioned.

"Nope, I wouldn't want you to be involved in my plan B."

Those were the last words we exchanged until she gave me a tour of her place. I asked a few questions and then she pointed me in the direction of the guest room and

257

gave me a copy of her door key.

"I'm gone, lock up if you leave please."

"No problem, don't forget to keep Pamela with you." I nodded at her N.P to get up and go with her.

The trip was last minute so I didn't technically have plans to go by but I knew there was a lot I could do while I was here. Nivea's condo was in the financial district at the waterfront. I didn't have a desire to see the Statue of Liberty due to the conflicting information about its history but since I never been sightseeing in New York I'd take I look. I walked over to Battery Park and put a quarter in telescope and tried to feel excited like the father at the telescope next to me was as he told his son the history he read in school books. Nothing sparked inside of me so I used the rest of the sunlight to walk the blocks that made up the financial district.

I passed the Exchange, visited the Museum of American Finance, had an ice cream while in South Street Seaport and let the sun set on me at the 9/11 memorial. I took the long way back so I could pass the charging bull. That 7,000 plus pounds statue meant something different for everyone who touched it. Kids saw it as the biggest penny shaped into an animal that they had ever seen in their life. Their parents might have told them, it was to bring hope after the 1987 stock market crash and the people in finance who visited it more than likely saw it as aggressive financial optimism. The way that most of them rub and cuff his nuts, whether a camera was flashing or not, you'd have think they viewed its scrotum as a symbol of virility. Not me, I saw it as the best example of how to monopolize on a given gift that the world will ever see. Nivea sent a text.

Dinner in an hour, ordered Chinese.

I hurried back to her place so I could jump in the shower before we ate. The living room, dining room, kitchen and hallway that connected them were now an extension of her home office. She had file boxes sitting on folding tables, everywhere. It was obvious they had shut her down for more than one rumored act of insider trading, she was utilizing too many references for it to only be that. I wouldn't ask what happened out of respect for her wishes but I would ask, "What can I do to help?"

She eyed me in relief.

"I need you to tell me how you knew I wasn't going to IPO at my party and then, I need to know how much you're going to charge me to look at these bullshit violations I'm being hit with. They're pulling shit out of nowhere left and right but I have files to co-inside with the dates and times." I looked around and before I could speak she said, "Everything here is on my computer too but I don't trust elevators," she pointed her index finger at the boxes and concluded with, "I prefer the stairs."

"I'll work Pro Bono and I'm going to wait to name my percentage based off the money you're going to make bouncing back. Now, don't you have some work to do?" I smiled and she smiled back. I think that's the first smile she's given since the hotel. I took the list of violations with me to the room. I didn't glace at them, I know if I did I would've skipped the shower.

"Dinner is served…"

Nivea almost dropped the plate when she walked in the room on me in my boxer briefs. It was the only piece of clothing I had put on after the shower. She turned her back to me quickly.

"I am so sorry. I saw you grab the list and assumed you were in here already working, I should have knocked."

"It's cool."

"No, it's not. I didn't have the right to not knock. You're a guest."

"Nivea."

"Yes, Dwayne."

"You've seen me in less."

She turned around slowly and said, "Oh yes, I do remember that."

An awkward silence moved like a breeze through the room as we both remembered that moment in dissimilar ways yet both of our thoughts ended with a laugh.

"You know I normally charge by the seconds for that."

"I was hoping you'd say that because I'd pay upfront for it by the hours. You're a blessed man, Mr.

Hollingswell." She placed my plate on the dresser and left the room.

I went through the first 6 charges and knew someone had a personal vendetta against her. The charges were outrages. They ranged from business to personal and the personal was connected to the business. It was more than a whistle blower running their mouth to the SEC, somebody was running their mouth low level to the state police to agencies dealing with Elder financial exploitation with her father and step mother listed as victims. She knew her father was battling dementia but hadn't known that he was listed as his wife's caregiver for multiple sicknesses she faced. When Nivea used their address, the state didn't question if the two were living alone and whenever either was asked who takes care them, they both said Nivea did to prevent being put in a nursing home. Nivea had two counts of that not to mention a handful of violations as a hedge fund manager that circle around them. The Insider trading was enough to get her fined and some jail time but if found guilty on elder abuse, her jail time will drastically increase.

I read, researched, and made notes until my eyes begged me to divert them elsewhere. I logged on to the dating site for a break.

I know the flower shop isn't open, what are you doing up?

I saw Brenda's online icon lit up, it was the prefect way to spend my time on break.

No, the shop is closed. I'm up doing inventory

and needed a break. How about you? Anything exciting in Nashville?

I had a lot shit happening around me but I couldn't complain. Elliott was in jail by the hand of the SEC and Nivea could be on her way.

Everything is back to normal this way. I'm up searching the web. Need to order some new equipment.

We didn't chat long yet her words left a powerful stain on my mind. She began talking about how there are a lot of people that don't appreciate what and who they have in their lives. When she said,

Appreciation is never letting go of the feeling or the desire you had before wanting or earning something. If you remember what it felt like not to have it, you'll never let anyone take it away from you.

Something about her words made me think of Nivea. She had been through a hell of a lot since we met. I got up to check on her.

"I was going to knock but..." I stopped talking at the sight of her sitting Native American style on the floor. She was next to her couch crying with her eyes locked at the view of Liberty Island. I crept up, sat down beside her, and pulled her into me to hold her from the back. Instantly she wiped up the tears from her cheeks and gave me a smile. I grabbed her chin, turned her face back towards the statue of Liberty and held her to sleep. Once she was out chasing z's I stretched her out, grabbed us a couple of pillows and we slept right there.

Nivea was gone when I opened my eyes but I had business to handle. First, I had to flag down a cab to take the NP to the airport. She had cared for Nivea the 48 hours that the doctor recommended and it was time to send her home. After waving her off I grabbed my bag and headed to my favorite spot across from the Stock Exchange and made a few telephone calls. I was able to secure a same day meeting with the Equity Research associate I met in the restroom while out with Nivea on my last visit. When that was done I called and made dinner reservation for Friday night at the steakhouse in the casino for Cynthia and me. That call took longer than the first seeing they had to call the owner before approving my last minute reservation request and lastly, I called to check on my office.

"How's everything going there?"

"Why, did you do something illegal I should know about?" Edward asked.

"Of course not, but I'll see you soon."

His question was out of character and it felt like someone was tugging at his strings. I had a feeling who might have been playing puppet master. I called the Federal holding tank to see if my visit with Elliott for the upcoming Saturday had been approved and it had. I was about to call and check on my mother to kill sometime but I couldn't believe my eyes. Heather walked past the window looking like every bit of a tourist. She seemed happy to be on vacation but she looked lonely. I snatched my belongings up and through them in back pack. I put some space between us and followed her. She walked the length of the block and then a smile grew on her face. At first, I thought she was happy because she had found her destination but I soon realized I was wrong. Heather was smiling at the man who was walking her way and his face lit up too. I knew I wouldn't be able to sit back and watch their interactions.

"How are you, Heather?" he said embracing her a little too long for my liking so I sped up just in case I needed to break the shit up.

"I'm excited to check out the office space. I apologize again for Mr. Hollingswell not being able to join us but he has confidence that I will make the right decision for the location of our New York office. Shall we proceed?"

I forgot that I had asked her to hunt for a location and I didn't think she'd travel to New York to do so. Seeing that she was kid free and banned from the office, she must have decided to take a vacation and do a little work. Her ability to be thorough without request is what made her valuable to me but her worth wasn't what triggered the jealousy. How her summer dress relieved the curves I tried hard not to look at, out of respect. I turned and walked away before she saw me in Neanderthal mode, on-hard and drooling.

Isaac Britton showed up to our meeting at the lounge almost an hour late and had to have been high. He was loud, boastful, and acting like we were frat brothers. He was taking the conversation everywhere but, in the direction, I needed it to go in. I had to take control.

"I asked for this meeting to finish up that chat we had on derivatives. You were telling me how you stay ahead of the curve."

"That's simply. I pull a Nivea Bowen every time."

"You pull a what?" I chuckled but was confused.

"A Nivea Bowen. That's where you sell dreams. I get investors like she gets potential fuck buddies to buy contracts of commodities for future dates at a set price and then I sell them by the hundreds. Just like she gets them to trick cash on her in the hundreds of thousands for future sucks and fucks at the price she sets," he broke out laughing and I tried to move on.

"So, what would you say is the main reason derivatives is a huge mover of the markets?"

"Security, they allow you to lock into an investment and play it safe by guaranteeing a profit. We all know that Nivea likes to be fucked and will let you do as you please with her for free. Whose pussy would be a better investment than hers to lock into? Even if you decide not to go all the way with her you'll still profit off her head." a bellow of laughter followed.

"I must be missing something. Is there a reason why you're involving Ms. Bowen in our chat? I'm lost."

"No, just making sure you understood my answers. That night we talked, I saw you sitting at the bar having drinks with her. You can calm down, I already had my fun with her plenty of times. I know how you people can get about your bitches."

"You people?"

"Yeah, you black..."

I was glad we had request a private room, no one was around to witness me knock his teeth to his taste buds. He spat the blood in his mouth to the floor.

"Hey buddy, that wasn't necessary. I like you..." I hoped he said you people again instead he said, "I like you for not being ashamed to be dating a known ho. She really..."

I walked out the room before I let his ignorance get my privileges to walk the streets taken away. I found a bar up the street and had a few drinks before going back to Nivea's. I hadn't decided if I wanted to knock Isaac's head off his shoulder for being racist or for bad mouthing Nivea. The fact remained that Isaac was another body I could add to her growing list of sexual partners. If I did want to pursue her, was I supposed to act like I hadn't gotten wind of her passed? I opened the door to her condo and got met by her friend sitting on the couch.

"She didn't tell me you were that damn fine. I'm Miya." The baby bump met me before I could reach her hand. I apologized and then stepped back. "It's cool, I'm not used to being fat either. This is my first and my last baby. Are you going back out?"

"No, I don't think so."

"Good because she got me sitting here waiting for her lawyers to come drop off some papers. If you're going to be here I can go. I work at a doctor office and those bitches get on my last nerve. I need some cuddle time with my boo if you know what I mean."

I knew what she meant but I didn't want to. Meeting her was enough to see that birds of a feather will flock together. I was going to give Nivea the benefit of the doubt but if this is her best friend, how could I?

"You can go ahead and go. I'll be here."

"Thank you and one more thing. Are you single? I'm asking because Nivea needs a man bad as fuck. She was messing with my other best friend, Zamora's husband, Evol for three years and now they ain't together because his wife found out. I thought her and Nivea were going to fight that shit out when I brought my boo over here but they talked. Anyways, she's a good girl but can't find a man for nothing. I told her I could introduce her to some of these balling ass niggas I know but that bitch picky. If you're single you should give her a shot. I think y'all look real cute together with y'all super rich, wall street investing asses... well, at one time Nivea was rich too but they just shut her shit down. I told her being a black woman in a game full of white..." I had to cut her off. If not, I don't believe she'd shut up.

"Yes, I'm single and I'll think about what you said regarding Nivea. Good night... what did you say your name was again?"

"It's Miya like the singer. Some people say I look like her but my man said I'm way prettier. When I'm out in public…"

"Good night, Miya."

I held the door open while she got her purse and finally walked through it. I was re-reading the charges against Nivea when my text message alert went off. It was the Church.

We need to speak with you face to face. It is imperative.

I wasn't due to return to Memphis until Thursday but if they needed me to return sooner, I'd be flying out in the morning.

Can it wait until Thursday?

It took twenty minutes to get a response.

Yes, we believe it can.

Not making a move when they reached out always made me feel uncomfortable but if the geniuses said it can wait, I wasn't mistaken that it could. I moved my research to the couch so I could watch Bloomberg as I worked. I switched to CNN when I heard Nivea fumble at the door. The story about her failed attempt to IPO days before the SEC shut her down had made global news.

"That's fine, book the flight. I don't mind the three-hour layover in Nashville. I need to get to California first thing Friday morning or my mom is going to come here. She's losing her mind each time someone tags her in a damn Face book post about me going to jail. Get me home, if she comes here I'll never get rid of her!" she ended her call and looked at me, "Is that blood splattered on your shirt and tie?"

"I think so," I said inspecting it myself. I knew Isaac was swallowing teeth but I didn't see were the blood flew at the collision. I continued with, "must be from that fight I witness on the subway."

"Welcome to New York. I think I've had every type of human fluid you can name on me at least once since I've lived here. Did you see that I made Bloomberg?"

"I did, but I turned it off."

"Well, I have somewhat good news I can tell you. The elder abuse shit was dropped so now I'm only facing the other four charges the SEC scrapped up on me. The shit there doing is still bogus but at least my lawyers can fight against the true wrong I committed and the false accusations."

"Yeah and it's a plus that you don't have any ties to the two firms involved. That will make it hard for them to prove it was insider trading."

"Well," she said taking a seat next to me, "that's the somewhat the bad news I was going to share next. I don't know one of the firms involved because they haven't released any information on it but I do know the other and there is a tie between us that will make it hard for me to fight that accusation."

"Don't tell me that you used to work there?"

"No, I didn't work there. I used to have a sexual relationship in college with the owner and made World Star not too long ago because his wife decided to test me at the coffee shop. We didn't knuckle up, we word fought and it ended with her husband sliding me his number. That too was caught on camera."

"Wait, so you were sharing information?"

"Are you crazy? No, I wasn't sharing information. The bitch... I mean, the wife is a technology geek. I think she either tapped into our trades or she has a bug planted in my office."

"You think she'd go through all of that because you had an affair with her husband? Wait, this isn't the dude you tried to attack that day, is it?"

"No, it's not and I didn't have an affair with her husband. I had him before they ever met but she will always keep an eye on me since he confessed that he showed up late on their wedding day because he spent the night with me."

"You're Toxic, girl!" It came out my mouth and it was too late to take it back. I couldn't hold my opinion in any longer. She was the predator playing victim and I almost fell for it. "First the burnt dude, then the married man with the girlfriend. You even did your thing with Isaac

Britton's racist ass and now the dude you're accused of insider trading with?!"

"Isaac, how do you know him?"

"Why does that matter? Look for the obvious and let the diversions go. I'm not judging what you do or who you do it with, I'm judging your execution when it comes to getting closure with them. I'd love to believe that what you have between your legs is good enough to have driven each one of these men crazy, I really would but let's be real."

She stormed off and left me standing there to stare at the back of her head until she slammed her bedroom door behind her. I thought about walking in on her to apologize but I could smell the weed smoke sipping from underneath her door. I grabbed the bottle of wine she had in the refrigerator and got comfortable on the couch. About an hour later she sat next to me and put her head in my chest.

"I am toxic, you're right."

"No, I'm wrong. Who am I to judge? You can't see it but I have a stain from my past I walk around with every day. I let it go years ago but those who were around me when I made it will never stop pointing at it. You got to pray on it."

"Will you pray with me?"

She closed her eyes, placed her hands in mine and we prayed together. I could hear her sobbing at my words to God but I think I needed the pray if not more than as much as she did. I was going through it too but only my soul could cry. After we shared the words, "amen" she looked me in my eyes deeply. While she stared into my eyes, mine were dishing the look back. It wasn't long before I was in between her legs stroking in and out of her with my arms cuffing her back. After praying to God to help her fight her toxins, I deep stroked in them without a life jacket. The devil had to have made me do it.

Nivea

I didn't want to wake Dwayne up but I needed to pee. After fifty-five minutes of love making he fell asleep with his extended cab parked inside of me on E. He was drained, he had to be because he dropped his load three times in those minutes. I could feel his gasoline slowly making its way down while pushing him out of me. I decided not to wake him until his dick detached us. I kissed his lips once we were no longer one and said,

"I need to use the bathroom."

Dwayne kissed me back and stood up drowsy. The night sky gave off enough light to show me everything I already felt he was working with. His silhouette included the ripples from his washboard stomach and the sledgehammer that hung below it. I was going to hold my pee seeing that the kissing had gotten him back hard. For another scoop of that, I'd risk blowing out my bladder.

"Yeah, I think I need to use it too." He grabbed his dick like it was a small child that he needed to hold hands with to cross the traffic filled street but I couldn't tell which of them was leading the way. I wanted to follow with my nasty ass but if I sneezed I'd cover the floor in pee.

I released the buildup and hopped in the shower. Usually it was mandatory to sit in the Jacuzzi after a session that long but Dwayne didn't have me sore. Unlike the last few I slept with he didn't aim to beat it up. He stroked me like I belonged to him as he wiped the tears from my eyes. Instead of all that, "whose pussy is this?" and "You like that, don't you?" that I'm used to hearing when a penis is invited inside me, I was given a beautiful silencer, his kiss. Love bird style kissing, the kind that led to prematurely confessing love when you mean to confess loving the feeling of the moment you're in. I could feel the words craving to come out of my mouth as our laps clapped, our tongues hugged and his hands caressed my skin softer than soap. I didn't let it out but it made me wonder if I should have because after he took me to God, I knew Dwayne was my King. There's two things real men do. One, take you to meet their parents when they know you are the right one and two, take you to God. I felt like I was now 50% away from the engagement ring.

I got out the shower and heard the shower in the hallway bathroom running. Dwayne left the door cracked so I peeked in. He had his cell phone in hand trying to connect it to a gold portable speaker he placed on the sink. A few seconds went by then a beat came on. It was slow paced with a heavy drum and piano vibe to it. He stood there for a few seconds nodding his head and where the voice of the artist was scheduled to come in Dwayne started rapping to the instrumental. His southern accent took over and I couldn't make out what he was saying. I heard him mention my name when talking about making love and something about going for the gusto, whatever that meant. It sounded good, even with the language barrier. It made me wonder what other talents he kept hidden.

"Are you okay?"

Dwayne was standing in my door with a towel wrapped around his waist. I could smell the scent of the soap mixing with his cologne. I wasn't shy yet his confidence made me feel inferior to him so I pulled my blanket up to my neck to cover my body. My self-esteem wasn't low but I did have a roll or two I didn't want advertised.

"Nah, don't try to cover it up now. I've already been in it," he dropped his towel in my door way. "and I'm about to get in it again if that's okay with you, Ms. Bowen?"

I grabbed the blunt out of my ashtray next to the bed, hit it twice and then offered it to him as I pulled the blanket off me to expose my underwear.

"I'm good, I want to be sober for this."

He kissed me and I put the blunt back in the ashtray without looking. It was something electrifying in the meeting of our lips. It felt real, like I was kissing my husband. Dwayne could have done anything he wanted to me and I wouldn't have put up a fight. He must have read my mind because he did whatever he wanted, whenever he wanted for the next 19 hours. It was 5 o'clock in the evening when we both had enough of the eat, sleep, and make love carousel we had been stuck on.

"They were huddled up talking about it and scared to tell you." he said randomly.

"What?" I laughed, I didn't have a clue of what he was talking about.

"How I knew your company wouldn't go public. They were at your party talking about it and practically playing rock, paper, scissors on when they would tell you. They didn't think I was paying attention but I was."

"So, you didn't have any inside information, you're just good at eavesdropping?"

"Why are you disappointed that I don't? how about you stop trying to play superwoman and handle everything yourself and talk to me. I might be able to help in ways you can't and won't think of."

He sat up and lowered the volume on the television. My mind almost jumped off track at staring at him sitting there naked.

"I want to know how I can beat this insider trading stuff. That's all I want to do. I thought you knew the SEC had been watching me and that it was them who made sure the paperwork was filed incorrectly."

"Oh, you thought I was a confidential informant or some type of finance rat? Sorry, I don't blow whistles. You hired a team of unprofessional professionals that you shouldn't be stressing about. They owe you and with this insider trading stuff, you should thank God you didn't go public. Your fines and penalties would be tenfold. Think of all the investors that would have pulled away. You fell off with this but falling of the porch is nothing compared to falling off a skyscraper."

I would have responded but his cell phone rang in

the other bedroom. Something about the look on his face when he heard the ring-tone told me he knew who was calling. He dashed out of the room, closed the door behind him, and I felt it was my turn to eavesdrop.

"Hey, Mama, what's up?" was all I heard him say before three minutes of silence followed. Then he said, "Yeah, it's her. I leave here in the morning and I'll go straight to see him. I'm going to deal with everything else Friday." There was a pause and then, "No, I'm with Nivea in New York helping get her stuff straight…no, I haven't told you anything about her but since you seem interested next time she comes to see me, I'll make sure to bring her by. Is that what you wanted to hear?" He went silent again, did some moaning as response, and then said, "You don't have to apologize, I love you too, and the next time he calls tell him I'll be there in the morning."

I was back in bed before he could open the door to his room.

"That was my mom, she was concerned because the money she asks me not to send came later than usual." He shook his head wanting me to believe his lie and followed with, "Gotta love mamas."

"Right, I'm headed home to mine Friday. Her friends saw me on the news and made sure to only tell her the worst that they heard about me. I have to get to California before she makes her way here. Besides not being able to put her out, I'm not in the mood to hear her tell me I need to settle down, get married, and have a shit load of crying ass babies."

"Sounds like my mama but she likes to mention my age. She says, Dwayne, you're 37 years old, it's time to make me a grandmother, don't you think?" He laughed and then said, "I haven't found a way to tell her hell no without being disrespectful."

"Like you said, gotta love mamas."

"But maybe your mama is right. Why are you scared of settling down with one person that isn't already tied to someone else?"

I threw my neck pillow at him.

"Men don't confess to being tied to women, even when they are married or about to get married. I don't hunt for men that are already taken, y'all come to me."

"Who's y'all?" he asked looking over his shoulder for someone else.

"Don't play single now because you hit it all day."

"And night, I hit it all day and all night. And I don't have to play single because I am. I'm not seeing anyone at the moment."

"I don't believe you, look at you."

"What does that mean? Because I'm handsome as hell, got money and got you over there shaking like a leaf on a windy day I have to be taken?"

"No, you don't have to be taken, you could be a player."

"I prefer to be a trader," he chuckled, "But all jokes aside, I did that relationship stuff and it didn't work out for me. There's a special lady I have my eye on but I think she looks at me like a brother now, I don't know. I might have waited too long to pursue her."

"So, you want me to believe you're not getting any pussy? You can come better than that, Dwayne!"

"I just got some pussy all day, all last night and I'm planning on getting some more before I call it a night. Before this with you, I mastered beating my meat. It isn't better than the real thing but I promise you, it's lets complicated and nerve racking."

"What do you mean by this with me? What is this?" I tried hard to get the whining out my voice but to no avail.

"You tell me. I told you when I met you that I don't do anything that ends in end, like girlfriend and you made it clear you don't do anything that sails away like relationships. So, what do you want to call it?"

I want to call it the real deal, is what I wanted to say to him instead I said, "I don't think we should call it anything just yet. I mean, we would have to come to an agreement on somethings, right?"

"Right! We'll name it something after 90 days spent like this."

"90 days? I thought Steve Harvey wrote that book for women?" I laughed before continuing, "We weren't supposed to have sex until the 90days was up."

"Well we did, I liked it and so did you. The 90 days is to see if we really like each other or if we're in it for the sex. I'm not being funny but while we go through this are you willing to be exclusive?"

The accent pillow went flying his way next.

"Yes, I can be exclusive but you really wanted to ask is if I can go without fucking anybody else. That's what you really wanted to say. Yes, but I will be traveling back and forth to Memphis quite frequently for all that," I said nodding at his swelling dick.

"Good, I want you to. There's less pillows you can throw at me on my bed. Now come give me a kiss."

I did exactly as my 90-day experiment asked.

*****

Dwayne had left an hour ago and I was dragging to get myself up. I had to meet with the SEC at the attorney general's office for questioning and wasn't in the mood for none of it. I wanted to him to stay so we could spend some time together out of the bed but life had to happen first. My house phone rang which was rare because my mother was the only person with the number.

"Hello?"

"Good morning, I apologize for calling you so early but can I speak to Dwayne please? He promised to call me once he got you back to New York and I haven't heard from him. I'm starting to get worried."

"Um, who is this?"

"Oh, excuse me," she laughed and mumbled something that I supposed she thought was a joke and then said, "This is his wife, well soon to be ex-wife once the divorce is final, but we are still very close."

"You're Dwayne's wife? How did you get my number if you don't mind me asking? And I'm sorry, I still didn't catch your name?"

"My apologies, my name is Cynthia Hollingswell and this is the number he gave me when I came to visit you at the hospital. I sat with you for about an hour but you were out of it. I really hate what happened to you. It's sad that you can't even trust putting your cup down anymore. It crazy that someone would drug you. How are you feeling by the way?"

"I'm better, thank you for asking, and for sitting with me at the hospital. That was very nice of you. I don't recall telling anyone that I thought my drink was tampered with at the bar. I actually thought that the guy I danced with had drugged me. Is that what Dwayne told you happened?"

She made a strange sound and I couldn't tell if it was laughter or if she was battling allergies. Once she got past the humor she found in my words, she said, "I hate liars!"

"Excuse me?"

"I said, I hate liars. Does my husband know that you have a problem with telling the truth and keeping your legs closed?" she asked and made the crazy noise again.

"I don't know what you're…"

"Don't lie to me you raggedy Wall Street bitch, I know the truth. You weren't raped, you were ready to commit it. I know something was slipped into your coke and rum because I slipped it in there. I should have used rat poison instead if I'd have known you'd convince my husband to take care of you afterwards. I don't know why I changed my mind about running you over that night. I guess I was scared I'd accidentally hit my husband by mistake."

"Listen, I don't know why…"

She cut me off again.

"No ho, you listen. Till death do we part. I made Dwayne the man that he is. I got him out of that hip hop gangster walking shit he used to wear. I showed him there was more than hot dogs and quarter bags of chip for dinner and that stroke he used on you, baby, that's all me. You're into finance, right? Well let me come into your world. I invested time and money into making Dwayne the perfect man for me. I gave him time to mature and held on to the position while he went through the process. I invested on the bull side, the upside and I'll be damn if I watch you or anyone else try to manipulate the market by bringing him down. So, take this little warning as me hedging but know, when I'm ready to sell my position, I'm taking my profits."

The call ended and I knew I should have ended it a

long time ago. She befriended me to build rapport so I wouldn't hang up when she snapped. I couldn't hang up because I needed to hear what she really had to say to me once she was in her feelings. I knew it wasn't 100% accurate. I grabbed my cell phone and called Dwayne but there was no answer, he must have already boarded the plane.

The meeting with the SEC at the attorney general's office was long, drawn out and seemed to irritate my legal team as much as it did me. I had been asked the same question four different ways every time they came up with a new question. I wouldn't rush to answer until my team gave me the okay. After spending almost an hour with them questioning why I bought the position on the day in question and me explaining that my analyst and momentum trader, Kishi spotted it as a good buy, I was then asked,

"What is your relationship with Stonewall Alliance L.L.P?"

"I don't have a relationship with Stonewall Alliance L.L.P."

The opposing attorneys and agencies looked from one to the other. The attorney general, the honorable Stacey Stockholm who attended Yale the same time as me and I can't recall there being anything honorable about the drinking and wild partying she used to do, nodded and the questions continued.

"Are you saying that you are not familiar with the firm?"

I looked at the head of my legal team Katrina, who also attended Yale with me and the AG and she gave me the same nod.

"No, that is not what I'm saying. I clearly said, I do not have a relationship with the firm not that I didn't know of it."

"You don't have a business or personal relationship with the firm?"

"I don't know why you want to take the long route but you keep asking the same question so let me help you out. I don't have a business or personal relationship with the firm. I did have a personal relationship with the owners. Ananias and Sapphira attended Yale with me, the Attorney General and two members of my legal team."

"Would you say Mr. and Mrs. Ananias and Sapphira Levi were your friends?"

"No, I would not?"

"So, can you please explain in detail the grounds of your relationship?"

The AG sat up tall in her chair and awaited my response. I could see the warm smile glowing and growing in her eyes as she grew impatient to hear my response. She must have attended their wedding.

"I had a sexual relationship with Ananias six out of the eight years I attended Yale and Sapphira had classes with me through out that time, we were never friends."

"That's understandable, how could she be friends with her future husband's past lover?"

"That's inflammatory and if we were in court I'd object. Ask the question, get the answers or I'll advice my client to deal with them in court. How do you expect her to feel comfortable if you're ready to attack?" Katrina said and the AG agreed.

"I'll ask another way, how did Mrs. Levi take the information when she discovered the two of you had been lovers?"

"She already knew before I sent Ananias her way. It was known throughout Yale that he and I were physical friends, we didn't try to hide or deny it."

"Is that why you told him five minutes after you bought your shares to buy in too? Because of the old physical relationship, you had?"

"I didn't tell him to buy into anything and I wouldn't have if the opportunity presented itself. I worked hard to build what I have and excuse me for being brash, but his dick wasn't good enough for me to risk losing everything I worked for over it."

"Was the owner of Zion Venture Capital good enough for you to take the risk for?"

"Come on now!" Katrina yelled out.

"I'll reword it, what is your relationship with the owner of Zion Venture Capital?"

The firm sounded familiar but I couldn't place it in my head at that moment. My legal team had only prepared me for questions about Ananias and Sapphira's firm. I hadn't been made aware of third firm involved. I whispered to Katrina, "The firm sounds familiar but I can't remember why." She nodded and then spoke up.

"My client was not aware of the information on third firm involved and would like to answer the question honestly but needs more information before doing so."

A man wearing glasses stood up and began passing out folders to my legal team. He handed me mine last then said, "Zion Venture Capital, owned and operated by Dwayne Hollingswell in Memphis, Tennessee. Does it ring a bell now?"

My mouth dropped.

Dwayne

Damn, I fucked up! Is what looped around my thoughts on my flight home. I knowingly and willingly raw dogged where probably half of the people of finance in the big apple been or was invited but the worst part about it is that I really enjoyed it. It was like the feeling you get after a long vacation where all you want to do is feel the comfort of your home, she felt like home. The way she matched my rhythm like a harmonious game of tug of war with her moans as background music had worth in terms greater than market value.

She was beautiful but that was vain. She knew how to satisfy me in bed which was vain too and knowing her background made it scary. What I needed to know was, did she have everything else? I wasn't excepting to give her a 90-day contract that fast but my dick panicked at the thought of her getting mad and not giving us anymore. If I sat back and let my dick do the thinking, she deserved a try.

When my flight landed and my cell phone powered on my text and voice mail alerts started buzzing back to back. One text was from the church reminding me that they needed to speak with me and all the others were from Nivea. I didn't bother checking them, I had too much pressing business and would call when I freed up. I had to get to the Federal Correctional Institution and see Elliott. If he felt the need to reach out to my mom, it was serious.

"Visitors for Elliott McLemore step forwarded."

I didn't see a face, all I heard was a broken-up voice through a speaker on the wall. I stepped to an electronic door and it opened. Elliott was sitting down and I could see he was past pissed.

"I thought we were brothers D? You told me I could trust you. If that shit was true please explain to me why I'm sitting in this bitch with no court date until the investigation on your company is complete?"

"No hellos, straight to the gut with it. Okay, the answer to your first question is, I wouldn't be standing here if we weren't brothers and you wouldn't have had my mama's number memorized in case of emergency if we weren't. That shit you said about trust and sitting in jail, from what I heard I should be questioning you on trust. You were arrested for using your girlfriend's online broker to trade after the SEC banned you, fuck that, after you promised if I helped you get off American soil that you wouldn't look at the markets unless it was for Zion Venture Capital. What happened to that?"

"You not telling me that bitch Cynthia was back is what happened." He lowered his voice but the anger still dominated his tone. When he mentioned Cynthia, I hung my head but I didn't know if it was out of shame that he had to bring her up or if I couldn't continue to look at him, looking like that. He hadn't shaved and it looked like he lost 20 pounds. His lips were cracking and his breathe smelled sick. Elliott was tough but jail could break the best of them. I prayed it wasn't breaking him as he continued talking, "So yeah, I made a few trades here in there in her name but never once touched the money, it was all hers. You and I know, the U.S dollar doesn't even get me to raise an eyebrow anymore. That pop the church told us about, I flooded it with everything she had and you know she got paid well. From $32,000 to $330,000. I thought it would make her smile and it did until later that night. She went to meet with an old friend and the next thing I know, she's telling me I got her committing fraud against the government and if I didn't turn the money in she'd call the SEC. My first thought was, the bitch isn't that smart, who taught her about the SEC better yet, who told her about my ban? To calm things down I put in a request to transfer the funds to my account but when she saw it she flipped. Next thing I know she's throwing my shit out. I get to work the next day and I'm being taken off in cuffs. Do you know why?" his silence made me look him in the eyes which seemed to be what he wanted so he could finish. "Because that bitch Cynthia planted that ho in my life to destroy me for helping your ass get on your feet five years ago."

"E…" I said but he waved me off.

"Nah, it's too late for sympathetic words. I need you to make all this shit right. I need a court date, I need that bitch Cynthia offed or I need you to do something that shows that you're your brother's keeper. I built that company with you and Heather. Now I hear you've fired her and I'm locked up over your ex, take a step back and look at how you're looking right now, brother. You pulled Edward off the streets and the SEC has him spooked. You need to handle this shit." He stood up and I spoke up.

"I'm going to handle what I need to handle and not because you have your chest poked out. I got you because we're family and that's what family does."

"Well, family, make this your last visit until I see some improvement. And as your business partner, you need Heather back in that office. Edward needs a sit down with the church, not you. That boy is doubting you're legit and it has nothing to do with loyalty, he just isn't built for tough shit. If that crazy bitch is back worse than before, you will need Heather and you know why. It's time to stop bullshitting with how you feel about her!" Elliott walked off without looking back.

My head was spinning on my way to the office. Cynthia was back and she was already kicking up more dust than she had years ago. I walked in the office with my head up and felt my heart break when I looked at Edward's mom sitting in Heather's spot. I wanted to walk up to her and fire her but the little Chinese man sitting in my lobby holding a box had caught my attention. He was wearing an old wooden Chillba hat that covered his face from the nose up. He looked like he had come straight here from a rice field.

Instead of firing Ms. Michelle, I asked, "How long has he been waiting for me?"

"That man has been here since I turned the elevators on this morning. He hasn't even used the restroom since he arrived."

"Give me a minute or two to get in my office and

then send him back. Let Jacob and Esau know I'm here and that I will see them once I'm done talking to him."

"Yes sir, and what about Edward? I left my personal feelings for my son at home but those folks really have gotten him shook up with all the talks of shutting you down for wrong doings. Can I pencil him in after the twins?"

"No, he has a job to do. You can remind him that's were his focus is needed and if he can't stay focus I'm willing to accept his letter of resignation."

My desk was covered in mail there was a pile of newspapers stacked on my floor next to the door. I hadn't had time to properly train Ms. Michelle but even with training she wouldn't be Heather. I picked up my office phone to dial out but there wasn't a dial tone.

"Hello?"

"Just a friendly reminder that we have a meeting tomorrow night at the casino," the sound of Cynthia's voice made me snap.

"I'm not going to make it; some other shit came up."

"You say it like it's negotiable. Don't show up and see what happens!"

She ended the call as my visitor knocked on the door.

"You may enter," I said standing to my feet while shaking the thought of killing Cynthia out of my mind. He placed the box on my desk in front of me and handed me a letter opener to open it with. Inside the box was another box a fourth of the original one's size. I opened it and dug around the packing peanuts until I felt what I hoped I wouldn't find, a key ring with a variety of keys.

"How long do I have?"

"They will arrive Monday at the open of business but you leave Friday at 10am out of Nashville. Tonight, is your last night here."

"And I take it that you and the fellas are not mistaken?"

"No, we are not mistaken, Mr. Hollingswell."

"I am assured, where do I meet you?"

"In Nashville at the airport at 10am. You will meet me at the American Airlines ticketing counter but we will take a private jet to Canada and be on our way from there. It saddens me to deliver this news but it is a part of the plan. Handle your affairs but please arrive on time. The counsel has made your arrival their first priority."

"I understand."

We shook hands and then I walked him to the elevator. On my way back, I looked at Ms. Michelle, slid my hand under her desk, and pressed the button. A button that I had installed but never wanted to touch. An alarm sounded and I watched heads pop up. Although we practiced the drill a hundred times, everyone looked unsure and asked if it was real. I could see the church making their way towards me.

"Is this the real thing?" Jacob asked.

"Yes, it is and you know what to do. You have until Monday at opening. What did you want to tell me, I'm sure it will fill in the blanks with this?"

As we walked to my office each person I passed asked if this was real and it tore me to pieces each time I had to say yes.

"They are trying to pin us with insider trading. There were two New York based firms that piled up on the UXYZ stock in the same time frame as us and the SEC found a small connection between all three of us, well four if you count Elliott trading under his girlfriend's name," Esau said.

When they told me what trades were in question, I knew the tie and I knew Spencer would make it out to be more than what it was, which was a coincidence between like-minded people.

"You see, D, my brother and I attended a few classes with Nivea Bowen of Bowen Capital Management at the New York Institution of Finance. Smart girl but a little too friendly." Jacob had to nod his head like he was remembering a situation where Nivea showed just how friendly she could be before he spoke again. "Anyways, we remained in contact with her via email but we have never spoken stocks. The last time she reached out to us was to invite us to her IPO party but that is it. We don't swear anything on our father's name but…"

"You don't have to. I believe you and it wouldn't matter anyways. Once the SEC reads the emails between Nivea and I and sees how much time we've been spending together, they are going to fine us and Spencer is going to do all he can to get me to step down."

"You know Nivea too?" they asked in unison. I've never lied to them and wouldn't, I needed them to understand the severity in this.

"Yes, I know her and I am also aware of how friendly she can get. We've been together every day for the last 6 days and there is a trail of proof too big to hide. Listen fellows, I'm going away until all of this blows over. Effective immediately, I am stepping down and appointing Heather as CEO. She will have everything in writing when she arrives in the morning and I expect you two to step up your roles around here. With instruction Heather will relocate the firm to New York and she has all the information on the staff regarding who is willing to relocate and what we will offer for those who don't. I have a lot to do fellas but I will be in touch. Don't change your numbers until I do."

I opened my office door and in unison the church said, "We love you, brother. We are not mistaken."

"I'm assured and I love you too, my brothers. This isn't goodbye it's only a lengthy see you later."

I closed and locked my doors and stared at my staff

through the glass. They were scurrying around like rats under a hot pot. I could hear the paper shredder going, computers restarting, and file cabinets opening and closing. I ran my firm legit, they weren't getting rid of incriminating items, I just had them making the SEC's work harder so I could laugh. I didn't have to leave the United States, but if I stayed, I could possibly face jail time. I wasn't going back to jail. I knew if I was arrested I could make bail but I still didn't want to waiver on my word when it came to my freedom. I didn't have to sign my firm over to Heather but why keep it? I had met my number years earlier and I knew she'd keep it going as long as someone needed a job. The insider trading and whatever else the SEC was about to throw at me was beatable. I wasn't in the same position as Nivea. My firm wasn't my meat and potatoes nor was it bread and butter. It was the placenta nourishing and maintaining me through my rebirth and it was time to cut the umbilical cord. I learned to feed myself and the only way I could prove it to myself was letting go of it all. I remembered reading somewhere in the Bible where it said a prophet won't be welcomed in his own home, I can say the same is true for an investor. The United States was coming after me just as much as they'd let me profit, maybe even more, so why should I stay?

I called Heather and she didn't answer so I went by the house. There was a car parked in the yard that clearly belonged to a man because I could see the fishing poles in the backseat. I thought about using my key and walking in on them, but after the plays I made with Nivea, I rang the doorbell instead.

"May I help you?"

A older gentleman came to the door and the smell of onions being sautéed blew past me. He was wearing an apron with a spatula in his hand.

"Yes, is Heather home? I was going to use my key but I noticed the car in the driveway."

"You must be Dwayne. Come on in, she ran to the store. I'm her father, Alex."

I didn't like the look that crossed his face when he said my name and I didn't have the time to chat. To be real, I wasn't in the mood to meet Heather's father. Not with Nivea's scent still lingering on my balls.

"I was just stopping by. Can you have her to call me please, I'm kind of in a rush."

"I certainly will and Dwayne," he called out as I turned my back. "when a father invites you in to talk about his baby girl, he doesn't want to hear that you're in a rush and a woman will only wait for the right man for so long. It takes that man to realize she's the right woman. I'll be sure to tell my daughter to stop waiting." He slammed the door in my face.

When I pulled into my parking garage I sent a text Chauncey,

It's the Art of War, come watch it at the car lot.

Five minutes later he text back,

TOXIN

Wouldn't miss it for the world cuzzo. I'm six minutes away.

When he pulled up he didn't say a word, he just hugged me. Chauncey was a fuck up but besides the relationship I had with my mom, he was the only one to treat me like family. I had told him my plans to escape it all years ago.

"If you get a text from me saying, it's time to wrap it up, I need you to stop what you're doing because there's shit I need you to handle for me and when I'm straight, I'll send for you to visit," I'd told him.

"You always on some spy shit cuzzo. Talking about, I'll send for you. Nigga, you ain't leaving me behind, I'm going with you," he'd protested.

"Nah, cousin. If I text you like that, I'm not smiling and you won't want to come with me. That means I have to make a quick exit. No room for tourists on my trip," I'd explained.

"Then who's going to protect you? You know you can't fight. Just because you beat up that heavy bag and do that karate shit that don't make you Mike Tyson or Bruce Lee. Last fight I remember you in, ole girl was beating yo' ass," he'd continued to protest.

"We were seven."

"Which makes it worse. You could have choke slammed the bitch and got away with it back then." He'd laughed and then his face had straightened up. "But seriously, cuzzo, if you have to make an exit are you sure you're going to be straight?"

"I'm not mistaken," I'd assured him.

"Cool, then text me some spy shit like, the art of war," that was his only request on the matter.

He hugged me for three minutes before saying his first words, "What you need me to do cuzzo?"

I let him go and stepped away. I opened my arms as wide as I could and turned in a circle slowly. "I need you to pick out two cars you want so I can sign them over to you."

He didn't look at them at all, he already knew what he wanted, "Let me get that G-wagon and that AMG."

"Say no more!"

We started our walk to my condo and I told him that I needed him to stay the night so he could drop me off in Nashville in the morning. No matter what I told him to do, he didn't disagree. That was the longest I'd ever witnessed Chauncey serious. He was silent as we approached the entrance. It was only 6 o'clock in the evening so I wasn't surprised to see Ms. Blakemore, but I was surprised by what she did.

She stood to her feet and hugged me tight and said, "I'm glad you're finally going home. There's nothing here for you but bad memories and lack of understanding. I've already scheduled for someone to move in your condo Sunday and the cleaning crew will be here all day

Saturday..."

Chauncey cut her off, "Hold on box lady, who told you that you can rent out my cousin's spot?"

"No one told me I could but as the owner of this building I can. Dwayne, you do understand that I'm allergic to rules and the judicial system. I can't have the Feds flooding my building to tear apart your place looking for something we both know isn't there, right?" She smiled and winked at me; I shook my head. "Is there anything else I can do you for you my love?"

I thought about it for a second and then said, "Yes, can I leave you with the titles to my cars? A car broker from Atlanta will come pick them up. If it's not a hassle, can he also bring you the money as he sells them and you hold on to it for me until I come back?" I smiled and winked but she shook her head.

"No, I think it's best I get a friend of mine to open a trust for Elliott with the money you make. He's going to need every dime he can get when he's done serving his five years. I'm guessing he'll only do three with good behavior. You see, Elliott wasn't as smart or as disciplined with his money like you. He took all of his money out of the bank in China when you sent Edward and put it all in UXYZ as if it was Monopoly money."

"And how do you know all of this?" I asked with a chuckle.

"Are you shitting me, Dwayne? I hope you don't think you're the only one in the Billionaire Boy's club, do you? You're not the only one Forbes purposely leaves off their world's billionaires list. I'm in the same council as you."

"I don't recall seeing you at any meetings," I said as I racked my brain not remembering seeing any women in the room.

"That's because you're smarter and more disciplined with your money than me too. You knew better than to take any oaths and pledges." She put her hands up and made her index fingers and thumbs touch to form a triangle and placed it over her eye. "I'm in a higher bracket than you thanks to my family line. I get invited to different meetings, let's call them member only summits, where I get privileged information on where every dollar of importance no matter what the currency is, is moved. Jim-Jim got torn a new asshole for writing back to some black guy who was in jail in Memphis and dropping all those jewels on the foreign commodities market. No one cared that he shared the information with you, but they all cared when you made ten times the money he had every touched with the information."

"Hold the fuck up," Chauncey interrupted, "I'm not the smartest fish in the box of fish sticks but I know ten times anything sounds like dough-boy bread. Box lady already said something about a billionaire's club and I watch those YouTube videos about the Illuminati, Skull and Bones, and the Free Masons so I know what that triangle shit mean…"

Chauncey was apparently running his mouth in

front of the wrong person about the wrong shit, at the wrong time, so I cut him off, "Get to your point, cuzzo."

"Okay, what I want to know is, are you some type of billionaire or something out the country, cuzzo?"

"Your cousin is a multi-billionaire outside of this bankrupted country and that's where the true problem lies. The Elite were pissed about some black guy, which is a nicer word than what they called you, making that type of money in the markets. Those who are ranked higher than me said not to worry about you because you were black, from the south, and you couldn't stay out of jail. They said you'd be like 70% of lottery winners who end up filing bankruptcy and lastly, you're black. It's no secret that the majority of black generations have to make their money from scratch because their forefathers failed to leave them anything to get started with. Then whenever some of you get a nice chunk of money, you become the family bank. Everybody needs a loan or has their palms out waiting for you to grease it..."

"No ma'am, Ms. Slave Master. I'm not about to allow that stero...sterotypic... you know what I'm trying to say, Dwayne. That bitch slick racist, she dogging our people!"

I could see Chauncey was bothered, but to me, it was informative. It was like getting a sneak peek into our enemies' minds to see my people through their eyes. I didn't want her to stop.

"Calm down, cuzzo, and let her finish. Ms.

Blakemore is a different sort, she's on the banana boat." I smiled but it was hard to pretend to be okay with the minstrel show and black-face. Egging her on to continue set my people back another 400 years.

"Like I was saying, those ranked higher than me, not me, Chauncey, believe that black people don't have any real financial literacy and that you guys are ballers. Got to have the big houses, cars, clothes, and chains with big screen TVs in every room. The way they saw it, Dwayne, you'd blow the money in less than three years. Here we are six years later and you haven't touched a dime of it. You were smart and continued to trade the futures market here and even bought yourself a seat at the Chicago Board of Trade. When you started your investment firm you ensured you'd never have to touch your foreign currency, but here's where you fucked up, you talk too damn much!"

"Excuse me?"

"I told you the bitch was on the cast of *Gone with the Wind*. She's probably the one who reminded ole boy in Atlanta of the segregation laws so Hattie McDaniel couldn't be at the movie premier!" Chauncey shouted.

"Who's Hattie McDaniel?" Ms. Blakemore asked.

"Don't tell her, cuzzo, because if she calls her Mammy and says it like the chick in the movie, I'm going to punch her in her throat."

I dug in my pocket and handed him the keys to my condo, "Why don't you go pack up whatever you want.

There are boxes in the guest room closet and trash bags under the sink. You can have whatever you want."

"Whatever I want? The computers and shit too?"

"You can have everything. Even the cash I keep under my mattress."

Chauncey was gone before I could turn back and face Ms. Blakemore.

"He's a funny sort, that cousin of yours. It's hard looking at him after watching him fuck your maid in the window. I'll tell you one thing, that boy has stamina," she laughed and the picked up where she stopped, "It's your mouth that's the problem, not the money. You promote up lifting, you talk about saving the world through ministry and even fought the school board on adding finance in the curriculum of elementary and middle schools for the under privileged."

"And why is that a problem? A lot of those stereotypical things you named would be abolished if they put my suggestions in place."

"Exactly, Dwayne, you're exactly right and that's the problem. I can't say too much but there are things in place that say what you're doing is wrong because it goes against the agenda. If you would have taken your payday with duct tape over your mouth the SEC wouldn't be trying to take you down, they wouldn't have made me move off my farm to keep an eye on you, and Cynthia wouldn't be back."

"What do you mean Cynthia wouldn't be back?"

The look on her face was ghostly after she let it slip from her mouth and she quickly grabbed her bag from the cardboard.

"Dwayne, my dear, I really like you but I've already said way too much. Since I value my life and am in love with my money I have to call it a night. Leave anything you have for me to do with the doorman. Now that you're going home, I can sell up my property here and go home too."

She walked to the elevators and I watched her hit the button. She looked around and then at me. The doors opened but she didn't get on. Instead, she walked over to the doorman's desk, opened what looked like a fuse box, flipped a few switches than said, "Why don't you take a ride up with me, Dwayne." I did as I was told.

I went to wake Chauncey up at 5 in the morning but he was already up sitting in front of the computer and by the looks of it, he hadn't been to sleep. He was on Black Professionals Meet Dot Love chatting with someone when I walked in.

"Aye, cuzzo, I was about to log in to my account but some chick named Brenda sent you a message about meeting in Nashville at the airport around 9 or 9:30. I told her yeah since you will be up there anyways."

"I'll be up there but on business. I don't have time to meet up with no dating site chick. I won't even see her again."

Brenda was alright in my book but now wasn't the time to add more to my things to do list. All we had was typed chats between us and I only gave her a thought when there was nothing else going on.

"I know, cuzzo, but she begged to see you. She said something came up and she had to leave New York for a while. With both of y'all fleeing away like spies, why not meet? I already told her you would."

"Then I guess I am. I'm going to go get the car, be downstairs when I pull up."

I played *Black Jesus* by Tupac on repeat as Chauncey used the ride to catch up on the sleep he lost the night before. The lyrics had me replaying my two hour talk with Ms. Blakemore inside her condo. The information she gave me, my money couldn't buy and the saddest part about it was my money nor anyone else's could fix the secret, toxic problems around me. I used to think that the decisions we made were what kept toxins around us which is true, but some toxins are a part of an agenda that was created before my ancestors were ever forced out of their country. I knew the United States' history was hid in lies and covered in blood, but to have my eyes opened to the world, the lies, and blood that devoured the Earth, I was taken back.

The sunrise played like a movie on the front windshield as I watched. The dark blue of the night had turned purple, and a few minutes later red then orange and yellow shined through the clouds. I always saw the beauty in the sunrise and sunset but now, after talking to Ms.

Blakemore I could see the lies in it. Those beautiful colors were proof of how us humans were contaminating God's beauty with our Toxins. All the colors I saw lacing the sky weren't made from God, some came from the exhaust of cars, factories, and the burning of chemicals we should have never learned to touch. I pulled up to the parking lot at BNA airport and wished I was preparing to board a flight to Mars instead.

"I told her you'd meet her outside by the American Airlines departing flight drop off," he said waking up at the sound of the car cutting off. "You wait by Southwest Airlines drop off and I'll go over there first, check her out, and let you know if she's worth meeting, okay? She said she will be wearing a red 'I love New York' t-shirt."

I could see Chauncey was excited but traffic was bad and it took me longer than the two hours we counted on. It was already 9:45, she might have already boarded her flight, and the reality had hit me that this might be the last time I was able to see my cousin here, in the United States. I wanted to spend my last fifteen minutes with him, not some internet chick. Before I could express it to him, he had disappeared. I waited five minutes for him to come back and he didn't, so I said fuck it and walked that way. As I got closer, I could see Chauncey exchanging words with a thick chick in a red shirt. I couldn't believe it when I realized it was Nivea. When she realized it was me, a smile grew on her face.

"Dwayne, what are you doing here?"

"How do you know him?" Chauncey asked and I

was ready to ask him the same.

"Because, I'm dating him Big Cee, Chauncey, Raymond, or whatever the fuck your real name is. How about you keep walking with your trifling ass!"

"Now I'm trifling? I wasn't trifling when you were cumming all over this dick was I? Aye, cuzzo, you don't want to fuck with this bitch. I already had her."

"Cousin?" Nivea asked before her jaw dropped.

"Yeah cousin!" he shouted and then looked at me. I couldn't say a word because I didn't know where to start. I knew it was obvious but I still had to ask.

"Are you Brenda?" She nodded her head and then I asked, "Nivea, how do you know my cousin?"

"That's Tom Lee Park," Chauncey screamed excitedly and my mind drifted to the story he had told me about fucking some girl he met online in Tom Lee Park as a limo with two small flags of China on the front pulled up. I lost my mind when she answered.

·"That's the guy I was with in Memphis."

As Mr. Zhang approached dressed in his all black business suit like I was used to seeing him wear instead of his rice field costume he wore to my office I cocked back and popped Chauncey square in his mouth. I couldn't believe he had drugged and raped her.

"Damn, what's your motherfucking problem, you gon' hit me over a bitch? You're ready to fight me over some pussy I tried to help you get, are you serious nigga? I didn't know that was your ho, but I'll tell you that bitch is for everybody. I didn't do shit but show up and she started begging to suck my dick..." I could hear Chauncey's words but my eyes were locked on Nivea. As he told his version of the story she never defended herself nor said that he was lying. He finished with, "And I'm telling Meme on you too nigga!"

"Mr. Hollingswell we must go, NOW!" Mr. Zhang said pulling me through the doors by the tight grip he had on my upper arm.

"Yeah, take that nigga away before I forget we're family. When you make it to where ever the fuck you're going you need to call me, nigga. I see I need to remind you that nothing but God comes before your blood. As a matter of fact, you made your choice. Fuck you and this bitch." Chauncey turned to the approaching TSA worker and said, "Is my shit busted? Does it look like I got hit by Mayweather or Tyson?"

Everything was moving fast but I had to know, "Were you raped or not?"

Nivea didn't open her mouth to answer but the way she lowered her head said enough.

Nivea

"Raped you, do you hear this?" Chauncey asked the TSA worker who saw the altercation between him and Dwayne. "My cousin bust my shit up because this bitch lied and said I raped her. I ain't one of these broke dudes that got to steal pussy, I'll buy it if I have to. I got some on layaway right now. Once I get her nails done, it's on."

"I didn't say you raped me, okay. I was drugged before we met up and I ended up in the emergency room the next day. When they found the date rape drug in my system they did the kit and found your sperm in me."

"So, I'm going to jail because you willingly gave up the pussy with Tom Lee's statue watching? Ain't this about a bitch. My mama said pussy was going to be the death of me, or lying... I don't know which one she said, but I'm sure it was one of those." Chauncey put his hands in front of him and made his wrists touch. "Man, you might as well lock me up because I know I nutted all in that thing. My toes were numb for two days after I beat her in. I thought I was going to have to get my shit amputated."

The TSA worker was trying hard not to laugh and hell, I was too. The situation wasn't funny but this guy Chauncey, was a character straight out of an urban fiction book.

"Sir, I'm not here to arrest you. I saw that you were assaulted and wanted to know if you needed me to call the police or an ambulance."

"An ambulance, you think my cousin hit me that hard? No, I don't need an ambulance but can you please do me a favor?" Chauncey dug in his back pocket and pulled out his cell phone. He was going through his contacts. When he found what he was looking for he hit send and tried to hand the guy the phone. "Can you tell my grandmother you saw Dwayne hit me in my mouth with a closed fist, over a fast tail girl who tried to do the nasty with both of us out of wedlock? Tell my granny the devil didn't come as a snake this time but as a pretty woman that's round in all the right places and a few of the wrong places but that's because she drinks a lot of cheap beer. Tell her my flesh was weak because I had forgot to pray before I ate dinner that day. I didn't think I needed to pray over those chicken nuggets because I only got four of them for a dollar. Now I know I was supposed to give thanks because Jezebel is trying to get me thrown in jail. My granny is a Jehovah's witness and she don't play about none of this worldly mess. Here, everybody calls her Meme and speak up. She don't like mumbling or soft men so don't tell her about your ponytail."

I was shocked that the guy took the phone and actually began telling his grandmother what he had witnessed. He did it with professionalism and care.

"You're not going to jail. I was drugged but I remembered everything that happened between us. I told the doctors that I consented to having sex with you, I just forgot to tell Dwayne."

"You and my cousin were dating, right?" I nodded

my head. "Then you didn't forget to tell him. You didn't want him to know that you were a little dick freak but he knows now and I bet he doesn't fuck with you anymore. He knows my dick has been in more than half of the women in Memphis including the clean looking prostitutes. My cousin ain't crazy enough to go in that thing after me." He shook his head and then asked, "So you remember how I had you up against the statue don't you? I know it's going to be hard for you to stop craving me but you're cut off, I'm sorry."

"Um, I believe she called you Pooh-sha-nuk or something like that. Anyways, she heard what you were saying in the background and said get your butt on the phone right now," the guy said as he held the phone out to Chauncey.

"See you're fucking up my family life!" He took his phone back and I used the opportunity to sneak off and head back to wait on my flight to board.

The flight from Nashville to Los Angeles was five hours but it felt more like ten. My mind was everywhere. I thought about my career, the IPO, my dad, and his wife, how the SEC was pulling no stops in their investigation of me, Evol, and although I tried hard not to, I thought about Dwayne. He had to hate me after hitting his cousin under false pretenses. I didn't lie to him and I only held on to the truth because I didn't think he knew him nor that I would ever run into the guy again.

"Would you like a drink or some pretzels ma'am?" the stewardess asked and I accepted both. I opened the pretzels and took a few out but didn't eat them. The name on the bag reminded me of something I had forgotten. Dwayne was Raymond which also meant that Raymond was Dwayne. I pulled out my credit card and bought 30 minutes of Wi-Fi so I could go back and read his messages. Dwayne and Raymond's mood and actions ran parallel which confirmed that they were one in the same. I decided to send my old dating site friend a fuck you message.

Hey Raymond or should I call you Dwayne now that I know the truth? I was on my flight to California and it occurred to me how you think I'm not shit and my life is full of Toxins but let's take a closer look at yours. Raymond told me how you lost your virginity between your mama's best friend's legs and might have conceived a child with her. Then I met Dwayne's best friend/ cousin Chauncey, oops, I forget this is Dwayne. Well your boy is trifling and admits to buying pussy. I strongly believe that birds of a feather do flock side by side so what do you spend annually on pussy Mr. "I don't do anything that ends, in end like girlfriend"? Oh, and the morning you left, your wife Cynthia Hollingswell called me to let me know that it was her who tried to run us over and that it was also her who slid the liquid ecstasy in my cup that caused me to sleep with Chauncey's low life ass. Not to mention that if you wouldn't have stopped by trying to hide from her I would have been dead or my brain might have fried. I recall Raymond saying that I had nothing to worry about when it came to his stalker, another lie. I know you can't see or hear me but I'm laughing at you.

TOXIN

You're walking and breathing fraud. You pretend like your life is so perfect but look at it. Yes, I might have a handful of sex partners you met but that's where my toxins stop. Can you smell that Dwayne? Those are your toxins I'm smelling not mine!

I sent the message and eased back in my window seat. My life wasn't perfect, nobody's life was and I didn't try to pretend like it was. The way Dwayne kept turning his nose up at me like he could take a dump and his shit wouldn't stink. I didn't expect him to respond so quickly; actually, I hadn't expected him to respond at all.

You have a lot of nerve to reach out to me with the goal of talking shit. Nivea, you lied to me about being raped, who drugged you didn't matter. I'm not saying it's right nor that you deserved it but saying you were violated when you weren't, that's fucked up. In 37 years, I've never put my hands on my cousin but when you said that he was the man you were with I snapped. I didn't see my cousin standing in front of me, I saw a nothing ass nigga that should have been in jail for sexual assault. Chauncey is trifling, I'll agree with you on that but what does that say about you if you consented to having sex with him? You were talking to him online before you ever met face to face. If you don't have any standards set for yourself what do you expect me to do with you? Your sex toll is up to six including me. A person who kills three or more people gets titled a serial killer so how many men do you think you can fuck before you get called a ho? I don't pretend like my shit is scentless but I do my best to try and cover up the

smell without using lies, you should give it a try sometimes. Instead of screaming rape because you decided to have sex in a park how about covering it up by becoming someone's wife and being their ho? Oh, and before I go, I do want to apologize for Cynthia calling you. She is a toxin that will take a Hazmat team to clean up. I really don't feel like I owe you an explanation but she isn't my wife. Just a crazy bitch that likes to lie about serious things like you.

My hands couldn't type fast enough.

You think you are so smooth but you're not. You know the SEC named you and your company as the ring leader in this insider trading case. Spencer made sure to give me a rundown of the shady people you have working there and the things that they have done. He offered to drop all the charges on my company if I helped him shut you down and I wanted to spit in his face for thinking that it was an option. I'm not a snitch or a liar, I'm loyal and as loyal as they come. I don't feel like I owe you an explanation either but since you don't know me I feel the need to share. I had a goal to IPO my company five years from the date I opened it. That goal included not getting serious with anyone until my goal was reached. I've never been in a relationship nor had a boyfriend or a man in my life. The fling you saw with Evol was a three-year dick contract. Was I wrong for sleeping with a married man? Yes. Will I be punished for doing it, possibly but there is only one judge and it isn't you, Mr. Hollingswell. That little 90-day bullshit you called yourself putting over us was the closet I've ever been to being locked down to anyone and as you see that only lasted two days. Since we are under investigation and I wouldn't switch up on you no matter what you think or feel about me, I'll make this my last time reaching out to you. I hope everything works out for us both.

Dwayne didn't immediately respond back. There was only three minutes and counting left to my over-priced session. As that number turned into 40 seconds his next message came in.

Ms. Bowen, I don't think or feel anything about you. I can't, you were a one-night stand.

There wasn't a need to respond, he summed it up with that message. I was a free cup of water during his drought. He needed to release and I accepted his pressure. It was hard to believe that any of this could happen post the magic that I felt in our kiss after we prayed but like my granny used to say, "The devil is the king of lies and emperor of confusion."

I made it to California a little after 1pm pacific standard time and lingered around the airport as a tourist. I wasn't ready to see my mama because she'd want to talk about everything that was happening to me and wasn't ready to relive it yet. Especially with someone who wouldn't understand more than half of the terminology I was using which meant I'd do a lot repeating. Seeing her face and being in her company would be nice as I went through this but today just wasn't the day.

I should have checked to see what events were going on this weekend because almost every rental car place was sold out. Truthfully, there didn't have to be anything going on in L.A for them to be sold out. It was the weekend and it was summer, more than enough reason to floss around in something you don't own to pretend your somebody in. I ended with a newer model Volkswagen and that was fine by me because I didn't plan to leave the house. Besides checking on the case with my lawyers my cell phone would be in do not disturb mode until I left.

My old neighborhood had changed drastically over the years that each visit home made me feel more out of place than the last. When I was growing up the area was predominately black until I got around thirteen and then it seemed like the Mexico/ United States boarders dissolved and I quickly became the only one on my street who couldn't speak Spanish. Coming home from college was an eye opener. Those who only could speak a few words in English before I left, could speak it more fluently than me. The new tradition called change had struck again because now my mother was the only minority left on the block. The lawmakers and investors got together and shook downtown up and where I was used to seeing bums laid out with a fast food cup in hand hoping for change, were the entrance to Condo's filled with the biggest celebrities the world had to offer. It was amazing to see the least desired area to visit in Los Angeles switch to the most desired.

I pulled into my mama's driveway and I could see some of the areas she spent the money I sent on improving. The house had undergone a full change in the landscaping with concrete being added in place and removed in others. The dirt that made the walkway to the front door was now beautiful titles of rock. The outside perimeter was covered in greener and the house had been resided in earth toned stones, it was beautiful.

"Nivea, is that you baby?"

My mom was in the kitchen cooking something that smelt good and I knew it was unhealthy when I walked in. Walls had been knocked down and the house looked spacey. Even with the changes she made that were visible from where I was standing, the feeling still felt the same. It felt like home. As my mom began walking my way, I felt the tears well in my eyes. I cried like her shoulder needed my tears to keep her alive. The rush of emotions came out of nowhere and the tears flowed more when I realized she was crying with me.

"Mama, why is it so hard for me? I did what I was supposed to do. I got my high school diploma, graduated from Yale at the top of my class, and built my business from the ground up, brick by brick. I didn't fail to plan, Mama. I made one plan and I stuck to it. Now it's all gone over a coincidence? Why is that supposed to be okay?"

I shouted at her but the anger in me wasn't directed at my mama, I was mad at myself because I knew everything was my fault. I made one plan in 12th grade and stuck to it without revising it with the change of times because I was sure it was fail proof. I selected and hired the people to IPO my company from the research I had done myself. I was so caught up in the possibility that Evol might have sent me the flowers that I didn't pay attention to Kishi's words even after she reminded me that I wasn't conducting business as usual. I decided that it was okay to sleep with whoever I wanted to so it was my decision to hide the truth from Dwayne because the truth was, I was embarrassed of myself.

I was learning that the simplest task in life could become the hardest like looking into the mirror. It would have been easy to take a look at myself and see the flaws but knowing that there are flaws makes it hard to do. My mirror broke years ago and instead of trying to define my reflection through the pieces, I threw the all the shards of glass away.

"Hush now, Nivea. No one said that what you're going through is okay and it's not okay until you decide to do nothing about it. I don't understand the ins and outs of your world but I know there is only one truth and you need to do whatever it takes to find it." She walked to the kitchen and I followed as she talked. "I didn't raise you to take handouts so I don't expect you to accept whatever life sends your way. You've always made a way out of no way; don't let this obstacle change that. You are bigger than your problems, baby."

"I'm the problem. I make bad decisions and I can't see that they aren't in my favor until everyone knows."

"That's because you love that word!" she snapped.

"What word?"

"I, you love to say, I. I did this and I did that. When are you going to realize there isn't a letter I in God or Jehovah? You chose to make decisions by yourself when God already said you can talk them out with him." She pulled the chicken out the grease onto a cookie sheet covered in paper towels and took a deep breath before asking, "When is the last time you ordered your steps in his word, Nivea? You can't keep making moves without taking it to the father first. Do you ever check the Bible before you make decisions?"

Her advice was on point but I wasn't in the mood to hear the truth from nobody. It's sad to admit but my attitude and my way of thinking is what got me in this situation to begin with. Knowing that wasn't enough to make me stop or feel less attacked by her. Since the thumb was pointing at me I pointed my index finger at her, "Did you check with the Bible before you decided to lay down with my daddy to have me?"

"No, I didn't," she answered without a trace of an attitude in her voice, "but I'd never call your birth a mistake, God doesn't make those. The mistake was my decision not to order my steps in his word, the very same decision I'm watching you make. Nivea, you are stressed and hurting, and the devil is hoping you keep coming his way because he's waiting for you with open arms. I'm not going to entertain the devil and I'm not going to help set the stage for you to do his work so go upstairs, baby. Your room is ready and I brought you a robe and some slippers. They are hanging in your bathroom with that bubble bath you used to love as a child that I would buy you from

Avon. Go soak and I'll come get you when dinner is ready."

She kissed me on my cheek and started humming, Take Me to The King by Tamela Mann. She left me feeling defeated. I must have had the devil in me if her speaking the word made me feel at a loss.

*****

Before I knew it, a month had gone by and I hadn't thought of returning to my condo once. With the SEC doing a thorough investigation into all three companies and the individual from Dwayne's company who went home and made the same trade with his girlfriend's online broker without her consent, there wasn't a rush to get back. It could take months to get to the bottom of it all and that was fine with me because me and my mom had built a bond and I was enjoying my time with her.

As a child, she kept me with her wherever she went and history was now repeating itself. We took turn-around trips to Las Vegas my first week home and went to Bingo together every Wednesday and Sunday nights. She read the Bible to me daily and hosted our Bible study chat afterwards. What I enjoyed most was that we honored the Sabbath together. From Friday at sunset to Saturday, we rested. I mean no work. We even prepared by cooking up all the food to get us through the Sabbath early Friday morning. This version of my mama, I wasn't familiar with. She always believed in God but now she lived for him. Since I had been gone I didn't get to see all the life changes my mama had made but I was impressed by them.

She told me, "With you gone off to college I went soul searching. I was lonely and thought it was time to finally get a man and guess what, I messed around and found God. I checked out the Kingdom hall to see what the Jehovah witness' were doing but something was missing. I loved their teachings but I didn't like all the gray areas so I tried Seventh Day Adventist next. They were somewhat better because they stressed healthy eating, the use of herbs but most of all the Sabbath which is a part of the ten commandments. I hung out there for a few years but I still felt like I was missing out so I did a drive by through the groups of Christianity. I hit up the Catholic church, Baptist, Methodist, Lutheran, Evangelical and the list goes on. I found likes and dislikes with them all so I decided to take what I liked from all of them, check it with the word and praise from there. I don't belong to any of them and if I'm asked I say I believe in Christianity."

My mama had a peace she never had before and with only hanging around her I had gained it too. I showered and dressed quickly to find out what she had planned for us to do today. Normally she'd tell me the night before but she fed me and urged me to get some rest. I didn't know I was tired until I laid down but apparently, she could tell.

"I'm all rested and ready for today's adventure," I

said sneaking up behind her in her bedroom and giving her a kiss on her cheek. "Where are we going first? Don't forget we need to drop off my rental car. Since I've been rolling around with you, I don't need it."

She had a neutral look on her face and I couldn't tell if it was leaning towards the positive or negative side more, hence the word neutral.

"The doctor, that's where we are heading to first."

"Are you okay, Mama?"

"I'm fine, I just want to know how long we have before my grandbaby arrives," she cut her eyes at me.

"Grandbaby, what are you talking about?"

"You got to get up extra earlier in the morning if you want to fool me, baby. You've been here a month and a few days and I have been with you most, if not all of the time. Where's your period? And while you think about where you might have left your menstruation at, look at the signs that pregnancy is waving at you too. If I feed you before 11 in the morning it makes you feel sick, you want to smell every scent that passes you, and that glow has nothing to do with the summer or that baby oil you soak in. If you're not pregnant then the doctor needs to tell us what's wrong with you because something isn't right."

It was July 16th and my last period was… shit, my last period was in May but even that was irregular. I was definitely late but stress can cause that, right? It didn't matter if I was late or not, if my mama said we were going to the doctor, then it was final.

What bothered me the most about our trip to the doctor was that I had finally forgotten about everything that happened before I made it to the West Coast. As we waited in the lobby for the test results, it all came rushing back.

In other news, Zion Venture Capital says Dwayne Hollingswell has officially retired as CEO of the Memphis based financial firm and has been replaced by Heather Rogers, the office manager who also acted as Mr. Hollingswell's personal assistant. The switch of power was effective immediately after the company was rumored to be involved in the largest case of insider trading the SEC has taken on this year. When Ms. Rogers was asked to make a statement she said, "I plan to reconstruct and elevate the company on new levels. As my first act as CEO I am moving our offices out of Tennessee to New York and the IPO of ZVC is in the near future. As Mr. Hollingswell's assistant I was privileged to his dreams for the company and I will make them our reality, he will truly be missed." We attempted to get an update on the SEC's ongoing investigation and all that Ms. Rogers was willing to disclose was, "I've been assured that if the SEC finds any wrongdoing on ZVC under Mr. Hollingswell's reign as CEO., that he will personally resolve the issue. Their ongoing investigation is not a concern of mine, thank you."

I wished there was a remote to change the channel or a button to turn the wall mounted television off but there wasn't. The entire time the reporter spoke there was a split screen up. On the left was a very nice picture of Dwayne and his contagious smile and to the right was the SEC carrying boxes out of his office like they had done mine. Looking at his face made me wonder, who the hell I was pregnant by? The thought of not knowing almost caused me to pass out.

"I don't understand why they couldn't just give you an ultrasound now so we can know how far along you are. It doesn't make sense that you have to go to your primary care doctor for a referral to an obstetrician and then let them set you up with one. If your period has been off there's no telling how far along you are. You don't feel any movement there yet, do you?"

My mama hadn't stopped fussing yet. To say she was excited that the test results confirmed my pregnancy she had been going off since they gave us the news.

"No, Mama, I don't and I don't want to talk about this right now."

"We haven't talked about nothing yet."

She whipped the wheel making a sharp turn onto the interstate and didn't say another word until we exited, "What do you have a taste for? I was thinking salad or sub."

"I'm not hungry."

"Great, one less mouth to feed. Guess me and my grand baby will be eating a salad without you," she smiled.

"Mama, this isn't funny."

"I'm not laughing and I'm not about to cry about it either. There's a baby coming whether you like it or not."

"Not if there's still time to get an abortion," I mumbled and she caught it.

"It's too late for the abortion. That was supposed to take place once you felt that unprotected penis inside of you. That's when you were supposed to abort the mission. Don't sin to clean up the sin."

We pulled into the restaurant she wanted to get the salads from and she asked, "What kind of dressing do you want on yours?"

"Blue cheese."

"I'll be right back. Go ahead and get out, we are going to eat and talk on their patio. Like I said, we haven't talked about nothing yet."

By the way she walked off I knew what she wanted to talk to me about. She wanted to know information on the father and I was ready to give it to her. What I wasn't ready for was the way she'd ask. "Mary was a virgin, what's your story? I don't see a ring on your finger so I know you're not secretly married. You haven't had a phone call so there's no boyfriend waiting for your return either, so how did you get pregnant?"

She asked how, when I expected her to ask by who.

"Like every woman excluding Mary, got pregnant. I

had unprotected sex."

She looked at me for a few seconds and then stabbed her tomato with her fork.

"Do you know who you're pregnant by? Let's start there."

"No, I don't," I responded holding my chin high pretending like I was okay with not knowing.

"Do you have any idea or a well calculated guess? The doctor said by your last period being in May they had to use that time. Can you recall who you slept with in late April, May and June?"

"Yes, I do. I slept with a married man late April, early May, and then I slept with a guy I met on a dating site who was unemployed and living with his cousin at the end of May." I had to laugh at myself.

"You think you're being funny, Nivea. If I was without sin I'd throw the first stone!"

My mama looked disgusted and saddened by my words. I wasn't aiming to be a bitch towards her but I made the bad decision, it was me who had to live with them.

"No, I don't think I'm being funny. It's the truth and I wasn't done answering your question. In June, I slept with a man known for buying prostitutes and a few days later, less than a week, I slept with a man you would have given your approval on. He was handsome, wealthy and he placed nothing before God. Too bad the two men were cousins, I actually thought I met my king."

Her hand flew across the table at lightning speed and I couldn't brace for the impact of her slap.

"What the hell is wrong with you? You're sitting over there smiling, proud to tell your mother that there are four men who could of father your child and I'm supposed to accept my daughter telling me that she slept with four men over three months all without a condom? You've lost your mind." I stood and she did too, "Nivea, plop yourself right back down in that seat, we're not done. I know you're going to run back to New York now so you're going to hear what I think and you're going to fix it, oh yes, this will be fixed. You already have intelligence, God gave you that, not those books you keep crediting your intelligence to. Those things are tools, like hammers and saws. They only work if you know how to use them. School was a tool for you and you knew how to use it so it worked but your problem is life. You let everything in it be a hurdle and you play it like a game. Look at me, dammit!" Her voice made the side of my face shake as she spoke. "This is your life, this ain't a game. You just lost everything I watched you lose sleep for years over because you dropped your guard. This ain't a game baby, you don't get do overs. There isn't an extra man that you can play with if you die. One mistake and you're gone!"

I couldn't swallow how my mama was talking to me which meant I was supposed to take it like rocks in the throat.

"I'm going to fix it, Mama,"

"You are still saying I, that's how I know you don't have what it takes to fix it. You can't fix it without God." Mama kissed me on my cheek and said, "come on baby so you can get back to the house and pack."

*****

"I told you I could get you in."

Miya had pulled a few strings at the doctor's office she worked at. The radiologist went to the same school as her and they knew a lot of the same people but they didn't know each other. She was quiet and Miya didn't know how to be quiet. She told her my situation three weeks after I made it back to New York. The radiologist declined to help hands-on but made sure the door was unlocked and the equipment was ready for Miya's use.

"Do you see anything?"

My stomach was covered in a cold gel and she was rubbing a probe over it. She started near my belly button and was now a millimeter above my pubic hairs.

"Yes, a big head and a steady heartbeat. By ultrasound, you're 8 weeks and two days pregnant. So, who's the daddy, bitch?"

I ignored the question by asking, "Can I see?"

She played with a button then a swishing sound

filled the room. Once she got the static out of it she turned the monitor and inside what looked like a gray triangle was a very small peanut shaped baby, my baby. Tears fell from my eyes as she printed off a few pictures.

"Here and you can at least tell me who you think the daddy might be. I could lose my job sneaking you in for a free ultrasound and you know I'm not supposed to be in the radiology lab this big."

Her hands fell to her on protruding stomach. She was five months pregnant but looked as if she was due any second. Miya was beautiful pregnant and the waddle in her walk was so cute to me. Since it was now safe to eliminate Evol, I could answer her.

"One of the Memphis, cousins. I'm hoping Dwayne. Is there a way to tell paternity before I get too far along?"

"You mean, can you get a DNA test done now so if it's not the daddy you want it to be, you can get an abortion and kill my god baby? Yeah, you can but why does the daddy matter when you're the mama?"

"Traits, characteristics, and the list goes on. I'm not thinking of getting an abortion but knowing who the father is might make me decide to." I had a flash back of how Chauncey was acting at the airport. The thought of having a baby by him was depressing.

"You were supposed to worry about that stuff before you had sex. How are you going to preach about the difference between niggas and men when you're battling between being a trifling ho or a woman? Look," she said changing her voice into a whisper, "If you want it to be Dwayne's baby, I can make that happen too okay? You don't have to kill the baby to win."

"I don't want to know what you're talking about nor how you can make it happen. I haven't decided if I'd let the father be in my child's life anyways."

"Oh, you haven't decided? I didn't know you had the power to decide if a man can be a father to his child or not. Damn Nivea, what happened to you? I used to think you were a good girl and now I find out you're fucking married men and cousins. You're talking about abortions and now you think you have the right to choose when a man can be a father. That doesn't even sound like the woman I know. I don't even know If I should believe anything you say anymore. Are you sure it's not Evol's baby?"

"I'm positive, now get this gooey stuff off me. All that water you told me to drink has me about to burst."

She wiped my stomach off and helped me sit up.

"The restroom is down the hall. I can't take anymore of you today. I'll call you later, I have to clean up in here before I leave."

Dwayne

"Zo lang ho!"

The greetings of good morning in Shanghainese still felt artificial to me and I'd been here for five and half months.

"Good morning, Feng. Can you please let Mr. Liao know that I will not need breakfast this morning? I'm going to step out."

"Yes sir, is there anything else I can help you with?" my butler and new right-hand man, asked.

"There is, tell Wei to bring the S650 Cabriolet around front and how about you taking that uniform off and driving me around today?"

"Yes sir!" he said excitedly.

When I bought my castle the service workers were included in the package. I wasn't a fan of using them at first but I quickly learned that they made life easier. No cooking, cleaning, yard work and no driving. It was like life before turning 18 without the parental touches of it. Besides, the house was huge and I didn't want to stay in it alone.

I didn't want to admit it but I was battling homesickness which was weird because I wasn't around anyone to miss. Here I was surrounded in beauty and missing the ugly sights of the city of Memphis. There wasn't any poverty or violent acts for me to see or hear about and it made me feel as though I had been kicked out the loop. The smell of fast food restaurants during lunch time rush that made me want to vomit by thinking of the deadly chemicals in it, was replaced with the scents of fine teas and burning herbs. I must have been losing my mind because I missed everything that I professed hate for and it worsened by the day.

"Is this attire suitable, Mr. Hollingswell?"

Feng had on what looked like the last ninja warrior karate suit and some wooden soled sandals. I saw people dressed like him on those Saturday afternoon karate movies but those people were short. Not saying Feng was tall but with him standing the same height as me, the outfit wasn't a compliment.

"You look fine but how about we go through my closet and see what we can come up with. With size shoes do you wear?"

I had on a slim fit polo, stripped Bermuda shorts and some penny loafers, from Brooks Brothers of course so for shits and giggles I gave him my terry joggers, a rugby stripped hooded sweater, and my leather crisscross sandals to put on. It was an improvement if comfort didn't come to play.

"Let's ride!"

We pulled up at the Shanghai World Financial Center which looked frighteningly similar to the new

World Trade Center in New York. The building has 101 floors in it and three are underground. It's the 8th tallest building in the world and it houses banks, insurance companies, securities and fund management, a hotel, and it even has a mall with a food court inside. It had become a daily ritual to pull up in front of it and watch the business world in action but that day, I had pending business inside.

"Did they install the new monitors in the back office yet?"

I asked my office manager Li but she didn't answer me. Instead she pointed at the surveillance cameras that monitored the small conference room.

"She arrived ten minutes ago asking for a meeting with Dwayne Hollingswell. I told her we didn't have anyone employed with that name but she said she knew we did because he owned the firm and she's his wife. She told me she'd wait here until we found you"

"Call security and have her thrown out."

"That's the thing," Li came from behind the desk and stood next to me, "I did and they left without taking her. I don't know what she said but they seemed scared of her."

"Why didn't you call me?"

"You said never to call you if they ask for you by that name since you are using your middle name here. I was checking the books for procedures to see if there was an in case of emergency clause."

"I'll handle it, thank you, and if they haven't installed those monitors for the new guy I have starting tomorrow you need to make that priority one."

BrC or Birthright Capital was my in the closet investment firm that no one should have known about besides those I told and that list was short. Elliott, Edward, Heather, and the Church were the only people I told and only when it became necessary to share. How Cynthia found out about it I didn't know but I would ask.

"Didn't I warn you not to stand me up? You must have forgotten who I am and what I can do."

"I don't care who you think you are or what you think you can do. That's why I stood you up, but I'm actually glad you're here. I really wanted to meet you at the casino but something more important came up. Since you're here, what was it that you wanted to talk about?"

I sat down in the chair next to her and moved it closer to her. I didn't stop until our chairs touched.

"Us, our marriage, and how all this time we've been spending apart has to end. We are married, Dwayne, and I've been a good wife. I gave you five years to do whatever, with whoever you wanted to do it. It's time to rekindle and start a family."

"Is that how you feel?" She nodded her head. "Then it saddens me to tell you again, that I don't care how you feel. I'm not playing your games anymore and I'm not moving to your beat. The days of you controlling anything that has to do with me are over. You're the devil and I'm spiritually ready to fight you because I know I don't have to battle you by myself."

"Listen to you, you almost sound like someone to fear. I always get what I want and if I label something as mine, then that's what it will always be. Don't think because I opted to give you a few years of freedom you're running something. You only have what I've allowed you to have."

"Bitch, you sound drunk. Everything I have, I got without you and you couldn't have stopped me from having it if you tried."

She cut me off, "I could have demolished Zion Capital Management when you first opened it. Now that it's closed how much longer do you think you will have this?"

"Longer than you'll live to see if you don't walk away while you can."

"A few million doesn't keep you fighting in the ring with me. Your money wouldn't last a full round up against mine."

I had to force my poker face to stay on so the joy I had inside wouldn't show. Cynthia didn't know my net worth and there wasn't a way for her to find it out because of the way I moved. I had read a book while I was in jail those thirty days on the risk and rewards of precious metals in the commodities market. For years I had been buying them physically with the bulk of my purchases being a couple of hundred dollars' worth of coins. I didn't care about the currency or the value written on it because with coins the values changed by the worth of the metal they are made from. After reading the book I reached out to a lot of the whales of finance but only one wrote back and it was nice and simple. His letter said:

Hey Dwayne,

Can't say I'm sorry or not about your current circumstance, I didn't witness the alleged crime. It sounds to me like you need more buying power if the numbers you were making before incarceration were that impressive. Get you a prime brokerage that's willing to give you a Portfolio Margin account for the leverage possibilities in it but don't do it in the United States. Find a country with a huge supply of gold and silver, make sure it is strong when it comes to export and importing and it would be a plus if they've recently had a recession or some other financial crisis. Hope this helps if not, read the post mark on this envelope. Good luck!

I didn't have to look at the postmark and I never have. China was dangled in my face too much not to choose it. China was listed as the largest holders of the United States 19.19 trillion-dollar debt. You don't have to read the Bible to know that the debtor is slave to the lender, don't pay your rent and see how that works out. I couldn't walk through my parents' house without noticing that 99% of their house was covered in made in China stickers and stamps. That meant they had a huge supply of currency and had to have a strong export/ import system in place. It took a quick internet search to find out their markets offer option contracts on silver and gold because they hold tons of it. I opened the firm in Memphis with Elliot's help and Heather worked hard to build up the clientele but when we saw our first profits, I went abroad. I opened a small three-man firm in China after buying the most affordable one bedroom I could find and did as I was told. I opened the brokerage here, broke into their futures markets and got my welcome package from the billionaire boy's club. Birth Right Capital is a corporation which makes it a person by corporate person-hood and in most cases a corporation has more rights than people. If I didn't want the personal information behind B.R.C publicized, as a person B.R.C holds those rights to privacy. I opted out of getting a salary from my company, I picked a dividend because they can be paid in cash. To make sure I didn't piss China off I didn't try to find a way around paying their high ass corporate tax. It wasn't because I couldn't figure a way out of them, it was because I wanted the peace and freedom that would come with playing by their rules. What I did was turn the bulk of my fiat currency from the dividends I earned into gold, silver, and non-market investments such as real estate and precious metals like rhodium, platinum, and palladium. I also stocked up on rare artwork that appreciated with time and stayed away from making purchases for depreciating items like cars, clothes, and electronics. The only way Cynthia would know my worth was if I took her on tour of my underground vault which I made sure was earthquake proof. And even if she found that, she would have to trace the identical moves I made in Russia for accuracy. It was my net worth and I could physically touch it whenever I wanted but I still didn't believe it was possible to retain. The funny part about it was if I Googled the richest people on earth, I'd see there are many more like myself and even more who asked to stay off the list. I wouldn't dare tell this psycho that.

"I don't care how much money you have, Cynthia, this has nothing to do with that. I'm never conforming to your bullshit again. I don't love you; I never did. You're beautiful so you caught my eye and after getting to know you I should have plucked it out for forcing me to sin. You're the devil, I'd never take you to God and profess you as my wife. Everything I said to you was a lie, I did it to get you to drop the charges on me. My mistake was using sin to get out of sin. I should have told you the truth and did the jail time so you wouldn't be in my face today." I got to my feet and said, "Get the fuck out of my office and don't bring your crazy ass back."

She leaned back in the chair, slid her heels off, and crossed her legs. I hadn't paid attention that she had been wearing glasses until she took them off.

"This is your last chance to play my game, Dwayne. What are you going to do?"

She sat a marriage license on the desk and I glanced at it but it couldn't hold my attention. The purple and black bruise that circled her eyes had me. When the conference room door opened I knew it was the police.

"Fuck you, I'd rather go to jail than conform."

"Let's see how you like prison in China. I hear they are one of the worst."

She started screaming, yelling, and crying like I had knocked fire to her. The shock value was missing because I had watched her act the victim role so many times that it didn't move me. I placed my hands out to the police and said, "I'm ready to go," in Chinese. They roughed me up all the way to the elevator doors.

*****

"Hey, I thought I asked you to get your guy to keep an eye on Cynthia for me? I just had to pay a couple of Shanghai Municipal police officers a bunch of yuan to believe my story over hers and the black eye she walked in my office with. I need him watching her at all times!"

I hid behind the adjacent building and called Esau until I saw Cynthia leave the building satisfied by my arrest.

"He is on the job and had been watching her but something came up that as your brother I thought was more important."

"What?" I sat down on the steps and waited to hear what new hurdle would plant itself in the way as I carried the cross to follow Jesus.

"Wait, I'll let Jacob tell you."

There were a few words spoken away from the

339

phone between the two that I couldn't make out and then Jacob said, "Nivea found out through a few mutual friends of ours that we worked for you and she started asking questions."

"Questions like what?"

"Nothing too serious. She wanted to know our role here and if we knew anything about the other firms involved in the insider trading stuff but that isn't why we put him on her. We found out through the mutual friend she was pregnant and withholding information on the father. My gut turned when I heard it, D."

"Just like my fingers went numb when you said it," I mumbled as he talked.

"It didn't take long for him to find out her due date or the fact that there's a few possible fathers for this child. He hasn't confirmed it yet but from what our mutual friend told us, she's named you as one. We hadn't planned on telling you until we weren't mistaken."

I hung up and called my lawyer in the States.

"Hey, Marcus, I need you to file an injunction, get a court order, or whatever needs to be done to have Nivea Bowen of Bowen Capital Management undergo a DNA test immediately. I need to know if the child is mine before it's born. I need it done like I requested it yesterday!"

Nivea

When I was comfortable thinking the world couldn't hit me with anything else, I got hit in the face with two fastballs and it wasn't my turn at bat. The first was finding out that my favorite twins on this Earth worked for the likes of Dwayne and the three were childhood friends. Their characteristics were very similar but similar isn't the same. I met the twins at N.Y.I.F and I knew the boys were something special, the special you find written in a story in the Bible. I'll admit it, I had that same feeling when I met Dwayne, mixed with a fairy-tale, millions have read, and that was the second fast ball, it was a legal notice from Dwayne's lawyer. It came with a kit from an international paternity lab, with legal orders for my doctor to perform a non-invasive prenatal paternity test on me. Dwayne's blood collection had been sent directly to the lab at my doctor's office and the only thing holding up the test was my willingness to provide the sample.

"I don't know if I want to know the truth, okay Miya? You don't understand what I'm going through!" I yelled as she put her gloves on in preparation for another free ultrasound. I was scheduled for an anatomy ultrasound but the baby wouldn't open its legs to determine the sex. Miya volunteered to find out if her daughter would be playing with her god sister or brother.

"I don't want to understand it like I've told you for months. You're seven months pregnant still shooting out toxins when it comes to my god baby's father. You're a sick bitch, Nivea." She followed with a chuckle, "When I'm done with this, you're going into the lab and you're taking that test so you can know the truth. It's not my fault if the results don't make it back to China, blame the shipping company."

Without care for the chill, she squeezed the gel on my stomach and placed the probe over my belly. Two minutes later she turned the screen so I could see it and said, "Let's find out who his daddy is, the world doesn't have to know."

For the next two weeks, I tried not to think about the test but wanting to know the results wouldn't release my thoughts. My focus was supposed to be on selling my condo and moving home with my mom but I couldn't let the toxins around me go. Between the SEC's turtle pace to make a decision and the paternity of my son, I couldn't enjoy the pregnancy. I was happy to know that within hours I'd have a resolution to one of them.

"Here, it came certified this morning and I met the mailman at the door. Nobody knows the results but the lab."

Miya handed me the envelope and then sat on my couch waiting for me to open it. I did and read the first paragraph. Instantly, I didn't feel the same.

"So, is Dwayne the daddy or not?"

"He is."

"Yes!" she said holding her stomach, "Now, let's go

have this baby before the excitement makes my water break and I have to push her out. I'm not missing this scheduled C-section for nothing in the world."

The waiting room was packed for the expected delivery of Miya's first born, Odyssey, with her and Man-Man's family. For them not to be married you couldn't tell it by their families, their unity spoke volumes. I tried to sit in a corner by myself but Evol and his wife felt the need to join me.

"Did you ever find out who you got knocked up by? I was glad to hear the time was off to add my husband to that long list of potential fathers. I heard it included at least one man from every firm in New York and Memphis. Finance pussy gets around."

While she laughed Evol stared at me like he would kill me if she wasn't sitting next to him. He stared at my stomach like they were from rival gangs. To snap him out of it I responded to his wife.

"Yes, I figured it out and I was happy too when I learned he didn't qualify. Hell, he doesn't qualify for anything else so I wasn't surprised." I stood up and walked off. I made it down the hall before I felt a hand on my shoulder turning me around.

"Is that how you do me?"

"Is that how you do your wife? Leave her sitting there while you chase after me?"

"Fuck her, I told your stupid ass that a long time

ago. It's you that I want but you got some other nigga's seed in you like that's not my pussy. Bitch, you're lucky I didn't knock you out when I found out. It's that Wall Street dude's baby, huh?"

Evol's eyes were red but I wasn't sure if the cause was anger or withholding tears. I didn't doubt that he loved me, I always knew he did, but it shouldn't have taken him three years to get rid of his wife which let me know that wasn't in his plans.

"Whose baby it is has nothing to do with you, just like my pussy," I added as I spotted his wife Zamora walking our way with tears flowing from her eyes. I took off in her direction and when we passed I said, "Your dog is off leash again."

She cocked back, held the pose for a second, and when Evol was in her reach she hit him right in the mouth as I kept on walking. Man-Man appeared in a set of disposable scrubs and yelled, "She's here and looks just like me. My baby is 8lbs 2oz, 21 inches long and healthy."

I was elated by the announcement but after that petty shit I decided to see Miya's daughter on another day.

*****

Being at the hospital with Miya and Man-Man's families gave me the same feeling I had after reading that

TOXIN

Dwayne was my son's father. Something in me activated and made me feel like I needed to tell Dwayne and give him the right to decide his next move.

I grabbed my laptop and sat on the couch. I thought about Raymond and what he said when he found out the child wasn't his but I needed to read it again. Dwayne had written:

...After going through all this I did make up my mind about one thing, when I have kids I'm never going to let them leave my side!

If that was true then he was the perfect man to father a child with even if we weren't together. I knew what I needed to do to fix this. I grabbed the results off the table, then snatched the letter from Dwayne's lawyer, and went to the post office to mail it to them. Who was I to decide if he earned the right to be a father to his son?

My mama said to fix it using more than my intelligence, and she was right, it's biblical. I remembered studying with my mother and stuff like this came up. It was new to us but it has happened before. Everyone experiences a different opinion due to their perception. Toxins are easy to spot but it's the perception you really should be watching out for. You only get to smell and taste toxins, with perception you get to feel them. They don't exist until you're in the action where judgment is necessary. You can get caught up in perception quickly because it's hard to make people forget a learned behavior.

*****

A week had passed and he hadn't made contact so I decided to make a visit. It wasn't thought out but I was getting closer to my due date and I wanted him to be in the room for the birth of his first born. I let my mama handle the sale of my condo. After telling her what I was going to China for, she understood. It was close to a twenty-hour flight but there were two layovers. The first was New York to Toronto. When we landed I powered up my phone after saying good bye to the pilot who tried to deny me the right to fly because of how far along I was in my pregnancy and he feared I would go in labor on the flight. It's funny how all it took was a thousand dollars to shut him up. I didn't have to worry about baggage because I'd only grabbed my purse and phone charger. If I needed anything I'd by it in China, why pay more to bring it from the U.S? I found a cozy spot by an outlet in the wall. I put my pillow in the chair and adjusted the neck roll around my neck. I unlocked my phone and went straight to the search engine. I needed to track that letter. I wanted to know if he knew. How he felt and if we could come up with a parenting plan. I didn't get to wonder long because Cynthia was in my face.

"Let me ask you something, do you really think I'm going to let you bring a baby in this world by my husband?" She laughed and did this thing with her shoulder. "You think I'm supposed to be cool with him slipping and getting you pregnant, like that's not my soul mate? Are you serious? Do you think I'm going to sit back and let this shit go, bitch I'm crazy!"

I slid across the leather chair as quickly as I could and stood to my feet as fast as the third trimester of pregnancy would allow me. I prepped for making first contact but she was being swept away. It was the twins Jacob and Esau swiping her away.

"Hey, sis, Dwayne wants to holler at you."

I hadn't seen my brother in years. Our brains and ranking in everything we did made us blood. What I had with the twins compared to nothing on this Earth but I knew Dwayne had me beat because their connection was through God. I knew they were on his side.

"I'm headed to see Dwayne now."

They looked at one another and then said, "I wonder if Dwayne knows that she's on the way?"

Dwayne

I got a letter to my castle addressed from Nivea. It was the results from the D.N.A test with a short, handwritten note, that read, "I'd like for us to discuss a parenting plan. Call me."

Under her words was a telephone number with a New York area code. I called, no answer. For nine hours, straight. I had the twins have their guy do a little research and he told me she had a layover in Canada. I told the twins to meet her there. I hung up before I found out where she was headed after Canada but I knew the flight pattern, Nivea was on her way here. The twins needed to intercept her. I hadn't decided my approach. The only thing that I was certain about was, I was going to be the best dad that I could to my son. I didn't know if I was going to try the family approach and see how it went. She was stressing over the riff-raff with her company and I wanted to make sure I was there with my own two eyes to be sure my son was being raised the way I wanted him to be. The only way I'd be sure would probably be to marry her or we would have to have a real good attitude about being roommates until he was 18. I had to be there every day and every night for mine because there was no one who could take better care of him like me but, God. My phone rang.

"Hello?"

"Hello, is this that nigga, Dwayne?"

The voice didn't sound familiar but he had a heavy

New York accent. It didn't take long to realize one of those dudes in New York had the heart to call me. I was ready to deflate his chest.

"Get to it."

"Get to it? Nigga, who in the fuck are supposed to be? Fool, this Evol. Nivea's old man."

Not being funny but what had the world come to when a married man tried to fight his side chick's child's father? Then he stated his name like it was supposed to mean something to me, just because he felt like he earned an honorable mention, I was going to brutalize him. Depending on what he said next I'd determine the severity.

"That's my bitch; you can keep your baby. She'll be back for papi."

He was a circus act; I didn't understand how Nivea kept attracting clowns.

*****

I was processing my thoughts but I kept hearing his voice, a voice I never wanted my son to know existed ring in my ears. I was shaking it off as Nivea's call came in.

"You had my brothers turn on me for you, you must be something special, Raymond, but I'm sure you and the twins would both credit it to God."

"Right, Brenda, I got the news. When is my son making his debut? I want to be there for it too."

TOXIN

I got word from her mother by email that she had been sick and the doctors didn't want her to fly all the way to China so I wanted to try to turn her around so she would fly back to New York and I'd take the risk of being seen there, but hours had elapsed. She was here, in China, on her way to me with my son. That's exactly how I would want it. I needed to get an understanding with her so we'd never have to get one again.

"I want to give this relationship thing a shot not only for me but if it came down to it, I'd do it only for my son. I'm not leaving his side, Nivea, so what's it gon' be? I'm not asking to play house either. We are going to do it or we not. If we're not, I'm still living under the same roof as him even if I have to find a way to get that backed through the courts. How do you want to live our lives?"

"Dwayne, I want to say give us a shot. I think we'd work out because we feel the exact same way about our son but we have a problem we need to handle before we do anything. You got a nasty ass roach problem and I don't know why you didn't fumigate, but I will. I couldn't make the decision to do it that easy as your woman. I don't have time to wait for an okay. I'm going to fix your bug problem; I don't mind using bug spray."

"You doubt that we would do that together?"

"Of course not, but the problem can't wait, Dwayne."

"It wouldn't wait!" I wasn't trying not to snap but I didn't think I'd have to bargain with her about trying this family thing out first. I wanted Cynthia too and I could still function completely while I hunted her, but who am I to tell her the feeling she had about the backyard was bad? It didn't matter if I felt comfortable walking in the backyard, she had to feel comfortable walking back there when it was her turn. If she wasn't comfortable, who was I to say what she felt was wrong? Unless it went against the word of God. "I don't think you get what I'm trying to say to you."

"You don't understand what I'm trying to get you to understand."

"Listen to what you just said, how am I supposed to understand that?"

Nivea must have lost her mind. I didn't understand what she was trying to say and I didn't think she understood her words either.

"Dwayne, listen to me. It can't wait, my water broke three minutes ago."

"Why didn't you say anything?" I jumped to my feet and started scrambling around to find my shoes. I was panicking like I was next to her. "Are you in pain?"

"No, not really, I'm more mad right now than anything. Something else is definitely going on."

"Where are you? I'm on the way."

The doorbell rang and I could tell Nivea must have been in pain by the way she laid on it. I rushed to my live feed and there she was standing at my door. Her stomach was round and so was everything on her face. It felt good to smile.

Raynesha Pittman Quincey Bowen

Nivea

Between the twins and I we must have called Dwayne a hundred times and couldn't get an answer. I even paid to use the phone on the plane to call and got the same results. The flight I booked claimed to be full but the seats were empty. I rode the plane alone.

I was hoping he could read in between the lines but I think the baby being on the way might have thrown his thoughts off course. I wish I would have been lying about my water breaking. They warned me not take that long of a flight and how smart was I to go against something that can be proven in over a dozen ways to be unsafe. When the cabin on the plane depressurized so did my tummy and the pains began to kick in. I thought it would get better on the cab ride there. When we made it, I wasn't sure if the cab took me to the right address or not because I was staring at a mansion. As far as my eyes could see it was stretched in beauty. I was admiring the beautiful pillars that lined the walkway to the door when my water broke. I didn't know if that was the normal way water was supposed to break or if that was a rupture and the baby's life was in danger. I didn't want to scare Dwayne but we needed to get to the hospital quickly.

"Just grab your keys and let's go, Dwayne. You won't be able to keep anything else."

"Hold on, let me grab my charger. We'll need to make long distant calls."

"You should call the police." I tried to keep the laugh in my voice but Dwayne wasn't getting it. I tried something else. "I know you said you don't open your door after 11 so if you want, I'll just go to the hospital alone and you stay here."

I could see Cynthia's shadow behind a tree not too far away from being in earshot. She had something in her hand and I couldn't tell what it was. I'd hate for me to assume it was nothing and he got shot. He needed to stay indoors.

"You're about to have my son, I think that's an exception to any rules I have, and why should I call the police? I can get you there faster than an ambulance."

His smile, he always got me when I saw him smile. There was a tickling in my throat, stumble in my walk, and my heartbeat felt hot and fast like I had just run track. His smile alone made me melt away. It was his smile I could see coming towards me through the opening in his door. I knew she could probably hear me but I had to protect him.

"Dwayne, don't come outside and call the police!"

Dwayne stopped in his tracks, reached into a flower pot he had by the door, and pulled out a gun.

"Come inside, Nivea, the door is open."

He gave the directions into the phone but he could see my face now, he could see it in my eyes.

"I don't think I should move and it might be best if

you don't come outside. She's holding something in her hands, I can see it in the shadow."

"Nivea, you and my son need to come inside right now."

His voice freaked me out so I slowly took a step up. Cynthia had tried to get me in Canada, I wasn't foolish to think she wouldn't do the same in China. I took another step up and shots went off.

Dwayne

Shots went off and I ran to the door, opened it, and pulled Nivea inside. After grabbing her by the shoulders and doing a quick glance over to see if she had been hit, I ran outside. The shooting had stopped and there wasn't any movement around me. I ran back in the house to check the video footage and almost tripped over Nivea.

"I don't think I'm going to make it to the hospital."

She was on the floor sitting in a mixture of blood and a watery substance clutching her stomach. I couldn't tell if she had been shot or if all the fluid was a part of the labor. We were quickly joined by my butler, driver, and maid all wearing their pajamas.

"Are you alright, Mr. Hollingswell? We heard the shooting and the police are on the way," Feng announced.

I couldn't respond, hell I couldn't even move. When the three men lined their eyes up with mine, they saw that the shooting was only a small problem.

"Dwayne, the baby is coming!" she screamed it out and the look on her face confirmed her words were true. I had seen enough movies to know that the face she was making meant she had already started pushing. I stood there frozen, not knowing what to do.

To be continued…

www.RayneshaPittman.com/Conglomerate-ink